Enemies Within

BRIAN PHILLIPS

DEDICATION

To my brother Joe, who proved that if you keep asking "is it done yet," it may eventually get done.

ACKNOWLEDGMENTS

I would like to acknowledge and thank the Springfield Writers Meetup for listening to pieces of this work and offering suggestions. I would also like to acknowledge the contributions of my beta readers / critics. This book would be a lesser work if it wasn't for the insight of Catherine, Matthew, Randy , and Colt.

THE RAT

The Rat used his long fork to slightly adjust a few of the small burning chips. The chips sat upon a stone plate, gently boiling the thick orange liquid in the flask above. Droplets of liquid dripped from the rim of the flask onto the small iron stand, sizzling when they struck. The room smelled like old tar and sweet spices. A single window stood closed against the wall. Strips of brown cloth were visible, jammed between the window pane and the frame.

He was being careful, very little of the smoke could be allowed to leak out.

The smoke wouldn't affect him anyway. The Rat had long ago become immune to its effects, but he wouldn't want any innocent passerby to come into contact with it. It would not do to alert the locals to his activities this night.

He looked up from his task, being careful, so very careful, not to nudge or disturb its perfect configuration.

"Eh? What's that? Something else to say?"

The other man looked up from the floor. His ivory colored

temple robes were stained with vomit, front and back. Gasping, the man tried to speak again.

"No, you don't understand."

Blood had begun to drip from his eyes, crawling down his face until the drops added red color to the top of his already stained robe.

"Phyllicitus, the goddess, she will find you."

Coughing took control of him. Each wheezing breath he took sounded like agony. The Rat gave him time to recover, moving over to his neatly organized pile of belongings and extracting a leather-covered journal. He began preparing an ink pot, then dipped a quill in it. All while watching the dying man drifting ever closer to the final black door.

Once his pen was sufficiently covered with ink, he spread out a layer of cloth on the floor. He sat on it, shielding his clothing from contact with the filthy floor, and began to record his observations.

The man spoke again, creaking out what might be his last words. "What do you want?"

"Want? Me? I don't want anything. I'm just here to record your final moments." The Rat scratched a note into his journal. "But I have these Friends. They want to know what you have been getting up to in that temple of yours. Can you give me any little tidbits that I could pass along?"

Coughing again, he tried to lift his head. "Don't do this. The Takers are going to come. They could take everyone in Home's Hearth. We have to try to stop them."

He began coughing uncontrollably, and shook his head, hoping against all odds that he could appeal to the Rat's humanity.

It was no use. The Rat had lost the human part of his soul long ago, even before the Takers, his Friends, had come.

The man began shaking violently. The Rat moved over to touch him, turning and repositioning him to gain a better view. Then he returned to his notebook and recorded what he had seen. He sketched the man's bloodshot eyes, noted points of interest with arcane symbols, and wrote notes in the margins.

"Before you leave me, I would like to thank you for your participation in my inquiry. I understand that these sorts of things are not easy."

The dying man could not respond. He tried to look up, but his eyes couldn't focus.

"I imagine you are confused."

The Rat opened one of his bags. It was a plain brown canvas satchel, its opening tied with a black cord. He untied the cord and reached in. He pulled out a long wooden container with holes drilled into it, each a hand span apart. He set it down and filled each hole with a perfectly crafted glass dish, and in turn, sprinkled different powders into each.

"Don't worry, it won't be long now. We just have to wait for the right moment."

Setting aside his journal and pen, he reached into the bag again and collected a pair of long gloves. The gloves looked out of place in this bare, wooden room. They were of the highest quality and decorated with glyphs of power. He spent a moment inspecting them, ensuring that they were entirely clean before opening a dark velvet lined box and picking out a short blade from within.

The man was almost gone. Moving the collection dishes closer, the Rat took his position and waited, donning the gloves in preparation for tonight's work.

The scent of cooking meat had penetrated into the room, mixing with leftover stink. A fire burned beneath the small metal trays. Five small chunks of meat, so recently a priest of Phyllicitus, cooked on metal braziers. The rest of him lay discarded in the corner, a bloody ruin of butchering. Burning crisps of heart, liver, kidney, throat, and brain contributed their smells to the foulness of the air. The Rat had just finished cooking them down to their basic elements, capturing their magic for his alchemy. Now those components were set aside, cooling in the room's air.

The Rat returned to his cleaning. A small bucket of hot water stood nearby. He dipped a cloth into the bucket and began scrubbing hard at the flooring, paying particular attention around where the body lay, trying to soak up as much of the blood as he could. Every time he finished a section of floor, he rinsed it with a foul chemical, causing evil-smelling clouds to rise into the room. The body had already begun to decompose under the harsh strength of alchemical solvents and acids. Its flesh bubbled as it was eaten away by chemicals, exposing bone and strings of resilient sinew.

The smell was awful, but the Rat paid it no mind. He had already calculated the exact amount of time that he could spend in the room without long-term effects, and he had plenty to spare before his night's work was over. He had used this dissolving solution many times and knew its behavior well.

His tools lay across the room, drying upon meticulously clean linen. Sharp knives, a short glimmering saw, bone breakers, and a meat cleaver lay upon a clean cloth. A newly emptied tub of cleaning formula stood upon the floor. None of the tools had evidence of the night's work, it had been expertly removed.

He collected his specimens and then hid the evidence, shrouding the deed in secrecy. By all indications, it should have been a profitable night. It wasn't.

No luck.

The young acolyte had yielded no information in the end. None of his flesh seemed vulnerable to the Rat's friends, the Takers.

He ravaged through the formula in his head, unsure of what he could be missing. Nothing. The spell wasn't enough, the alchemy wasn't triggering correctly. It was always difficult to deal with the followers of the gods. It was especially difficult to deal with the followers of a healing goddess like Phyllicitus. Her powers were ambient throughout Home's Hearth. Her priests gained health, stature, and sometimes just dumb luck, merely by living there.

His Friends had no inspiration for him today. They seldom added new insight when it came to crafting. As cunning and wise as they were, they were not crafters. They were not alchemists like he was.

Cleanliness is next to godliness... Having no further plan for the night, he continued to clean.

Smiling at his dark humor, he continued his task. The hours of the night slipped away until the room was completely spotless, and all his tools and samples had been collected in the metal tub. Its bent metal handles were a shoulder's width apart, making it perfect for its job of carrying and hiding alchemical tools.

Digging into the contents of the tub, he pulled out a cloth bundle. He unrolled the bundle, then changed into new garments. He discarded his old clothes into the tub, then donned a thin brown shirt and short trousers. It was the sort of clothing a common working man owned.

Now that the mess was cleaned up, he began to deal with the smell. He opened the single window enough to allow more wind into the room. Letting the breeze in, he watched as it broke up the vapors and prevented them from seeping through the floorboards.

Placing a perfumed blanket across the top of the tub, he opened the door and began carrying it across the creaking wooden hallway and down the stairs. The downstairs was quiet, lit with only a few candles when he arrived. The common room of the inn was empty except for a single woman sitting in a chair beside the great stone fireplace. She groggily looked up as he entered, her long gray hair hung limply across her shoulders. She had been beautiful once, the Rat considered. Now she was just lonely. Her husband was long gone, a victim of the last Taker invasion. He died at the hand of the Eisenvard, one more killed for the sake of purifying Home's Hearth.

"Late night, eh? You've been working hard up there. I didn't see you at dinner," Jezzine, the owner of the inn, said.

The Rat smiled and replied softly, "Yes, unfortunately, it didn't go as well as I had wished. But now, well, it's done. I thought I would let myself out."

"Don't care for a drink before ye go?" Jezzine asked. She always wanted to spend time chatting away. She was both a fool and a busybody. He felt the Friends urging him to leave, to be about his business. But he ignored them. He knew that he had to seem normal at all times, and the Takers didn't know how to do that very well at all.

Instead, he gave her a tired smile. "That is a wonderful idea. I'll take you up on that."

She stood and walked behind the bar, picked up a large clay jar, and poured the strong-smelling liquid into a cup. He set the metal tub down on the floor, staring down at the child's blanket decorating its top. Animals were sewn into the fabric, showing a green deer, a brown bear, a kitten frolicking with puppies, and in the corner, a crow. He shook his head at the childish renditions of the First Gods. Reaching down, he adjusted the blanket to cover the rib bone that had emerged from beneath.

He needed to keep that covered, as it could be embarrassing.

"Business been good?" she began.

"Well, yes and no. We don't have as much demand for the medicines since the goddess returned. That is good for everyone, but there are days when I miss how easy it was to make a living healing the sick."

"Miss the days when only the rich got medicine, eh?"

"No, it's not like that." He shook his head with a slight smile. It was like that, he just didn't want to admit it. "I do fine enough now. The temple pays me a monthly fee and I fulfill their orders as I can. It is rarely slow in my shop. Their healers use a lot of my herbs and potions, so I stay in business. I'm just saying that it takes a lot more work and a lot more late nights."

Nodding at him, she raised her glass. "To Phyllicitus."

He raised his glass in return, then drank down the spicy liquid. It burned in his throat.

"Any news from the temple?" the Rat asked. "I've heard

rumors of a battle in the countryside. Is there any truth to that?"

The Rat doubted that the temple had heard of that battle yet, but it never hurt to check.

"A battle? With who?" Jezzine asked.

"Raiders, I heard."

"I hadn't heard anything about such a thing. Who do you know that I don't?"

"My source can be unreliable. It's a constant stream of gossip that I won't trouble you with."

"I quite enjoy gossip."

"Not this kind. It's all politics."

She made a sour face. "Oh no, I despise politics. That's why I love living here. Home's Hearth has its goddess back now. No politics are needed."

The Rat smiled back at her, genuinely happy with her naiveté and willingness to ignore the obvious. "There's always politics, we just don't always get to see it. As long as there are people, there will be games of power."

They spent another ten minutes catching up on the news of the town. The old lady was very familiar with who was sleeping with who, and which couple was having relationship challenges. She delighted in telling stories of the struggles of her neighbors, especially when it resulted in one of them crawling out of their neighbor's window in the middle of the night, naked.

Eventually, the Rat ended the conversation.

"It was great to catch up. It's late though, and morning is coming all too soon."

She placed a hand on his arm as he bent down to pick up the tub. "You'll be returning then?"

"I'm sure of it. I will see you in a few weeks at the most." He smiled at her to reassure her. "Have a pleasant night."

Walking out of the inn, he joined the night. The street was newly paved with cobblestones. Clouds covered the stars so that the only light came from torches burning at the end of each block. He began walking, unsure of his direction, waiting for his call.

He could have stayed there without a problem. Jezzine would have welcomed him into her bed. But that would have meant introducing her to his Friends. They were not the sort to concern themselves with human relationships. Any embrace from him would have ended with her being taken. It wasn't time for that yet, not yet.

The call came before he walked two blocks. As he passed a broad avenue, he felt the need to turn right and walk down it. It was a simple emotion, a desire with no reason behind it. That was how the Friends communicated. They didn't use words. They used feelings.

He turned right. Walking and turning, walking and turning, he threaded his way through dark streets and back alleys carrying the tub filled with human remains, never once encountering another person. Within an hour, he found what he was looking for. A group of carts stood parked outside of a livestock yard. One of the carts had a bold red line painted across its left side. The Friends verified that this was what he was looking for by filling him with confidence when he saw it.

He approached and pulled back the cover of the empty cart. His arms had begun to ache as he carried the tub. He was glad to deposit it into the cart. Retrieving his blanket, he moved the specimens contained in the tub into his satchel and looped its strap over his shoulder. He finished by replacing the cart's cover and walking away.

The Takers could be so very clever at times. The owner of the cart never knew why he was dropping it off there. Someone would come tomorrow and take it away, disposing of the bones and leaving the cart where the owner would discover it. They were quiet, efficient. The Rat respected that.

Smirking, he walked through the streets toward his home. The sun was beginning to rise when he arrived. Unlocking the door, he opened the shuttered windows to the street. Early rising workers walked in the street, already beginning their morning tasks. No sleep today, but no matter, he seldom needed any sleep lately, since the Takers became his Friends.

Pulling down a set of tools, he began his morning work. He cut up the cooked samples into small chunks with sharp knives and then used the mortar and pestle to reduce each of them to a paste, adding in different ingredients according to his needs. Then he took out twelve small jars and filled them with the pastes, mixing them with different salts and oils from his workbench. He used an ink quill to write on the side of each jar. When finished, he began cleaning.

It was two hours later when his door opened. A tall young man wearing a dark green traveling cloak walked into his shop. A short sword was belted to his hip.

It was an unusual customer for his shop. Independent healers were becoming rarer, and this man had the look of youth about him. The Rat was suspicious because most people went directly to the temple instead of coming to alchemists, at least since Phyllicitus had returned. The Rat's curiosity was piqued.

The young man walked across the room, looking back and forth, trying to discover if they were alone. The Rat bowed slightly, motioning him forward. The young man moved in a cat-like way, lithe and silent, keeping alert. His long straight red hair stood out as it hung against his light brown shirt. It was finely kept, hinting at a life unused to manual toil.

"What can I help you with today young master?"

The young man shot him a look of disdain. He reached his hand beneath his cloak and pulled out a dark green bag along with a piece of paper the size of his hand. "I've been sent for a pickup. Do you have the order?"

Then the Rat saw it. A silver ring decorated the young man's right hand. A large skull shape extruded from it. He began to panic.

How did the necromancers find him? Why didn't the Friends warn him?

He had a dozen plans set up to escape the city guard, the temple, the priestesses, even the goddess herself if needed. He had nothing prepared for a visit from a White Hand apprentice.

The apprentice continued, annoyed by his surprise and delay. "You are Federick Spate? Alchemist? I believe my master sent you a message regarding this order four days ago?"

Four days ago? That was when the Friends asked him to collect the priest.

Then he felt it. The Takers were calling to him, telling him not to worry, to just give the young man his order. He looked at the paper and quickly memorized its contents. Then he walked into the back room and collected the twelve newly sealed containers. His heart beat fiercely as he walked back into the room. He sat each of them down in front of the apprentice and began to describe their contents. The young man held up a hand, stopping him. Then he transferred the jars into the green bag one at a time, treating them carefully. The Rat stared at him as he packed the jars, committing every one of his features to his own near-perfect memory. Red hair, light freckles, five feet and nine inches in height, slightly nearsighted, the list went on and on.

Before leaving, the apprentice produced a single golden coin and laid it upon his counter. "I do hope this will be our last business arrangement, but if necessary, I want you available. Can you do that?"

It didn't sound like a question, more like a command. The Rat simply stared at the young man until the Takers told him their will. "I'll be here when you need me, you can count on it."

"Good"

The apprentice left without another word. The Rat moved to start packing, to execute his escape plan, but stopped when the Takers calmed him down. In a few minutes, he could think again.

A White Hand Apprentice had come to his shop. Where there was an apprentice, there would be a master, he considered. What will we do with him?

The Rat didn't have a clear plan yet, but he began working on one. First, he would need to discover who the master necromancer was.

A COLD WELCOME

She hated standing in line, and she hated being hungry.

Chamise stood six places behind the lucky person receiving their free meal. Her stomach complained jealously.

No one starved in Home's Hearth, even those that the goddess wasn't very pleased with at the moment. Even if you get exiled, the goddess feeds you. That was her, exiled. Even Eisenvard got fed it seemed, if begrudgingly.

"Next!"

The line moved forward one pace. A rag-covered old man limped past her, carrying his hard-loaf covered with stew. The scent drifted past her nose, triggering her stomach.

Her stomach growled again. She didn't want to admit hunger. She also didn't want to admit pride. She was above all of that, wasn't she?

She had arrived in town the previous day. The horse had managed to get her here faster than she expected. That meant a lot of riding, a small amount of sleep, and no hunting.

She wasn't the hunter though, she was the hunted. She

remembered the White Hand master named Easter, his ornate robes, his black ring, and the dozens of huge dogs that followed him. Miller had told her that White Hand masters could return from death. She had murdered the one named December in the tower—a nasty, despicable man.

She shook her head to dismiss the old Eisenvard thought. Some people just needed to be killed. It was best for all. That thought was straight from her past, taught to her by her father. A few miles from here, it stood carved into the walls of the Eisenvard keep.

Unless Goddess Phyllicitus had burned the building down in the past three years. Anything was possible.

She knew December was going to be returning for her though. From what Miller had told her, he was the sort of man who took things personally.

If he hadn't stabbed Miller, she would have let him live. After December had betrayed them in the tower, she had to do something. So given the lack of a better idea, she killed him.

But December was a necromancer, a death-wizard who knew the way back from the final black door. He would return from the dead, then come for her.

"Next!"

The line moved up again. A young girl passed by her with a basket of muffins and tomatoes. It was more than enough for a single meal. She thought about stopping the little girl, charming her a bit, and asking for a bite. Her pride got the better of her and she stayed in line, steadfast.

She moved forward. As she stepped, she moved her shield closer to her body, out of the way of people passing by. She still wore her boiled leather breastplate. Her heavy mace hung from her dark arming belt. Gloves were tucked into the belt beside the mace. She looked completely out of place in the poor line. She was dressed for battle and it didn't fit in this peaceful town.

She wasn't happy. Her strong face scowled as she stepped forward again. Brushing her shoulder-length blond hair out of her face, she steeled herself for today's indignity.

She regretted not hiding her weapon or finding a place to store her armor. She should have kept low-key and mixed in with the crowd. The war gear made her stand out in this town. Weapons were rare in the populace. The guards carried clubs instead of swords. She felt like a rabid bear in the middle of a litter of kittens.

Miller had said they would be expected, though. This food line wasn't much of a welcome.

She had been greeted by a temple acolyte when she arrived at the temple steps. She told the greeter the simple truth, that she was here with an apprentice wizard, and that she was helping fight the Takers. It only took a few moments before she was rushed into the temple, and found herself in front of Sister Fidelity, a stern middle-aged woman who seemed to be in a rush, and she didn't seem to care about Takers whatsoever.

Sister Fidelity? She thought it was more like Sister turd-face.

Sister Fidelity hadn't wasted any time in her interview. She asked about Miller. Her questions made it sound like she knew him, or at least of him. It got strange when she began asking about Aileen.

Chamise shook her head. She hadn't planned on being questioned for more than a quarter hour just about Miller's Mistress.

"Next"

It was going well until she had been recognized. Sister Fidelity was a little more scornful than she had anticipated. Sister Fidelity remembered the Eisenvard in all their glory. She also remembered the dark coven of necromancers. Eisenvard and White Hand wizards didn't mix well in Home's Hearth, apparently.

Chamise took another step forward toward her meal. There had been no bed or meal at the temple. Now she stood in front of the old priestess giving alms to the poor. The old woman's hands were wrinkled with age and hard work, yet her skin was completely free of spots or blemishes. The goddess blessed everything in Home's Hearth, especially old women.

The priestess scowled at her. All of a sudden, Chamise didn't feel any benevolence coming from the priestess. All she could detect from her was an annoyance.

"The temple sent word ahead. I've been waiting for you. Where have you been?"

"Standing in line."

"Haven't seen an Eisenvard in a long time. Are there any more of you?"

She tried to offer a friendly smile but ended up with a smirk. "There's only one like me, with or without the Eisenvard."

"No need to be cheeky, girl. I haven't been an Eisenvard in a long time. I'm just trying to get a little information."

Chamise swallowed her pride and tried to appear friendly. "I'm not here for any trouble, I'm just hungry."

"Of course, of course. What does the goddess always say? Come to me, I shall feed you and make you my own."

The priestess reached back and picked up a single potato from the long table behind her. It had been stacked together with other healthy delicious food. Oranges, tomatoes, and plumbs stood piled high, available for picking. Chamise was offered just a single twisted old potato, the least appetizing thing there.

With that poor offering, the old priestess made it clear that Chamise wasn't welcome here. It was a slap in the face.

"I remember your kind well," The priestess uttered under her breath.

Chamise waited a moment, not reaching for the food, just focusing her light-blue stare at the elderly priestess, daring her to say anything more. She was exhausted after weeks of running, starving, and fighting to get here. It felt like an insult. She could feel anger rising in her heart along with a strong sense of injustice. This would not stand.

Before she could walk away, her temper had her in its grip. She slapped the potato out of the old priestess's hand. It hit a wall and exploded into a shower of white and brown, covering the priestess' arm, parts of the table, and a few people in line.

Chamise stepped forward, putting her face next to hers. "Apparently, you don't remember us at all."

Then she spun on her heal and walked away. Her gaze forced people aside as she left, daring anyone to stand in her way.

She scolded herself, talking as she walked away. "I knew this would happen, I knew it. I've only been here a single day, and it is all coming back. I shouldn't have come back here, ever."

The path back to Ingalls seemed appealing, but she knew how difficult it would be going it alone. The roads were safer now, but it was never good to travel alone, especially as a young woman. It invited disaster.

She walked through the town, trying to calm down, ignoring her grumbling stomach and healing wounds. The battle at the tower had left a few cuts and bruises on her.

If she left Home's Hearth, Master December would track her down and kill her, probably while he was fresh from the grave. If she stayed, she would have to do something extreme to satisfy the temple, probably give oaths to serve Phyllicitus. When she thought about it deeply, she knew that she would rather walk back to Ingalls than swear oaths. Phyllicitus had already rejected the oaths of Eisenvard. She wouldn't see her as any different than the others.

To the gate with the temple and their oaths.

Looking up, she spotted the city market. It was closing its stalls for the night. A half dozen merchants remained. They were packing up their wares and covering their booths with hanging tarps.

When she was a little girl, she would sneak to the marketplace at night and try to beg sweets from the bakers. The bakers had always been kind, as they were going to use the leftover bread to feed pigs anyway. She headed that way.

Half of the merchant tables in the market stood empty. She moved quickly through the market, weaving between tables and looking for opportunities. A long table held bread trenchers covered with steaming meat, its juices soaking into the hard trencher bread. It smelled wonderful. The stall next to that had beer casks. A crowd of twenty people gathered around the beer table. It looked like this was going to be a popular spot in a short time, and their day was just starting.

She moved on.

She passed by a table of apples. A one-armed man behind the table looked at her oddly, but didn't speak to her, or comment on her warrior attire.

"You willing to trade a few apples? I've got no silver, but I may have something in my pack..."

The man scowled back at her, showing three broken teeth beneath an unkempt beard. "Hard times, eh? New in town?"

"Yes, all of it. I've been hard riding for a week, and now I'm starving. Tried the poor line, but it didn't go well."

Surprisingly, the man nodded back, understanding her dilemma.

"The goddess isn't very welcoming to warriors, eh? Seen that before. Sometimes she likes to give us a cold shoulder until we leave town. She can be kind of unkind in that way."

The man didn't ask for anything, just handed her an apple, then handed her three more.

"Bandits?" he began, unsure if he should pry into her business, but delighted at the prospect of a new story.

"Worse. My father was Eisenvard. I'm getting the extra-cold shoulder."

An unexpected smile shone from his face. "Your father, eh? What was his name? Maybe I'll remember him."

She looked again at the crippled man. He seemed to stand taller now, engaged with their conversation instead of simply waiting for apples to sell. He was tall and gone to fat. He could have been a warrior in his youth, a formidable one. Now he was an older survivor.

Wasn't that the goal? Survival?

"My Father? Sir Torques de Silva. His friends just called him—"

"Silver. You're Silver's girl?"

His grin got even larger. "Don't tell me, let me remember, let me remember…"

He stared at her for the space of ten heartbeats until it came to him.

"Chamy!"

She nodded and gave him a short bow. "At your service."

"It's so good to see you. It's been so long… since… since…"

He stopped talking.

"Since my mother. Since the judgment."

Pausing, he chose his words carefully. "At the time, you know, it all seemed so right. Now I'm old, crippled, and I'm not so sure anymore."

"That's what father told me," She said with anger and pain laced into her voice.

He continued. "It was a shame, a horror really. She shouldn't have died over that, shouldn't have died at all. It broke your father, but I guess you know that."

This conversation wasn't heading where she wanted it to go.

"It helps if I don't think about it. Thanks for the apples."

She turned to go, but the man called out.

"Got a place to sleep?"

"I'll find a place. I'm not in the mood for more poor lines or charity."

"Good words, I agree. How about some advice though?"

"Alright."

"Most of the Eisenvard buildings are gone now. The strong house is still around though. The goddess allows people to play games on the grounds, and the priests store books inside the old keep. It isn't hard to get in, and you won't need to beg for a bed. No one lives there, but a few of us are still around."

Nodding, she looked back at him. "That sounds perfect. Thanks." She didn't like the idea of mixing with the old Eisenvard, but she had little choice right now.

THE TEMPLE

Miller walked up the white marble stairs toward the Temple of Phyllicitus. The entry priest stood on a platform four steps above him. He didn't get halfway there before the priest held up his hand, motioning him to stop.

"Apprentice Miller?"

Miller knew they were expecting him, but this seemed a bit precise. He wondered how long they had been scanning the crowds and checking the gates for his arrival.

"At your service. I'm here to see the high priestess, or Goddess Phyllicitus if she has time."

"I know who you are here to see. I'm sorry, but that isn't possible. The goddess has personally denied your request for an audience. For what it's worth, I am sorry."

The priest seemed familiar. Miller felt like he should know him. It had been three years since he was last here and he couldn't come up with a name to go with the face.

He tried again. He didn't want to be turned away so easily. At the very least, he would have to report back what happened. He didn't want to seem like a complete dolt.

"I'm not here on a lark. Listen, there are Taken out in the countryside. I've been running from them for the last month. How about a little kindness here? Or is the goddess finished with that sort of thing?"

The priest hung his head, none too pleased with blocking Miller's way. Miller could tell that the priest would much rather simply let him in.

"If there were any way I could, I would. But the goddess has already sent word ahead. She isn't interested in seeing anyone from your order, anyone."

"I'm not anyone, I'm just me. I'm not here to represent the order, I'm here as a favor from Aileen." He neglected to name her by title. It turned out not to matter.

"Exactly the problem. Your mistress", he uttered the word with a hint of contempt, "is no longer welcome here. She has chosen her new family and we wish her the best of it. But according to Phyllicitus, we are no longer her family."

Stunned, Miller struggled with what to say, but couldn't find the words. Finally, he settled on, "That's cold."

The priest only nodded his head in soft agreement.

A name emerged into Miller's mind while he looked up at him. "Brother Fannon. Please. I won't beg, but it is very important. Aileen wouldn't have sent me if it wasn't. You know that she still has love for the goddess, and she still holds the temple in high esteem."

Brother Fannon didn't respond immediately. With an indecisive look on his face, he wrung his hands as he thought through all the avenues available to him. Eventually, some form of plan emerged and he made a decision. The grimace on his face showed his uncertainty with his path.

"Please allow me to fetch Sister Fidelity then. Perhaps she can explain. She also has authority to allow you entrance if deemed necessary. Will that do?"

"Oh, well, alright. Can you summon her? I'd like to get checked in and start my work early tomorrow if possible."

"Work? Not sure what you are referring to. I'll let Sister Fidelity explain if you don't mind."

What? Not sure? He thought about the Takers marauding about in the bodies of highway guards, farmers, and who knew what else. Miller wondered what Brother Fannon wasn't sure about. He also wondered why Brother Fannon wasn't inviting him in himself. Something had changed in the last three years. He thought about how slow the bureaucracy was at the temple. With the goddess back, he expected decisions to be made more quickly. Now he felt like he was just standing around, waiting while the bureaucracy worked its way toward its goal line.

Just to test Brother Fannon, Miller took another step. The priest gestured toward him. Miller felt the spirit channels flow. He was preparing some sort of spell, maybe a nasty one. He looked at the stairs and at the temple walls. Enchantments had been expertly overlaid into the stone. The Temple of Phyllicitus was a welcoming place, but only when it chose to be.

Three years ago, this was the only fortress that could hold back the Taken, the White Hand, and the First God of the far north. It didn't look to have gotten any weaker.

"Sorry, didn't mean to offend. I was just trying to judge how serious you are."

"I'm serious," Brother Fannon snapped back.

"I see that. I'll just wait on the benches if that is acceptable."

"See that you do." He asserted coldly.

Miller bowed and retreated down the stairs. He walked ten minutes to the outer lawn and found a bench. Birds flew overhead, moving branch to branch through the garden. White feathers, gold symbols on their wings. He marveled at the birds, they were new to Home's Hearth. He had never seen their species before. He gazed about trying to spot other exotic animals or even just changes within the courtyard.

There was a lot to look at. Twenty statues decorated the perfectly manicured garden. Short grass grew ankle high across the area. Patches of white and yellow flowers flanked the garden, giving the illusion of islands among a green sea.

Eventually, after a full hour on the bench, a priestess emerged from the temple. She stopped to talk with Brother Fannon, then walked down the stairs to join him.

This wasn't looking good, Miller thought, as Brother Fannon turned away and returned to his duties. Miller gazed at the approaching priestess for a long moment, taking in her long straight brown hair, her proud stance. He didn't know her but she had the air of someone used to giving commands.

The priestess had dressed plainly in a standard white temple-dress with a tan apron. Ink stains decorated her hands, betraying a life spent writing. She had an unusual golden broach pinned to her robes. It was shaped like a bird clutching an acorn. The shining gold stood out plainly against the white and tan silks.

He stood patiently and respectfully as she approached. After the affront he had given Brother Fannon, Miller didn't want another. The priestess stopped for a moment to stare closely at his face, at his clothing, at his entire appearance. She didn't waste time with social niceties.

"You're Miller, from the White Hand?"

Her intensity put him on the defensive.

"Ah, I'm Miller." He raised his hand with the apprentice ring on it. The silver shone in the sunlight.

"Last time I was here, no one commented on the order. I was just Miller, and I was just here to help. What happened? I've been away for two years. I haven't been keeping up."

"That's the problem. None of the White Hand have. You helped to solve the Taker problem then did what you always do. You retreated. You left others to clean up your mess."

"I'm sorry. I didn't know that was going to cause a problem. In our defense, no one ever talked about creating a permanent presence in Home's Hearth. The goddess herself would object."

Miller continued. "Our order is, well, we are a lot smaller than you give us credit for. The temple had the ability to do what needed to be done. We didn't. We had the magic and the luck to figure out how to identify the Taken. We eventually got skilled enough so we could recover a few of the Taken. I think the decision our masters made was the right one. It would have been nothing but trouble if we had stayed."

She shook her head slowly back and forth. "I could almost believe that if you hadn't destroyed the Tweed family in the process. You killed the ruling family and burned down their entire keep."

Miller remembered the pit. Takers had infested their castle and infested everyone. He remembered the fear and the dark. He remembered going room to room with only a feeble bit of magic to cut through the inky darkness. Only spellcraft kept him from being swallowed up alive.

He said, "Believe me, nobody enjoyed that. But it needed to be done. I was there. I saw it. It was a nest of Takers, it had to be burned out."

"Phyllicitus believed that we could have saved them. You helped build the cure yourself. Why did you have to kill all of them? Even the children?"

"Aileen had that same conversation with the other masters. She tried to convince them that the family could be saved. She even sent emissaries." Miller paused to remember how those men had narrowly escaped with their lives. "It was bad. There was something there and Mistress Aileen feared it. She said it was worse than just the Takers, it was their den.

"She cried when she made the decision, but she made it nonetheless. The other masters agreed, and that was that."

Her eyes softened as she looked at him. She formed her question as if it was the most important one she had ever asked.

"Any regrets?"

"Yes, I regret all of it. I wish none of it had ever happened."

They passed a minute in silence before Miller tried to change her focus. "These Takers aren't gone. They've just gotten smarter. You know that, right?"

"Yes, we started to suspect that earlier in the year. There have been too many odd occurrences."

"Yet you will not allow me in the door? Won't allow me to help?"

Instead of replying, she stepped forward, then reached down to take his hands in hers. "We know you apprentice. Whether we allow you an audience with Phyllicitus or not, we expect you to be helping in every way possible. I know Aileen personally. Unless something drastic has changed, I suspect she will throw her support in as well."

"But Phyllicitus?"

"It's hard to explain, yet easy at the same time. Phyllicitus is the Goddess of Love. Aileen was sworn to her. She was family. She left, and then never returned. At first, Phyllicitus expected her to visit every few months. As the months went on, she began to understand. Aileen wasn't just leaving to help against the Takers, she was leaving to get away from Phyllicitus. Aileen had fully converted to your order, and that hurt the goddess more than you can know."

Miller tried to hide his surprise. A goddess is throwing a tantrum? Now?

"Don't the Takers have priority over hurt feelings?"

"You are thinking about this wrong. I ask you this—how can a goddess of love, not love? Can you imagine a deeper pain for her than to be ignored, to be cast aside by those who once loved her?"

"I don't generally think about a true goddess getting hurt like that. I always imagine it has to be some world-changing event to do that."

"No, Phyllicitus is fine with earth-shattering events, it is the heart-shattering ones she has trouble with."

Miller let go of her hands but didn't walk away.

"I just spent a month on the road to get here. I've been fighting Taken the whole way. I ran into a company of bandits that had been completely infected. All of this happened while the temple was supposed to be watching. I'm telling you, things are going wrong. The Takers are preparing to return. We need to get organized and stop with all the drama. I need your libraries. I need your crafters. I need the same support I had last time, only more of it."

She pointed her index finger back at him. "And I need you to gather your order's strength and do some work on your side. Learn what these things are, and how we can stop them again. Get us some protection, some method of discovering them. And above all, get Aileen to come here and fix this whole thing. She is the one who planted this weed in our garden, she needs to be the one to pluck it out."

He thought for a moment. How was he supposed to do that? He had no idea.

He nodded back to her. "I will talk to her. I don't have much influence, but I think if she hears it from me then she might come."

"She needed to come back to the temple a year ago. The temple won't be much use to you until Phyllicitus is appeased. We can't offer you help or shelter, but we don't have to exile you from Home's Hearth either. Meet with Aileen and tell her what we need."

"I can do that. I do need some help though. I have a young woman in my care who has been taken. We've got her sitting inside a magic circle now. It seems to be working. I need a place to protect her though, one without a lot of necromancers skulking around. Can I at least use your crafting hall?"

Her eyes widened in shock.

"You mean you have an experiment subject? Keep your twisted White Hand projects out of our city. She is in your care, so she is your responsibility. Keep her out of our city, and while you are at it, take that horse of yours with you. You don't get to use the goddess for free stabling."

"Wait, you have my horse?"

WHAT TO DO ABOUT BRITA

The long hall lay empty. Most of its contents had been moved out. Its tables, benches, and chairs had been recently gathered onto the grassy yard. A small table had been kept in the room to serve as a writing desk. Just this one serving table and its 8 chairs remained from the original furniture. Outside, set on top of the growing lawn, the remaining six great tables and more than sixty chairs sat abandoned with grass growing beneath them. Thick sheets of brown canvas covered the furnishings haphazardly, as though preserving the wealth of this old hall had been an afterthought. A great chair, taller than a man, lay discarded on its side. Grass grew high around it, hiding most of its glorious carvings.

Replacing the furnishings, a dozen trunks and three empty buckets stood at the far end of the hall. A pile of blankets lay strewn on the floor.

Miller pushed open the thick door to the hall. The iron hinges complained loudly as they had not been maintained for years. An armed guard stepped in front of him, crossbow drawn, pointing at his heart.

"It's just me Cerna," Miller said, holding his hands open, letting the guard see that he was unarmed.

Cerna nodded and motioned him into the hall. As Miller stepped forward, the sound of his steps created echoes on the bare wood floor. The remote sound of sobbing greeted his ears. He stopped after a dozen steps, just before crossing the white circle painted onto the floor.

"How long has she been like this?"

"She's been crying for an hour. The crying is better than the screaming. She kept being loud, making crazy sounds, begging. She wanted something, but I couldn't tell what."

"You wrote it down?" Miller said, gesturing at a small table with a single ledger on its surface.

"It didn't make sense. No use."

Miller turned to face the tall man, shaking his head back and forth. Cerna towered over him by at least a hand span. His gut had grown since the days he had ridden with raiding armies along the border passes before Phyllicitus returned from the places between, but he was still dangerous.

There aren't many people that the Eisenvard would reject because they were too violent. Miller guessed that made him highly recommended to the White Hand.

"You understand what we are doing here right?" Miller gestured to the sobbing young woman sitting on the bare floor, her arms hugging her legs in desperation. "This woman has been taken, she is possessed by something we don't understand. It's up to us to figure out how this happened, and hopefully, to discover a way to stop it from happening to others."

Cerna grimaced back at him. "No, it's up to you. My task is to make sure that if she leaves the circle, she dies. If anyone comes to visit her or try to grab her, they die too. That is my only job."

Frustration welled up inside of Miller. "I did ask Master Easter for someone who could write. You can write, can't you?"

"Sure, but I'm not anyone's secretary. Write your own notes, schoolboy," Cerna growled, "or hire a scribe to sit with me. I've got a bigger job than that." He laid his hand on the hilt of his curved sword. The thing was impressive. The blade began at the hilt and grew in thickness as it traveled toward the floor. The sword was formed into a curve designed to easily cut meat into smaller pieces, especially meat that just happened to have two legs. Two small cloth charms hung from the black leather handle. It was a heavy thing, yet designed for speed.

Miller wanted nothing to do with it. He stepped back. "Look, I'm not trying to be difficult, but we are doing something to save lives."

"I already have a life-saving job. If that woman gets out, I am going to save everyone's life by chopping her head off. And oh yeah, there will be a lot of blood, and if the blood gets beyond my clothing then Master Easter will end my life. Stop wagging your tongue like you are in charge. You had better remember your place, apprentice. I can kill you on the spot and none of your masters would care."

That sounded like the kind of orders that Easter would give. Guard the woman at all costs unless she tries to escape, then minimize the damage. Cerna would be little if any help. Miller returned his hands to the open position, raising them, trying to show no threat to the man.

Cerna spat words at him before he turned away. "That's right. Keep walking. If you give me any more problems, I'll let you talk to Easter about it, after he digs you up from the three graves you will be buried in."

Where did Easter find this maniac?

Instead of pursuing the conversation, he turned toward the woman. Her sobbing had stopped, and she looked up from her place on the floor. Miller smiled warmly at her, then gazed down to inspect the large white circle painted on the wooden floor. Two concentric circles lay upon the floor. One containing the other. A series of 14 binding runes occupied the gap between the circles.

Miller paused to take in the scene, opening his channels and feeling for the flow of magic. It was strong in the circles. Strong currents of magic flowed between the circles, enough to keep any spell out. It might even be strong enough to seal her away from the Takers. But Cerna had said that she was screaming.

Brita sat at the center point watching him, tears streaking her face and blouse. Her voice was broken with sadness when she spoke. "Did you see her?"

He could only shake his head. "It didn't go well."

"But you said that your master could get you in."

He showed her a rueful grin. "I did get in, then I was escorted out. So much for the word of a White Hand master, eh? Who knew?"

Who knew indeed? Aileen should have gotten him an audience. Nothing even close to that happened. Aileen had been a priestess of Phyllicitus for years before Easter convinced her to join the White Hand.

Brita crept toward him, her lovely straight black hair reached down to the floor. Brita's lips were dark red. Her green eyes watched him as she looked up. Her ample bosom threatening to pour from the white blouse. "You said that you could save me."

The image captivated him for a moment. She was enticing and beautiful. His heart yearned to help her.

She was also taken. Something lived inside of her, issuing orders, listening to their secrets.

"We haven't even started, so you don't get to give up. Master Easter will be here soon enough, and things will happen."

Her eyes rolled up in their sockets.

"Here we go again," Cerna announced, a hint of mockery in his voice.

Miller scrambled over to the small table. She had already begun speaking nonsense before he could get ink on the quill.

"You don't understand! Sideways! Sideways!" She grabbed her head with both hands. "It feels like I'm not on the floor! Oh Goddess, where am I? Why won't you come get me? Oh! The leaves! Don't touch them!"

"See, crazy as a soup sandwich."

Miller didn't look up from the ledger when he replied to Cerna's slight. The image of awoken plants came to his mind. Miller remembered how they danced within the cracks between the worlds. Shuddering, he snapped back. "Crazy, maybe. Or maybe she can just see things we can't."

###

Someone knocked on the door.

Cerna picked up the crossbow and removed the retaining pin, transforming a piece of inert metal and wood into a killing machine. He walked to the door and peered out a small spy-hole next to it. Satisfied, he opened the door and pointed the crossbow down at the floor, well away from the man entering.

Miller turned to face Master Easter as he arrived. Easter's skin had tanned since Miller had seen him last. Small wrinkles had appeared near the corners of his eyes. He walked into the room slowly, as if careful not to accidentally slip and fall. His cheeks inflated, then deflated as he entered, as if entering was some kind of finish line he had been racing toward for weeks.

Easter was tired and travel-worn. Miller looked at him closely. He looked like he had not rested in days. Easter's silken red cloak and brown fine leather pants seemed to survive the journey with little impact though. Even his white shirt and the dozen brass buttons along his pants bore little evidence of mud or even grass stains.

His face seemed to carry the marks. Fatigue dimmed his eyes and new wrinkles decorated his face.

The leader of his mistress's cabal had just arrived to visit with an apprentice. All Miller could think about was how lucky Easter's apprentices must be without all of the laundry duties to occupy their time. Once Aileen had started wearing those nice jet-black dresses, his laundry duties reduced as well. She preferred hands with more laundry skills than his. All it took was ruining one expensive dress to end the personal early-morning sessions where she lectured as he scrubbed. At least, he considered, she never made him wash the undergarments.

Two large mastiffs entered the room behind Master Easter. Cerna tensed, unsure why the dogs were there, in the long hall. Even Brita, from her nest in the center of the protective circles, looked up in alarm.

"How is our guest? Are we attending to her well?" Easter began.

Reading the unspoken message from Cerna's silence, Miller replied, "Well enough. She may require some, well, improvements though." He continued on when Easter didn't reply. "Being a woman, well, the bucket is difficult."

"Yes, of course. I'll leave that issue in your capable hands."

He walked over to the table and began leafing through the journal. "Interesting. Maybe not useful, but interesting."

"It is early."

"Yes, it is early yet. More things will follow. Speaking of that, how are your supplies?"

Cerna spoke up quickly, enumerating the number of hams, bottles of beer, and baskets of fruits he had stored. The supplies would last four people a month, a week if one of those dogs stayed with them.

Easter gazed over at Miller. "I see some gaps in the journal. What happened?"

Miller was startled out of his daydreaming. Cerna had plainly not kept up with the journal as he had asked. For a moment, Miller thought about casting blame on Cerna but dismissed the idea. If he did that, then they would be at each other's throats the whole time they spent together. Cerna was likely to cut his throat while he slept if he tarnished his reputation with Easter.

"As I said, Master Easter, we are just getting started. I do advise getting a full-time scribe for this duty. While Cerna is here the entire time, the pens are not easily reached when she begins her bouts. Cerna's passion for the blade, I fear, may not translate to the quill."

Easter shook his head in silent frustration as if he had expected this result. "Don't worry about that. I'm assuming we will be moving into the temple soon enough. Did everything turn out well with Phyllicitus? Any issues?"

Miller gritted he teeth and prepared for the worst when he replied. "Other than Phyllicitus rejecting any notion of us working together, no."

Easter looked stunned. "What?"

"She is upset with my mistress. I gather she had been expecting a visit for some time and didn't get one."

Easter's eyes grew wider. "Are you kidding me? We have Takers moving through the community, changing their ways and building their plans, and we have no way to stop them. She is upset that she didn't get a special visit from her favorite pupil?"

Miller could only shrug. "I have no idea how a goddess thinks."

Cerna could not resist putting a barb in. "That's why you're still an apprentice, boy."

Easter's gaze fell on Cerna and ended his glib remarks. "We don't have time for this."

"I know. But what would you have me do? I managed to speak to Sister Fidelity. She sympathized but couldn't do much."

Easter didn't reply. After a few moments of silence, the two dogs left his side and began moving across the room, smelling, exploring. They were upset and looking for something to do, some target for their sharp-toothed attentions.

Miller thought about the dogs. He wondered if their anxious moods were coming from their master. That led to questions about how the dogs were linked to Easter. They seemed to know his moods and his will without any trouble. He considered opening channels and looking for the signs of spellcrafting. But if Master Easter took offense to his inquisitiveness, it might go badly for him. He set the idea aside.

Easter began moving toward the circle, stopping within an arm's reach, and looked over at Brita as she rose from the floor.

"And you? How are you enduring?"

She stood, then curtsied, as if she were preparing to dance. "Pain hasn't started yet, but will on the morn. I like your puppies. They remind me of barns."

"Barns?" Easter cocked an eyebrow in confusion.

She began hopping up and down, counting forward and backward across all the numbers she knew. It only took thirty hops.

Miller moved to the journal and began writing.

Exhaling, Master Easter made a decision.

"We need the temple. We might as well kill this girl right now if we don't get their help."

"What? No," Miller began, unsure how to convince Easter otherwise.

Cerna reached for his sword hilt, sad eyes looking toward her as if to apologize before cutting her down. Easter held up his hand. "Not yet. This is Aileen's mess, she needs to clean it up."

Easter walked toward the door. "Stay here for now. I'm going to bring back the right people to fix this."

Miller began to bow. By the time he had looked up, Easter was gone. All Miller saw was his two dogs following him out the door.

Cerna shut the door and looked back toward him, adjusting his metal open-faced helmet and brushing his graying brown hair out of his face.

"I'd say that went well." Cerna grasped his sword hilt. "It's always good when blood doesn't have to be spilled."

Miller's eyes grew wide as he thought about how close they had come to outright murder. Murder for no point whatsoever.

"Indeed."

Miller stared into Cerna's face. Small beads of sweat had emerged from his forehead. Cerna was worried. Perhaps, Miller thought, he wasn't such a heartless brigand after all.

A MISSING HORSE

Miller lifted up the metal bucket. He had no idea where the masters had found it. It was dark, bent in three places, and looked like it had been used as a target for catapult practice.

One of the dents was clearly a boot print. Someone had mistreated this poor bucket. It was time someone put it to good use, Miller thought.

He looked over at Brita. She was surrounded by a quickly drawn magic circle. Glyphs and symbols lay etched on the floor, chalk dust smearing pathways where the ritual was rushed.

They were a just a few hours' journey from Home's Hearth, far enough to be away from the crowds and bustle of normal life. Master Easter continued to worry about the Takers though. It was as if he expected Takers to jump out and attack at any moment.

Miller thought about another of Easter's pieces of wisdom. He claimed that it wasn't paranoia if they really were out to get you. That seemed to apply to the entire Order of the White Hand, regardless of the Takers.

Brita would need a bath soon. She had been riding with the Taken for weeks and it showed. The smell of horse dung and campfires hung from her.

Miller breathed in deeply, trying to recover from the earlier drama. Fresh air filled his lungs. Though Home's Hearth was fairly clean as towns go, there was no replacement for country air. This inn had been a lucky find. He walked around the inn, searching for the calm pool of water behind it. A horse corral was there, four horses stood in the corral.

He stopped. His horse wasn't among them.

He remembered bringing the mare into the corral and leaving her with the other horses. He had told the stable boy to watch his horse and to find him if anything happened.

The stable boy was gone and so was his mare.

A rare profanity escaped his lips. It seemed appropriate given his challenge.

Walking around the corral, he looked for tracks. He knew that there was little chance that he could track anything—he had little skill at tracking, but he didn't have any other ideas. There were hundreds of tracks from a dozen horses, all laid since the last rain.

Miller stopped to stare at the mess. Nothing he knew could unravel this. There were too many tracks, too much information. He recognized defeat when he saw it.

Out of desperation, he began to call out.

"Stable boy! Stable boy!"

A few moments later, a young girl rushed out from within the inn. The girl appeared to be no more than twelve years old. She wore an apron stained with the remains of a hundred meals. Her long auburn hair hung past her shoulders in twin braids.

"He's gone to the front fields. Can I help you?"

"Where's my horse? She's a mare, brown mane with a white spot on her head."

"Oh, that horse."

The girl began fidgeting, wringing her hands together nervously.

"Yes, that horse. Where is it?" A hint of anger was starting to creep into his voice. She took a step back.

"Your horse is fine, sir. Dorton, he's the stable boy, see, my brother, he's off to fetch her."

"Why isn't she here?" Miller spread his hands to accentuate the point. "This is where I left her. I told Dorton, or whatever his name is, to come find me if anything happened."

"Well sir, um, nothing kind of happened."

"Kind of? Where's my horse?"

The girl looked up at him. Her brown eyes were fearful as if sensing trouble. After a few moments thought, the girl arrived at a plan.

"It's hard to describe. I'll show you. Follow me, please."

The girl led him past the corner of the inn. A wide field lay there, sunlight glinting off the long grass. It could have been a wheat field, but only grass grew there, undisturbed by farmer or plow.

It would take a half-hour to walk across it. A thin line of elm trees stood on its opposite side, breaking the field into portions.

He saw the mare on the far side of the field, just a few steps from the tree line. The stable boy, a ten-year-old with hair as hazel as his sister's, stood there trying to work the horse. He struggled with a bridle, trying to force it on. The mare would have none of it. Somehow the mare had ended up in a perfectly good grazing area and she would not be moved, thank you.

"You've got to be kidding me. You let her out?"

The girl quickly denied the charge. "Oh no, sir. We wouldn't do that. She must have jumped the fence."

"Jumped the fence?" Miller thought about it. The fence stood as high as his shoulders. There wasn't enough room in the corral to build up speed to make such a jump, even if it tried to run the inner perimeter first.

But this mare was a different kind of horse. He was getting accustomed to unusual behavior from it. It was smarter than any other horse he had ever known. Somehow, it seemed like the horse understood any situation and chose to be on his side.

The girl continued, assuming Miller didn't believe her. "I know. It would be amazing, but I think she jumped it. We left her in the corral to drink from the pond. When we came out to check on her, she was in the field. Dorton ran off to get her but she got spooked, I think. He's been trying to catch her since we started cooking about an hour ago."

He thought about the young boy out there in the field. The mare towered over him. The boy would grab her neck and attempt to force the head harness on her. She would wait until it was almost fastened upon her head, then shake her head vigorously, releasing her from the harness and knocking the poor boy to the ground.

"She's very difficult to handle. It's not Dorton's fault."

Miller nodded. He could see what was happening. The mare was toying with the boy, playing with him. She must be bored.

"She isn't difficult. She's just bored. I'll go talk to her."

He set off across the field. The young girl followed behind.

"Please don't be cross with Dorton. He didn't lose your horse."

"I'm not upset with Dorton because he's out with her in the field, I'm upset because he didn't come to get me." They continued walking through the grass leaving a trail of trampled stalks behind them. The girl didn't respond. She knew that he was right.

Dorton saw them coming. He stayed by the mare's side waiting for them.

Thoughts of the horse filled Miller's mind as he approached. They had been through a lot together. She had saved his life on more than one occasion. She was the fastest horse he had ever ridden, and the smartest.

Past conversations about the First Gods bubbled up from his memories. He fondly recalled Aileen teaching some of the finer points of the Raven God. It was more than a supernatural bird, it was the personification of justice, of wrath. Those tales were not pleasant. Aileen had spent two years in Jarlsland fighting against border raiders back when the wars flared. The raiders turned out to be worshipers of a First God, some incarnation of a reindeer. He had chuckled at the idea of a war against a supernatural reindeer. So had Mistress Aileen at first. What she hadn't counted on was that it wasn't just a god of a reindeer, it was a god that possessed the power of winter itself. To make matters worse, the reindeer god had some kind of shaman who followed it and raised an army of Northerners to raid into Home's Hearth. The shaman could summon winter spirits, trolls, and ice magics as well. The city had barely survived their attack against Home's Hearth. Hundreds of people had died. Even today, Mistress Aileen would hesitate to battle that reindeer god.

And the reindeer god didn't die. It was an embodiment of nature. Somehow, for some reason, it had accomplished its goals and simply left.

Takers had moved into the lands surrounding Home's Hearth just a year after that. He remembered when the White Hand had sent him to Home's Hearth. The order wanted to find a way to detect the taken people. It turned out to be simple. Somehow the Takers could be disrupted with farming spells. Spells that guarded crops against insects could render a taken person completely confused. They would meander about without any direction, lost in whatever dark place their mind had been taken to. Eventually, a taken person would fall to the ground, clutching themselves in pain until the spasms passed. Sometimes, albeit rarely, the taken victims would permanently recover. A strange cocktail of potions to fortify the mind, and farming spells to chase out the Takers had worked, at least for a few years.

Now the taken people had changed. The Takers had found a way to counter the mental potions and farming spells. It had been easy to discover who had been taken. Now just a few years later, it was impossible again. That meant that any person, at any moment, could be an enemy. Brothers could turn against you. Parents would kill their children in their beds. Miller needed to find some new way to detect the taken and to defend against them. Three years ago, it was mere luck that had yielded a solution. He had no idea where to even start his search now.

Three years ago at the end of those times, the Takers were blunted by a combination of White Hand magics and Eisenvard swords. The White Hand culled hundreds from the population, deciding who lived and who died. The Eisenvard went into villages, burning anyone who they even suspected of being taken—no trial, no spell, just fire.

Phyllicitus had returned shortly after that. The Takers had retreated. Phyllicitus returned just in time to put Home's Hearth back together.

And now, three years later, he was standing in a field about to beg a horse to stop toying with the help. Miller shook his head at the humor in it.

Dorton stood still, waiting on him, his faced screwed up in concern. The mare had stopped her game and stood quietly as well. Dorton saw an opportunity and started to approach the horse. The mare shook her head back and forth and turned away.

"Don't bother. She's toying with you. Haven't you figured it out yet?"

"You're a bad horse," the boy called out in frustration.

"You're the one who let her out. It serves you right."

"I didn't let 'er out. She jumped the fence."

Miller looked back toward the corral. The other horses moved around within its confines. The fence nearly to their heads.

"Look at that," Miller said as he pointed to the corral. "How could she jump that?"

The iron logic of the ten-year-old clicked into operation. "I don't know, but it did. Bad horse!"

Miller shook his head in weary resignation. "You've got to be joking."

Then he turned to the horse. It stared at his face as if daring him to take the boy's side. He reached out toward the boy and motioned for him to hand over the bridle.

The mare turned aside and clopped away, putting thirty paces between them. It seemed content with the current arrangement. There would be no corral tonight.

"Have it your way," Miller said as he turned away. He carried the bridal with him. If the mare didn't want it then it wasn't going to happen, no matter how hard he tried. Some battles, he reflected, just weren't worth fighting.

A MOLE

The Rat awoke on a gray morning. A soft rain fell outside, coating Home's Hearth with a thin layer of clean water. He felt the Friends trying to communicate with him—the pushed feelings of urgency. They wanted him to react but he had no idea what they needed.

Neither did they. That frightened the Rat. He had grown dependent on their directions, following them no matter the path. He heard their thoughts, jumbled with a hint of panic.

There weren't many things that would cause the Friends such distress. He thought of the options and came up with two.

The Temple of Phyllicitus may have discovered his experiments. His work converting priests to Taken went on making progress every day. Experiments should begin soon. If the temple discovered his activities, it would become difficult to acquire another test subject.

Or it might be necromancers. The Order of the White Hand, reviled by all, had a habit of showing up uninvited. Home's Hearth provided a unique advantage to the Friends. The goddess didn't have a very good relationship with them. Somehow, she felt that the exploitation of the dead wasn't in keeping with her principles.

He hoped to find a way to drive a wedge further between the goddess and the White Hand. If he could take a priest, then he could extend his influence into the temple.

An electric jolt shot through his spine. The Friends weren't interested in his politics. They wanted Phyllicitus. They thought they could take her and bring her into the family. The Friends, those disembodied voices, could then help her as well.

The Rat harbored some doubt. He tried to commune with the Friends. He needed to explain that the powers of a goddess were unique and lay outside the understanding of mankind. But these were not humans. They didn't seem to care. If anything, that just made them want her more.

He heard the shop door push open. Someone wearing wood-soled boots stomped into his entryway below. It was early for customers, but not so early as to be worrisome. He pulled a woolen tunic over his linen shirt, protecting himself from the morning's chill.

The Rat combed his hair quickly and left the room. A short hallway lay outside his door. He called out to the customer.

"One moment. One moment."

He heard a familiar voice call back from below.

"Rise and shine alchemist. I've business for you today."

It was the visitor, the one with long red hair who collected his unusual ingredients. He hadn't received any communication from the Friends regarding an impending visit. Whatever caused their distress had evidently caused them to miss an appointment. The Friends could be distracted like everyone else. The day wouldn't be a complete waste. He learned something new already.

He walked down the stairs at a leisurely pace, not wanting to alarm his visitor. The young man stood near his bench of ingredients, inspecting the labels of each as if he were in a common store. Only the temple bought ingredients anymore.

There was no point to having a display.

The Rat kept his display of ingredients visible in the window though. He wanted his neighbors to remember who he was, and what he traded in. It was amazing the types of things people would turn a blind eye to if they thought you were an alchemist or a spellcrafter, he reflected. Common folk had little appetite to involve themselves with such matters.

"Strange. I didn't get an order from you," the Rat said as his feet left the stairs. The red-haired apprentice scowled at him impatiently, as if bothered to be dealing with lesser folk.

"I'm here right now, aren't I?"

"Yes, and that is unusual in itself. What can I help you with?"

"I need to ask you a few questions about the last delivery."

"Hmmm. I seem to recall that our deal was not to ask questions."

"Not those types of questions. Pay attention, churl," he said haughtily, showing his silver apprentice ring as he spoke. This apprentice was accustomed to a certain level of fear. The Rat didn't feel it.

"Your business then?" The Rat said, his patience beginning to wear thin.

"I'm to ask you about the status of your work, and whether the elixir has been completed."

His eyebrows raised up, showing surprise.

"The elixir? What has he told of that?" It could be a bad sign if the master was talking about his project. It would not do.

"He said that you were brewing an elixir, one that would help our channeling. And if it were ready, I was to bring it to him."

Now the Rat really was surprised. The elixir had nothing to do with magical channeling. It was a formula that, if completed, would allow the Friends into the bloodstream of protected people. One drink of that and a priest would become vulnerable, perhaps even a necromancer.

"And what was your master planning on doing with such a thing? It's highly experimental, unproven, and perhaps even poisonous."

"That isn't your concern. Your concern is to give it to me. I will deliver it to my master. He told me that the price you asked would be met."

"Indeed?" The Rat didn't have any idea who this master was, but they seemed to know a lot about his business.

"Indeed. Now quit stalling and fetch it for me."

"Very well. It will be a few moments to bottle it."

The Rat turned into his workroom, out of view of his young red-haired visitor. Passing a meticulously clean workbench and a stack of metal boxes, he went to the back door. He slowly opened the door, trying to be quiet, then walked out. His alchemy tower stood outside, a wooden four-story structure used for burning the most noxious substances. He ignored the tower and walked out the back gate onto a small road.

Two children sat across the road. A young boy with a protruding belly held a knife and a piece of wood. Shavings decorated the ground beneath him as he carefully tried to carve the wood. His sister, standing beside him in a red dress, looked up in alarm as if they had been caught breaking some sort of rule.

"You two are awfully young to be playing with your father's tools," the Rat said, even though he had seen them here many times, trying to build toys or carve animals for sale in the market. Their father was a master craftsman and his carvings were sought after in the market. These two were always trying to make a few coins when their father couldn't see it.

The boy screwed up his face in mock fury. "Bugger off, you old brewer."

"Yeah. Bugger off," the sister added.

"Oh, sorry. I thought you two would be interested in a few silver coins this morning." The Rat held out his hand. Three silver coins, each larger than his thumb tip, lay there.

"Hey now. What's this?" the boy said.

The sister's face had transformed. Her eyes grew wide. Her mouth opened wide.

"It will require some bravery though. I've got a young man in my shop now. He's some kind of apprentice. I need to know who his master is. I'll give you these three coins if you follow him and see where he stays. If you discover who he works for there will be three more coins for you."

That was more money than they would earn in half a year. It didn't take them long to decide.

"Sneaking and spying? Easy. We'll do it."

The Rat smiled. He held his hand out toward the children. The young girl walked up and picked the coins out of his hand one at a time, weighing each one before she tucked it into her pouch.

"He will be coming out of my shop through the front in only a few minutes. Get ready. Don't be seen."

The boy dashed off. His sister ran close behind him. The Rat grinned at their retreating forms, wondering if the children would survive this ordeal. If that apprentice served who he suspected, those children would be earning that silver.

He shook his head, thinking about whether Phyllicitus's power could preserve them. He considered how her power was so easily taken advantage of to serve his own ends. This would not be the first time.

But if that apprentice served White Hand necromancers, everything was about to change.

He turned back through the gate and closed it. Then he stopped at the base of his alchemy tower. Fetching a ring of keys, he inserted the largest into an iron lock and turned. The lock opened, dropping and pulling the attached chain with it. He opened the door and walked in.

Closing the door, he took three steps to the center of the room. A staircase led upward, but he ignored it. Instead, he bent down and pried a floorboard up. He knew the perfect place to touch it so it opened easily. The newly opened gap exposed a two-foot deep enclosure. A metal rack of potions stood there. Eight braces held potions on the holder. Two of the potions were his final best work. The magic didn't function yet, but soon his experiments would lead him to success, he could feel it. Another two of the potions were his earliest attempt. They resulted in little more than questions and failed experiments. He reached down and took one of his earlier attempts.

He thought about what would happen to any fool stupid enough to try it. Perhaps it wasn't a death sentence, but they might wish it was. For a moment the Rat considered giving the young apprentice one of his more mature potions. A grin spread on his face. He put the earlier potion aside and replaced the floorboard before he picked the portion back up again. With the flawed potion in hand, he left the tower, relocked the chain that held the door closed, and returned to his shop.

Another customer had entered the shop since he had left. She wore a temple robe. He recognized her as one of the healers in the temple.

"Here you go, sir. I had one left."

The apprentice smiled back, aware of the ruse. If this priestess knew what the Rat was giving him, they were already doomed. He held out the metal tube, wax seal toward him.

Then the Rat turned away from the apprentice as he walked out of the door. He smiled at the priestess.

"Now how can I help you this morning?"

Frantz walked out of the Rat's shop, potion in hand. He smiled, happy at his luck today. Master Darjeeling had told him of the secret work that the alchemist toiled at. A potion that could increase his ability to channel flows would be a treasure. With his master's trial approaching, it would be invaluable. Even though an apprentice never knew when the trial would come, Master Darjeeling had told him that his Frantz's time would be soon.

Turning right, onto the broad avenue, he walked quickly back toward where Master Darjeeling awaited his return. Only four other people walked the street this early, intent on their morning business. He walked briskly, eager to make his report and finish with this business. The vial in his right hand would give him the power to easily pass his trial and achieve his master's ring.

A sound caught his attention. Rapid footsteps moved over cobbled streets. Someone was in a hurry. Frantz slowed his walk, trying to hear better. He didn't want to be distracted by his own footsteps. After a dozen paces, he heard it again. It sounded like someone had dashed across the street, just a few blocks behind.

It could be local townsfolk hurrying to complete their morning's business. But it might be something else entirely. He needed to be sure. Turning left at the next corner, he gazed about, looking for somewhere to hide. It didn't take long. A fenced yard stood just past the corner. A wooden fence four feet high stood decorated with roses, obscuring the house behind it. A gate stood closed facing the road. It had been locked with a simple bolt from the interior of the garden. He gazed through the gaps in the fence, searching for the bolt. It only took a moment to find it, open an elemental channel, and pull the bolt free with his flows. He opened the gate and stepped in, then closed it behind him. He ducked down to gaze through the slats.

A young boy ran to the entrance of the street. He stopped, gazing down the street in search of some prey. A moment later a young girl joined him, breathing hard with her exertions.

Frantz grew interested. It was innocent enough, two young children playing in the streets of Home's Hearth. There were no coincidences though. The boy gestured onward, farther along the street. They sprinted off down the street, in search of their quarry, leaving an empty street behind.

Frantz opened the gate and stepped out. The two children didn't notice the apprentice necromancer channeling dark powers behind them. The young boy began to slow, his breathing grew heavy.

"Hurry up!" his sister shouted.

"Go ahead. I'm not feeling so good." The young boy

stopped, then grabbed his stomach in both hands. "I feel like I've got to chuck."

She didn't like the look of her brother. Gar had grown pale. Sometimes dire premonitions would strike her as they did this time. Mostly they were like fleeting daydreams, gut hunches that amounted to nothing. Here in the goddess's city, there was little that could hurt her, or so she believed. The fever of the chase kept her in its embrace. She decided to continue the chase and ignore her irrational fears.

"Come on Gar! Don't be a loser!" his sister teased, then ran down the street without looking back, unaware of whose mercy she had left her brother to.

The young boy leaned over. With a squelch of pain, he began vomiting. His hands went down to touch the street, to hold himself up. Frantz continued the spell, driving sickness into the young boy's guts. His body rejected the sickness by jettisoning all his stomach's contents.

The boy grew weaker though, as if his very life's strength faded away.

Frantz smiled at the young boy's predicament. Every heave of the boy's stomach resulted in a fresh splash of vomit, and a thimble full of the boy's life force being transferred to Frantz. It wasn't a large portion, Home's Hearth made spells such as these difficult to cast, but it was enough to re-invigorate him after an early morning. Before he broke contact, he took a moment to memorize the boy's aura. He was curious if the boy was under any influence beyond stupidity. Frantz could guess who had put the boy on his trail. Perhaps, he thought, turnabout would be fair play in the near future.

Another moment, another sip. The seconds passed by and Frantz grew a bit stronger. The steady drip of life-force filled him with energy. He got lost in the experience. The flow ended soon enough, leaving nothing behind. Shrugging with disappointment, Frantz turned and walked away.

The body grew still as the boy's breathing ended. A few moments later, the sound of shoes pounding on the street filled the air. The sister bolted from around the corner, breathing hard. She saw the boy laying in the road.

"Gar?" She called out.

Gar didn't answer. The young boy was passing beyond the final black door into the beyond. Only a few moments of life remained.

She sprinted to his side, bending over to push him. He didn't move.

"Gar?" The girl's voice became a plea. "Answer me. Get up. Get up."

She pushed his body again. He didn't respond.

She began to call out to the empty street.

"Help!"

A few moments passed with no response.

"Help!" she yelled again, louder.

She didn't wait long, Gar needed help immediately. She began to scream at the top of her lungs.

A door opened as a woman walked from behind a gate, covered in roses.

"What's happening?"

"My brother, he needs help!"

The woman dashed up to them, scooping up the boy into her arms. She didn't pause as vomit and blood smeared across her arms. "Come with me, girl!" She turned to walk briskly down the street heading toward the temple.

"Help! Please help us!" The woman called out at the top of her lungs. Three more people arrived to help. They helped her move Gar out of the street and toward the temple. Within ten minutes they were entering the temple, carrying the boy's dead body.

Sister Fidelity wrapped her arms around the girl, holding her tightly. She had sobbed for fifteen minutes, unrelenting, and then had finally calmed down as she moved from the horror of her brother's death to absolute denial of it. She shook in frustration and grief. Sister Fidelity kept her in the close embrace, whispering into her ear.

The sister asked gently, "What's your name, dear?"

"Hurriet."

"I've got you, Hurriet. Don't worry. I've got you."

"Gar" was all Hurriet could say. Her voice sounded far away, as if she still could not believe what had happened.

The great door opened. Sister Mercy walked into the room, a page of parchment dangling from her hand. Sister Mercy waved it in the air to dry the fresh ink as she approached. Sister Fidelity didn't want to release Hurriet yet. There was too much healing to do, but this visit was important.

"Sister."

Sister Mercy replied, "I have what you asked for." Four short years ago Sister Mercy had been sent to learn the arcane. Healing crafts and spirit bindings were not the only magic that the temple spellcrafters practice. There were other terrors in the world. They prepared to face them all.

She held up the paper so Fidelity could see. Five magical symbols decorated its surface. A bold red circle had been drawn around one of them. It was the symbol of death, of plague, of necromancy.

A chill went up Sister Fidelity's spine. Sister Mercy was an expert at discovering the telltale signs of magic. Spells and rituals could leave signs behind if one knew where to look.

"There is no doubt?"

"No. The signs are all there. It wasn't even hidden very well. Whoever did this didn't care if anyone knew or didn't know that they could be found."

She exhaled, blowing the air from her lungs as if she could push out the day's stress. Necromancers were a lot of things, but bumbling wasn't generally one of them.

There were necromancers in the city, directly in opposition to the goddess's wishes. There had always been talk of necromancers snatching away children, but she had never seen it with her own eyes. Now, here in Home's Hearth, they had taken one of their own. Something would have to be done.

But she had Hurriet to take care of now. She needed to get the girl back to her parents. Other temple priests had been sent ahead to break the news. She was sure the mother and father would want to see their girl soon.

"Thank you. I will talk to the goddess about this."

Sister Mercy bowed, sensing her dismissal. She turned and walked from the room. Fidelity continued to hold the grieving little girl.

REUNITING

Chamise walked through the gateway. Carved vines etched in flaking gold covered the arch, lending a sense of wealth and luxury now long gone. She paused to rest her aching legs as she gazed at the surrounding gardens. The grass, once beautiful and well kept, had become a collection of weeds pockmarked with bare earth. She let her pack sag onto the ground, allowing the weight of armor, weapons, and two apples to leave her shoulders.

She guessed that the goddess wasn't too concerned with this part of the city.

Ghosts of her past reached out from memories. Her father wasn't there anymore, but she could feel him calling out from across the years, from beyond the grave. She remembered playing with him in this place. Just a few years ago it was called the central training ground. Now she could only call it 'the old lot.' It lay empty, surrounded by ivy-covered walls that needed a little work and a lot of gardening.

I never wanted to come back here, she thought to herself. Never.

She needed a place to stay. She also needed a place that didn't come with the price of begging. The stone building across the yard offered a free place to rest her head. She would not beg from the temple. She had tried to find a room at three inns and boarding houses. All had refused her a room. They apologized to her, but the temple had sent word. She wasn't welcome. It was clear she wasn't wanted in Home's Hearth.

That didn't stop her. Instead, it stoked a wave of anger inside her. The temple is supposed to be looking out for the greater good, she thought. Now Phyllicitus has them looking at their own shoes. They could try to avoid the fact that the Takers have regrouped, but avoiding it will not help. Chamise knew that they didn't have time for these games. She cursed inwardly. Nothing has changed. It looked exactly as it had before once the glimmer of wealth had worn away.

She walked across the lot to the old Eisenvard keep. Someone had removed weeds surrounding the entrance. A brown pile of discarded plants lay strewn about close to the stairs.

Well, someone still seemed to care.

Trusting in the advice of the one-armed Eisenvard she had met in the market, she walked up the three steps and grabbed the door. It opened. No one had locked it. The halls of the Eisenvard were open to any who would dare enter.

Walking into deserted stone hallways caused a shiver of apprehension within her. Crates of old records stood piled up where scowling armed guards once stood. The duties of protecting the hall had been relegated to old papers that would never be read.

"Welcome home," she said.

Her words were lost in the entry hall. A few echoes caused the moment to last, but like the Eisenvard themselves, it was soon gone.

She adjusted her pack and turned to the right, walking down a wide hallway. The stonework of the hall was covered in sculpted plates, each carved with the lessons and legends of the

Eisenvard. Each word on those plates was part of the credo, the essence of the Eisenvard.

Within the credo, the oaths of the Eisenvard stood cut into the stone. Carved faces looked out into the hallway, each one placed two paces from the other, like faces looking from the past, the first of the Eisenvard, the first holy warriors.

Words. A wall of words. She wondered how much trouble these simple words had caused over the years.

She paused in the hallway, re-reading the credo for the thousandth time. She didn't need to. Her father had taught them to her well. She wasn't a little girl now, she had become a Free Mage, she wielded the power she inherited from her mother. Now she had new eyes. She wanted to read words again and get a fresh perspective.

Each set of words had been carved onto its own stone panel and set into the wall. The words had been said at some point in history. Each panel had the name of the speaker and a date was carved after it. She moved from panel to panel, reading, analyzing, then began to understand.

The main message of the credo told her to raise the sword, to defend the weak, to attack the dark magic and those who used it. When she looked at the dates, she saw a different story though. The early dates told a story of defending the weak. The later dates talked about killing all spell-crafters, all magicians, all witches.

She wondered what had happened to cause that. The Eisenvard tried to follow all of this, every word. They never paid attention to trends, or to the history. The words were holy, and that was the end of it. In the end, it hadn't been enough though.

She never remembered the Eisenvard trying to hunt down priestesses of Phyllicitus though. A few were training in the magical arts. Most learned healing magic, a few even learned crafting magic and fine arts such as painting and sculpting. A select few were given more serious magical skills—the ability to steer lightning, control darkness, or curse an enemy. Those had worked to bring Phyllicitus's word to faraway lands.

Aileen had been one of those. Not for the first time, Chamise wondered what the necromancers had offered Aileen to lure her away from the temple.

A scratching sound emerged from further down the hall. Her gaze snapped toward a sharp corner in the passageway. The sound of steps emerged.

She chided herself. She was in Home's Hearth, in the bosom of the goddess. What could happen?

She decided that being prepared would a good idea.

Pulling up her bag with her left hand, she gathered her courage and moved forward. She reached in to grasp the mace handle with her right, making sure the pack would not interfere with its quick use.

A tall man walked around the corner. He stared at her. His eyes widened a bit, surprised to see her. He held a wooden staff in his hands, ready for a fight.

They looked at each other in silence, taking each other's measure, finding weapons, assessing strengths. He wore a threadbare coat, inside out. Someone had done a poor job dying it brown. A thick belt encircled his waist where he had a knife entirely too large for eating with.

"What are you doing here?"

"I'm walking. What are you doing here?"

"I live here. You need to leave."

She shook her head. It looked like a fight. This place and its troubles never seemed to end—the constant conflicts, the jockeying to be top dog. Not for the first time, she wondered why she was here and why she tolerated all of this.

The man gave her a cocky smile, gesturing with his staff to indicate where the exit was.

She was tired, annoyed, and game for a fight. She didn't want to hurt the old man, but she wasn't backing down either. Instead, she released the mace handle and took hold of her pack in both hands. In an instant, she was in motion. She barreled forward, shoving her body into his staff. He scrambled back to regain his range.

She swung her pack overhead, bringing the weight of her gear, armor, and apples down on him. He grabbed the staff and blocked the blow, just like a trained Eisenvard. But Chamise knew his moves. She had studied them herself. The pack struck the staff and managed to block his vision in the same move. She ducked low, moving quickly beneath his guard, releasing the pack to fall upon the ground.

Then she was on him. His legs were spread in the classic staff defense and she grabbed them. Moving with force, her entire weight behind her, she tackled the man to the ground. His breath shot out of his lungs when he impacted against the cold stone floor. He partially lost his grip on the staff, holding on with only his left hand. She scrambled on top of him before he could react, pinning his arms by straddling his chest and holding them down with her legs.

It wasn't the pose of a gentle lady. It was one that would win a fight though.

He moved to heave her away. The dagger appeared in her hand, then it was against his throat.

"Fight's over. You lost. You know the rules. The hallway is mine."

The man stopped, gazing up at her. Suddenly, he burst out laughing. "Well played! Well played! I thought you were a vandal. I am so sorry."

He continued to laugh as Chamise stood up, offering him a hand to help him from the floor. His laughter stopped as he stood and looked at her again, taking in her age, and her womanly curves.

"You're a little young for knowing about Lord of the Hall."

"I was fourteen when Phyllicitus sent us away. I played plenty of Lord of the Hall."

He gazed down at her from his towering height. Nodding, he continued. "I only remember five girls of that age. You are?"

"I think you know."

He nodded, his face grew serious. "Silver's girl. The witch."

###

Miller felt the brush of her consciousness. He knew that Aileen was searching for him. He put down his dice and looked up in apology. Cerna scowled back at him, unhappy at the prospect of losing even more coins.

"She is preparing to contact me. These things don't usually take long."

Instead of Cerna's gruff voice, a sweet high voice replied. "Go ahead, we'll be fine. The dice aren't going anywhere."

He nodded and got up from the table. Brita smiled at him from her small bench. The new furnishing, a short side table, stood in contrast to the bare room within the circle. The small table was large enough for Brita to play at dice but not much else. She also had a small stool to rest on. They had moved it as close to the edge of the circle as they could without damaging it. Cerna had insisted that if she was going to play, they had to see the dice.

No cheating was allowed, even for the Taken.

He felt Aileen's will strengthening, the warm embrace of her call gently lulling his mind into spirit channels, back to a place that only existed in Aileen's imagination. She seemed hurried. Miller didn't even search for a chair, he simply sat on the floor. There was no use being sent into a trance, then waking up to a cracked skull because you fell. Even the simple things can kill you.

The world started to fade away as he sat. Then he was in her room. A comfortable sofa and three chairs were scattered about the room, forming a ring facing in on each other. Aileen stood at their center, dressed for travel, armored, and armed with her soul blade—a terrifying weapon that he had helped forge. The steel held a small part of her soul, fused with the strength of a lightning bolt.

"Are you still in that house with Brita?"

"Yes. Nothing has changed."

She looked back at him, trying to hide the annoyance from her eyes. "Nothing other than Phyllicitus acting like a spoiled brat, you mean?"

"Well, yes. I didn't expect that to happen. She's been helpful before. Do you have any guess at to what is going on?"

"Absolutely. She's pouting."

"Pouting?"

"Yes. Just like a fifteen-year-old girl that got left out of the party. Pouting."

"I don't know what to do. I feel like I've failed everyone." He thought of Brita, and how his hopes were so high when he had first arrived. Now her cure seemed farther away every day.

"Not your fault. Don't take this out on yourself. Something is broken here, and I don't think you are going to be able to fix it by yourself."

"Master Easter was here. He seemed a little upset about it all."

"Trust me. Easter has already contacted me. Somehow he talked me into coming to Home's Hearth to straighten this mess out."

"You don't like Home's Hearth?"

"What? Oh, I love the city, I love the place. But there are a lot of memories there, a lot of entanglements."

Miller heard the sadness in her voice. He wondered what had happened here to make her so melancholy whenever she came back. Did she miss it? Or fear it?

"I would really appreciate it if you came. I could use the help with the research as well. I could also use some more supplies. We aren't getting any support while we are outside the city. It's just too far. I wouldn't have thought five miles would make that much of a difference. It does."

"Don't get the wrong idea. This Brita problem is yours, not mine. I'll help where I can, but I won't be around much. I have to deal with Phyllicitus, and, well, other issues."

"Other issues?"

"So, I may not be coming alone. There will be a few more

masters to keep us company."

"More masters? How are we even going to get one into the city? Let alone more?"

"Won't be a problem. Trust me."

Trust me, the goddess will see you. Miller had heard that before. He didn't reply. She didn't seem to expect him to.

Aileen changed the subject. "So, I've got some apprentice work for you to do before we reunite. I'm guessing that I'll be there in three days."

Multiple questions struggled to come out of his mouth before he settled on the single word. "Alright."

"You are to practice your disciplines. Every day. At least three hours a day."

"Disciplines?" They had finished those lessons a year ago.

"Yes. Disciplines. There could be up to five masters coming on this trip. I want your mind locked and calm, and your mouth closed. Let's not give the other masters any reason to look down on us, shall we?"

"I've dealt with masters before. Don't worry. I won't shame y—"

"Disciplines. Three hours daily. No skimping. I'll see you in three days."

Three days seemed quick to Miller. There would be little time to chat and catch up, no time to plan their next moves.

"Before I go. I need to tell you this," she continued.

He watched her try to relax but she fidgeted with her hands. She always fidgeted when she was nervous.

"The other masters will be watching both you and I. Relationships between the masters can be, well, complicated. No matter what you see or hear, you need to stay calm. If we need to talk, we can sneak away and talk."

That didn't sound good to him. He wondered what they would need to talk about.

"I've got to pack. I'll see you in three days."

The magic began to fade away. He slowly became aware of himself within the old hall. Brita was singing a nonsensical tune and rolling dice. She wasn't winning, but no one expected her to.

"Good news, maybe."

Cerna didn't hesitate to reply. "Anything we should know about? Or are you practicing for your master's ring by being annoyingly mysterious at every opportunity?"

He stood and walked back toward the table, grabbing the back of the chair to lean on as he approached. He waited for a few more dice rolls before he updated them on Aileen's plans.

Miller said, "Aileen is coming here. She should be here in three days."

"My coins are on Easter. He twisted her arm and got her out of bed finally?"

"I guess so. She told me to expect up to five masters. I guess that includes her."

Silence.

Cerna's eyes widened. "Five?"

Brita interrupted. "Five? Is that a lot?"

"It took three to wipe out the Takers in the final battle. So yes. Five is a lot. They don't usually gather in these numbers outside of the conclave."

HAZEL

It had only been a day since Gar had died. A hollow feeling crept into Hurriet as if part of her life was forever gone. That part had been her brother Gar. Now she stood at the back of their lawn. A fence separated her from the road that her brother had played on so often. He had only been ten years old when he died alone and abandoned.

She glanced up at the tall tower in the alchemist's back yard wondering if the man knew what had happened to her brother. The alchemist had urged them both to be careful. A terrible feeling gnawed at her heart. Gar died too young, and of nothing. She wondered if the alchemist knew something more than he had told them. She had never trusted that man. She didn't know why, but she always wanted to flee when he got close to her. She had always let Gar talk to him.

Now she regretted it. Her father had told her that alchemy was a dangerous trade and that people who practiced it might as well be sorcerers. They commanded forces beyond the normal world. The tower represented that craft. Some nights when the wind was calm, terrible smells would descend from the tower down to the streets. Gar wasn't afraid of the odors, but her mother would always call them inside nonetheless.

Her mother was broken, balled up in her bed unwilling to leave her small room. Father said little as he took over the household duties. It was as if nothing happened, except that he stopped talking almost altogether since then. Their home, so recently one of light and family, was now a broken thing. She wanted Gar back. Sadly, not even Goddess Phyllicitus could do that.

Across the street, the back gate opened. The alchemist emerged, pausing to close the gate behind him. Her arms began to tremble with fear. She wanted to talk to him, to accuse him, to scream at him. It never happened. Instead, she called out from behind her fence.

"We followed that man for you."

The Rat stopped, then turned to peer into the fence. "And why didn't you come back as I had instructed?" He sounded impatient.

"Cuz Gar died. He died right in the street, all alone."

Her voice began to crack with held-in sobs.

The Rat turned and walked toward the fence, toward her. She took a step back.

"Oh goodness," the Rat said as he stopped his forward motion.

"Who was that man we were following? Did he kill my brother?" She spit the words out as if she had memorized them, but they were from the heart.

The Rat paused before answering. "I'm not sure. I wasn't there. Was your brother injured? Have a bump on his head?"

"No."

"Did you hear anything? A struggle perhaps?"

"No."

"So what makes you think that he was murdered? I mean, when was the last murder in Home's Hearth? Since before the goddess returned, I'm sure."

"I've just got a feeling. Something about alchemy, magic, stuff like that."

"We should talk more about this. I have to run an errand. I'll be back later tonight. Come by later and we will talk. Let's see if we can sort out what this is all about. If necessary, I will seek out someone to help." The Rat grinned at her. "Then maybe we'll bring your mother and father into this. Oh, indeed, bring them along as well."

A shiver ran up her spine. This man was not to be trusted. His cold eyes met hers, peering through the fence. She feared she was doomed. If she brought her parents by, they would be doomed as well. She had been good at looking into people's souls, determining their worth. This man had no soul. Her heart began to beat in fear. She shouldn't have spoken with him, she thought. She should have just run away. This was Home's Hearth; it would have been fine.

The Rat turned away, returning to his business as he walked down the road. "I'll stop by tonight. Until then, let's just keep this between us two."

Hurriet watched him go. He didn't look back, simply kept to his business. Three dozen steps later the Rat turned right, into a narrow alley. She kept still to listen as his steps faded away toward the Crafter's Street. She was angry. Her intuition screamed at her, accusing her of leaving Gar to die. It also told her that if she hadn't left, she would be dead as well. For the first time, the intuition seemed to hold more truth than the rest of the world. She needed to pay attention to it more. It seemed crazy to allow her daydreams into her daily life, but there wasn't much else she could do.

Gar was dead now. Mother had gone to her bed. The sound of tears filled the home. Father had stopped talking. It was as if he had stopped feeling. In a similar way, so had she. Somehow the world had grown less wonderful in just a day.

She turned left and began walking along the fence line. The fence stood taller than her, but not by far. Ivy crawled up the sparse planks nailed side by side, each a hand wide and two hands apart. She and Gar had nailed every one of these planks up. He wanted a pig to live in the back yard. Mother didn't approve, but that didn't stop him from his preparations. Gar always prepared for things, especially the things he was trying to get out of their parents.

She reached the end of their back yard. The fence turned left and connected with the back of the house. The house was a good house. This neighborhood was filled with craftsmen. Her father was one of them, a successful master leather worker. His tanning yards had been moved outside of the city boundaries because of the smell, making his presence at home all the more remarkable. He worked hard. Hurriet loved him even as she wished he would spend more time at home.

Now that her mother was grieving, he would be around more, as much as he could. She wondered if the alchemist would come to her house to speak with her parents, to tell them about Gar. As she turned back, intent on continuing her pacing, a jolt of fear struck her. In a moment of clarity, she instantly foresaw what might happen when the alchemist returned.

The alchemist had sent both of them, Gar and herself, to follow the red-haired man. He didn't react as if he were distraught, or even the slightest bit guilty for sending them into that deadly situation. He seemed resigned, dismissive. Somehow, in her imagination, she could see him coming back to their home tonight and finishing the job, leaving no witnesses. She glanced up at the tower. An alchemist could take bodies away during the night, feed them to his potions, and they would never be seen again.

Goosebumps sprung up on her arms as she thought about what could happen. Visions of an empty house came to her mind. The house stood, devoid of any occupants, abandoned and deserted. She didn't know if the alchemist would do the things that she imagined. Gar had always told her that preparing ahead of time was the best way to come out ahead. She decided to take his advice, if only for a small while.

Hurriet had no idea how long the alchemist would be gone.

She didn't want to be home when he returned, if only to have enough time to think. She went to the back door of the house and went inside. She could hear her father speaking gently to her mother in their room and decided not to interrupt them. If her intuition was right she should leave them as they were. The alchemist would surely come to the house and ask about her. She didn't want them to have anything to hide.

She went to the kitchen and took a burlap bag, then filled it with eight pieces of dried meat, three pears, and as an afterthought, a two-day-old stuffed pastry. She felt sadness as she left through the door. She went to the back fence, climbed over it, then walked down the street.

At first, her footsteps led her toward the temple. She thought about seeking help there. The more she thought about it, the less she liked it. The priests would take her seriously, and probably act to protect her. Her mother had always forbidden her to visit the temple though. She said that the goddess would bring her into the temple and most likely keep her. For some reason, Phyllicitus liked young girls with imaginations and her mother wanted no part of it. She wasn't desperate yet, so there was no point in exposing herself to the temple.

She knew what she needed—a plan. Gar always told her to have a plan before she did anything complicated. After the plan, she would probably need some help.

The two-track country road led through rich fields of barley and wheat. The Rat walked confidently through the well-patrolled countryside. With the goddess back in Home's Hearth, there was no danger of encountering robbers. And of murders, well, that depended.

He stopped to inspect some purple flowers that had sprung up from the side of the track. They would be useful for preparing basic potions. He stopped and picked them. After he counted the number of petals and leaves on each plant, he stored them in a small leather tube hanging from a shoulder strap. Walking on, he kept an eye out for new things to collect. The tube bounced against a flask at his waist, making a hollow sound when it did.

It only took another hour of walking until he found her.

The farm woman stood a hundred paces from the road, shovel in hand. She toiled in the soil, her muscular arms churning up the brown dirt, using the shovel as a makeshift hoe. The woman seemed unafraid of hard work. She struck at something in the dirt with the shovel over and over, growing angrier with each blow. The Rat couldn't see past the waist-high wheat, but he could hear her curses. Whatever she was digging wasn't giving up easily. She combed her dark, sun-damaged hand through her rich curly black hair, wiping the sweat from her forehead.

Smiling, the Rat turned off the road and began cutting through the field. Twenty yards in, the woman stopped her digging and turned to face him.

The Rat called over to her. "Do you need assistance?"

He kept walking, carefully looking side to side. No one else was near.

"No. I've got it. Keep walking, stranger. This stump doesn't need your help, and neither do I."

The Rat grinned. He tried to look friendly, but he had to pay attention. He had thought this would be simple, now he was beginning to reassess. Most people had let their guard drop since Phyllicitus had returned. Indeed, most of the dark parts of life had retreated since then. There were a few that would never let their guard down. This woman was clearly one of them.

"Don't get the wrong idea. My name is Mortimer. I'm from Home's Hearth. I'm here to collect rare herbs for the temple. I'm looking for these purple flowers; have you seen them? I have an example that I can show you. Will you please help me?"

It was only a little bit of a lie, but the Rat was good at lying.

He kept walking toward her. She looked at him, taking in his traveling clothes, his well-kept hair, his gentleman's manner.

Halfway there, he tried to get just a little closer.

The woman appeared to be thirty years old, and in good physical shape. She looked exotic, bringing images of places far away. Her voice had the ring of a local. She seemed to be a hard worker. She wasn't that tall though, if he could get close enough then he could take her, and if her family was new to these lands, even better.

She turned and ran, throwing the shovel to the side and sprinting away from him.

The woman had good instincts. The Rat wanted her even more.

He reached down to his belt and grabbed the hand-sized flask hanging from it, releasing it from its thong. He didn't try to follow the woman. Instead, he raised the flask to his lips and sipped. The Rat replaced the flask, tied it securely to his belt, and resumed walking toward the fleeing woman. She was more than a hundred yards away before the alchemical formula began to work. He felt a slight sweat all over his body. Then he felt warm. His heart began to race and his hands began to tremor.

The Rat knew that she would not escape.

A burst of energy suddenly washed over his body. He didn't hesitate. He sprang into a run. This wasn't his normal pace or the normal pace of any man. The potion had done its job. He sprinted through the waist-high crops faster than a horse could gallop. The stalks whipped at his hands and clothing as he passed through. He gained on the woman quickly. Just as he approached, she turned to face him, knife in hand.

The Rat sped up even faster. He approached, smashing into her with his shoulder. Pain lanced into his arm as the dagger drove in. Blood sprayed out all over his clean shirt and the woman's face. He didn't care, he could barely feel it anyway. Fast as a snake, he grabbed her hand and pulled it away from the knife.

She screamed and kicked at him, striking his legs with the soles of her solid work boots. He continued to move quickly, grabbing the knife and jerking it out of his arm. More blood flowed.

The Rat slashed at her with the knife. She wasn't fast enough to do anything about it. A cut appeared on her face, crossing half her cheek and splitting her lip. She screamed and thrust a thumb toward his eye. With the potion, he was fast enough to avoid it. She grabbed for the knife and he purposefully dropped it. The woman didn't hesitate; she moved in to recover it. When she did, the Rat grabbed her by the hair and pulled her up into a close embrace, forcing her face close to his bleeding arm wound.

They went down to the ground, wrestling for some advantage. The woman grasped for the knife. The Rat simply held on. In five minutes, it was over. The woman suddenly stopped her struggles and stared out to the horizon, unconcerned about the man who held her. The Takers had her in their sway. He relaxed his grip, breathing hard after such an intense struggle. Then he pulled away far enough to be respectful, but close enough to hold her upright as she sat on the bare ground. After a few minutes, she seemed to notice him. She stared at his face, confused.

"Shall we try that again? I am in need of some help, and I feel that you are an excellent candidate for the task. Let me take you away from this life of toil. Come with me?"

He stood and reached for her hand, grasping it to pull her up.

She was silent, still bewildered about what was happening to her. The Friends could take someone quickly. She was trying to resist. The Rat knew it would be to no avail.

"So what shall I call you?"

She replied in a dreamy, unfocused voice.

"Hazel. I'm Hazel."

"Indeed, you are. And I am Mortimer. Right now, you are probably feeling a little confused, that is normal. You will feel better in a few days. Things will be odd, but you will discover that soon enough. Let's start walking, though. Home's Hearth is at least a day away."

"Home's Hearth?"

"Yes, Hazel. I'm taking you to your new home."

A GATHERING OF MASTERS

"We have company."

Cerna stood up from the chair he had been sitting in for three hours, stretching his muscular arms.

"Who is it?"

"Not sure yet. It's still raining. It's hard to see clearly."

Picking up his weapon, Cerna moved to stand next to the doorway. The curved sword was a nasty piece of business. Cerna looked like someone who knew how to use it.

Miller noted Cerna's caution. It would be hard to take him by surprise. He seemed always ready to fight.

Cerna had been keeping watch for the past eight days, waiting for the masters to arrive. Miller finally understood why Easter brought him in. He was always watching, always alert.

"I think I know our visitor. Judging the size of him, I guess it is Master Darjeeling." Miller was relieved. Master Darjeeling had embraced madness long ago, but somehow, that made him more personable and easier to talk to. The other masters got darker, more murderous, as they aged. Master Darjeeling had become, well, happier. Half the things he said were tinged in madness, the other half humor. Darjeeling loved to eat as well. His rotund belly was easy to spot from a distance.

Then Miller remembered the experiments he had seen Darjeeling perform. Darjeeling liked to play with others, like toys. He was usually having a good time doing just that. Of all the White Hand masters, Darjeeling had the greatest familiarity with madness, and he used it like a tool, infecting others with illusions. Darjeeling never attacked with sword, he always attacked with an opponent's own mind.

Darjeeling approached the door. Miller pulled it open further to allow his girth easy entrance, but Darjeeling stopped dead in his tracks.

"What are you doing, Miller?"

"Opening the door for you." Miller stared at him, preparing for the madness.

"And did I knock?"

"No, but you did approach the door."

"There are customs at stake here, boy. Now close the door so I can knock and be allowed in. That way I can get out of this cursed rain."

Miller shrugged and closed the door. A few heartbeats later, a knock sounded. He opened it.

"Miller my boy! It's been so long! May I come in and get dry? It's as damp as the cat's bath day out here."

He motioned Darjeeling into the hall, stepping out of the way. Miller wondered what cat's bath day was, and who gave their cats a bath in the first place.

Darjeeling walked into the hall. He didn't even look to the side before he addressed Cerna. "Hello, Cerna. How have you been?"

"Well enough, Master Darjeeling. Well enough."

Darjeeling was a heavyset man with a thick second chin and black stringy hair, currently wet from the rain. He wore a black cloak coated with wax to keep the rain away. He stood in the hall, dripping, looking from corner to corner as if in fear.

He wore a cloak to stop the rain, but without hat. Miller noted his incomplete preparation. Darjeeling never seemed to change, always on the verge of making sense, but never quite there.

The silence stretched long, and Miller became uncomfortable.

"Can I get you a drink?"

Darjeeling only raised a finger to silence him. His gaze fell upon Brita. She cowered at the far edge of the circle, eyes wide in fear.

Cerna announced a new visitor. "Someone else is coming. It's getting busy around here."

After five minutes, a younger man opened the door and walked into the hall. He didn't knock or wait for an invitation. Instead, he struggled with a large pack on his back, its weight challenging his strength. Setting the pack heavily on the floor, he pulled off his wet cloak and looked for a place to hang it. Miller recognized him, then reached out a hand to take it from him, but he shied away, preferring to hang it himself.

"Oh, you have such nice hair," Brita said, pointing at the new arrival. "It reminds me of baby blankets and stars."

Miller knew this apprentice. They weren't by any means close, but as apprentices in the same cabal, they had dealt with each other before.

"Hello Frantz. Care for a glass of wine to keep the chill away?"

Frantz stared at Darjeeling, trying to anticipate any orders. Darjeeling continued to stare at Brita, turning his head at different angles, as if she confused him.

Miller looked at the newly forming group. There was way too much staring going on for his comfort.

Shrugging, he went to the pile of supplies, fetching a bottle of red wine and three cups. Cerna held up four fingers, and Miller grabbed another. He looked over at Frantz, clearly cold yet unwilling to discuss his discomfort in his wet state. Miller grabbed a fifth glass. He served Frantz first, giving him a cup of wine for Darjeeling as well. Apprentices got the job of checking for poison, and Frantz didn't hesitate. He began channeling to find any strange additions to the wine. After a nod, he drank a sip from each. Miller turned from them, pouring another cup for Cerna, then walked over to Brita still cowering on the far side of the circle.

"Are you all right?"

"Sure. Scary. Something isn't right with him." She pointed at Darjeeling.

"I know. Don't worry, you'll get used to it."

He set her empty cup on the floor, then poured it half full of the deep red wine. Setting the bottle aside, he set his hand at the base of the cup and channeled, creating a small gap in the protective circle. She smiled at him as he slid the cup into the circle.

"You know, I think you will make a fantastic father someday."

Miller tried to act like it was a joke, something humorous to pass the time. Brita looked perfectly serious though.

"Hardly, being in the Order and all. I've heard that I don't get that option. Masters can't have children, and apprentices aren't allowed families."

She smiled, arching her back to show off her form to its full advantage.

"No families? What about the families that you started with? Apprentices aren't hatched, are they?"

"You leave all that behind when the order takes you in."

"Why would you do that? It's your family, right?"

"Because if you don't, the order kills your entire family. That little fact makes it easier to leave your family, even when you love them dearly. Leaving them also makes it more difficult to commit to the cause. Filters out the unmotivated, or at least that was the original idea. You really need total commitment to become a master."

"You don't want to be a master anyway, silly. You want me!" Brita smiled with a tease in her eye as she sipped the wine. He stared back at her luscious form, her deep green eyes, her long black hair.

Sadly, she was more right than she knew. Miller continued his daydreams, staring at her face, her curves. He sighed. It was unfortunate, he thought, that they had these, well, complications.

He allowed himself another moment to fantasize. An un-taken Brita, a small ranch with horses, children, making love every night he could.

Then he thought about where they were right now, and why Brita was here. Brita had been taken, yet his young heart yearned for her. This was how the Takers got close to people.

"I've got to check on my horse."

He turned away as Brita started making whining noises. "Don't go! We need to pick out names!"

Making up his mind not to interact with her fantasies—his were alluring enough—he went to fetch his cloak. Cerna smiled at him as he left the hall, silently mocking the situation Miller had found himself in.

Miller wanted to escape. "I've got to check on the horse."

"I'll bet." Cerna said, a crooked smile shining from his face.

He put on his cloak and went outside. It continued to rain outside, but not strong enough to stop him. It was a short walk to the barn. The grass was wet and the trail in front of the hall had transformed into mud. There was no point trying to avoid it, as the barn was completely surrounded with a muddy paddock at this point. He moved through the brown sticky mud, dragging clumps of it into the barn where the mare stood, patiently staring at the door, waiting for its bag of oats for the afternoon.

"Sorry I'm late. People started arriving. It's getting crowded in there."

The mare walked over to him and he began scratching its neck. After a few moments of scratching, Miller walked over to the stack of bags and pulled one up. Opening the bag with his knife, he poured it into the feed trough. The knife was almost the length of his forearm, thin, and useful for a variety of tasks including opening burlap bags full of oats, or sliding between chain mail links.

The thin knife, the poniard, glimmered in his hand as if it had somehow trapped sunlight long ago and hadn't released it. The runes on the blade countered its smooth edge with their rough scrawl. This knife might be a piece of art, but it did its job. It had managed to kill a White Hand master.

Here he was, opening up canvas bags of oats with Chamise's knife. A mage-killing tool enchanted to murder any spellcaster who received the pointy end of it. The spellcraft was basic. Sharpening, heart-seeking, and speed had been woven into the tool. He shook his head. The knife had nothing that would destroy a White Hand, but it sure could put holes in things. Especially apprentices.

The mare began to eat as he dropped the bag and put the knife back in its scabbard. "So she's in Home's Hearth. I guess I should give her the knife back. What do you think?"

The mare didn't reply. It seldom did.

"Yes, I agree. No use making a decision until we see her. She might still be upset."

The battle at the tower had been enough to upset anyone. Master December had turned the graveyard into a small army of walking corpses. The Protectors were not ready to battle the dead, and it showed. They managed to cut through the village and enter the tower. But that had been December's plan the entire time. They never left the tower.

He thought about the scene in the entryway. Severed limbs and pools of blood decorated the entire room. It was a nightmare. Chamise had been there the entire time.

He shuddered.

"Well, either way, I suppose I'm going to be nice to her. Someone has to make this better. Maybe a nice dinner?"

He didn't bother tying the mare to the post as he left her to the meal. The trip to Home's Hearth taught him just how intelligent the horse was. If the mare wanted to leave, she was going to leave. There wasn't much he could do about it.

Bidding goodnight to the mare, he left the barn and trekked back through the muddy paddock, returning to the hall. Easter had managed to arrive without Miller noticing. One of his large dogs sat on the floor, staring at Brita across the circle's boundary.

Easter stood speaking with Darjeeling about the upcoming conclave of masters. Politics always came into play as soon as there were more than two people in a group. The Order of the White Hand had been created three thousand years ago, and the politics were deep and unrelenting.

Apparently getting killed didn't get Master December excused from his trial though. As soon as December returned from beyond the final door, he would be standing before the conclave to answer for his missteps. Miller wondered if all of this was part of some grand strategy that Easter had devised. Miller imagined what December would say to the conclave. "Look at me. I killed a bunch of your apprentices, but I also died to save one of our own apprentices. Let me go, will you?"

As the dead were only mere apprentices, Miller expected that sort of defense to work, at least for a little while. From what he had seen, masters tended not to get worked up when an apprentice or two died. It wasn't uncommon for masters to murder their own apprentices. December's crime was to kill dozens of them without regard to who their masters were. All of the masters seemed enraged over this, as if they didn't care about the lives of individual apprentices, but they cared deeply whether they had enough apprentices in all.

The room had added a few more people. It was starting to get loud as a half dozen conversations took place at once. Easter had brought another master that Miller didn't know very well. The new master stood alone, wearing his dark robes like armor. He was a huge specimen of a man, more than a head taller than Cerna, and muscular like a warrior. His mahogany skin stood in contrast to everyone else in the room, but his suspicious eyes were in common with the other masters. His bald head shone like a helmet as he scowled at everyone without regard to rank or age.

Miller tried to remember a name. He thought that might be Master Gates. He wasn't known to be a friendly man, but he was said to be highly competent.

Easter was motioning Miller to approach while standing near the table, fingering through the pages of Brita's log. Brita had retreated to the farthest edge of the circle, trying desperately not to be noticed by pulling a blanket over herself, and singing a child's lullaby.

"Yes, Master Easter. How may I serve you today?"

Easter looked up as he approached. He pointed down at the book, its pages opened to show neat columns of words on the left page, and doodles of lines, curves, and words on the right.

"This handwriting. It's yours? All of it?"

"Yes. I did my best. She hasn't been making a lot of sense, but I managed to write most of it down."

"I like what you did here." He turned the page to display another failed thought-experiment Miller had conducted. Words were written down on the page, and lines showed connections between them. Each line had marks indicating how many times they had been used together.

This wasn't the first time Easter had looked into the journal. Miller wondered what he was looking for. Perhaps signs of progress? There would be little in that book.

"I was trying to make sense of it. I hoped there was some sort of pattern. I couldn't find any."

"Yet," he replied, offering a friendly, if insincere, smile.

"Indeed. Yet."

"Keep it up. You may find something eventually. Out of curiosity, what did you hope to find? Did you have any specific signs in mind?"

"Not sure. Some kind of code maybe?"

Before Easter replied, Cerna interrupted the conversation by standing down from his watching post and walking to the door, opening it wide.

Aileen stepped in. Somehow, while traveling here, she had managed to acquire another dress that would just as accurately be called a work of art. It held different shades of black and dark green in a net of handwoven stitchery. The dress had small hand-sewn birds, crows maybe, sewn into it like a set of patches. Were it not for her athletic build, the low bodice would have shown the world much more of her form.

Miller gazed at her for half a minute, feeling his heart race, yearning to abandon Easter and speed to her side.

He whispered to himself, "Thank the Goddess. You're here."

He felt happy, confident, as if everything was now going to work out. For the first time in months, he felt safe. Somehow, everything could turn out all right after all.

She looked across the room, spotting Miller. She didn't move toward him, or even call out. She stood there staring at him, her hands fidgeting with the waistline of the dress. He felt her eyes looking into him, seeing all of him. Something was wrong though. Her stare was intense. She was normally relaxed, even among the other masters. Here, in this place, she looked on edge.

The fifth master walked into the room. Miller's blood ran ice cold. It was Mistress Sword, clad in hunting leathers and tall boots. Mistress Sword always preferred clothing that was less fashionable, and more flame-resistant. Her skill with crafted fire was well known within the order. Many apprentices had their share of burns from her. Sword's cruelty with it was equally famous.

Mistress Sword, as she preferred to be called now that Aileen had made that title her own preference, was gorgeous. Her face was unmarred by life as a master, with the exception of the cruel gaze she used to view the entire world. Today she favored brown leather hose to keep the damp at bay, beneath a thin tan skirt that kept the ensemble in the almost-normal realm.

She wore a short black coat decorated with metal studs. She wore it to keep the rain from her shirt, or whatever else she was wearing beneath it. She would have fit in with a group of foresters or hunters. She was neither. She pushed back her unruly mop of curly brown hair, giving her the look of some ancient queen of the forest. Miller had seen paintings of the First Gods and their followers from long ago. Mistress Sword would have fit in among their number admirably.

Right now her fashion sense made her look either daring, or crazy. In truth, she was both.

Sword's eyes met his and he remembered every hateful, spiteful, sadistic thing she had done to him. He had been in her service when he was first inducted into the order. Emotions washed over him. He felt hatred and fear.

Why is she here? She isn't even in the cabal. Why in the name of the Raven God is she here? Miller thought.

He tried to calm down. He wondered angrily about Easter. How could he let Sword into this? It was too important, and Sword was too unstable.

Almost of its own will, his right hand found the hilt of Chamise's dagger. The cold metal somehow gave him comfort. The master's ring on Sword's finger testified to the futility of his thought. Masters of the White Hand don't stay dead. He could stab her with this dagger and solve the problem, but only for just a few weeks.

Darjeeling walked over, dodging around people in the filling hall, to stand beside him. He gently set his hand on Miller's shoulder. Miller felt the anger drain away, like water pouring from a bucket. He had a faint sense of spirit channeling. Darjeeling was doing what he does best, mind-tricks.

"I see you." It was all Darjeeling would say. "I mean, I see you."

The anger had deserted him, but in its place, a sadness had grown. The two of them, Aileen and Miller, stared into each other's eyes from across the room. She looked blank, like she wanted to be far away. His eyes pleaded with her, begging that it wasn't so, that she hadn't brought Sword only to torment him. He never wanted to see Mistress Sword again. He didn't know why she was here. He just wanted her to leave.

But Mistress Sword was part of the Order of the White Hand. She glanced over, looking Miller straight in the face. Then she gave him a tiny smile and walked up behind Aileen. Aileen was frozen in his gaze when Sword reached around her, gently touching her stomach with her hand. As Aileen became aware of the touch, Sword leaned in and kissed her on the cheek. Instantly, Aileen broke contact, stepping away from her.

Miller rocked back with the shock of it. He knew that Aileen had been raised in the temple of the goddess. The priestesses were all expected to know the art of love, in all of its flavors. Sword touching her so intimately overwhelmed him. Miller started shaking. He could feel his heart tearing with pain. He couldn't think, it hurt so much. He felt himself being guided forward. Aileen and Sword stepped aside as Darjeeling guided him out of the hall. He hadn't breathed since he saw them embrace.

Now he know why Aileen wanted him to come here alone, Miller thought to himself; it was pretty obvious.

He didn't turn when the door closed behind him.

Inside the hall, it had become quiet. The other masters noted Darjeeling's exit and the despondent apprentice he took with him. Master Gates only frowned deeper and shook his head in disappointment and annoyance. Easter walked over to stand in front of Aileen, reaching up to remove a tear from her cheek with his thumb.

"Did that go as planned?"

"Not really. I was trying to avoid this. It would have been better for everyone to keep this secret until he won his ring."

"Do you really think that would have made a difference?"

"I think it would have given us the time to recover. Now, I don't know." She looked at the closed door, her eyes searching for some clue what the future held.

"Why didn't you talk to him? We all saw this coming."

"I couldn't think of the words. I know that sounds weak. I just didn't want to hurt him."

Sword couldn't resist a snide remark. She smiled an evil grin.

"It won't matter anyway. He didn't get his ring, it's just a matter of time. He's dead meat walking."

The soft laughs of Brita filled the empty air between them. "I've been taken, and I'm not that cruel."

He didn't remember how he got there, but Miller found himself standing in the empty field, a hundred yards from the hall. Darjeeling and his apprentice Frantz stood next to him, trying to keep him calm.

"It's hard when your feelings get attached. Best to push through."

Darjeeling's wisdom, as obvious as it was, glanced off of him like he was made of steel. Frantz offered Miller a wine cup decorated with carvings of flowers and rose petals. He drank from it greedily.

The cup was filled with brandy, not wine. He didn't mind.

It burned as it traveled down his throat. Miller was beyond caring. By the time he was ready to talk, the cup was empty. Frantz had already begun refilling it when he began. It had been an excellent brandy, with flavors of plum. Frantz lifted a small bottle and refilled the glass.

"Mistress Sword. She was, perhaps, exceptionally unkind when I was her apprentice." Miller began as he took another sip, trying to hold back the worst of his words. The words that could get him killed.

Frantz smirked. "I've heard tales from other apprentices. I've been told that it's like living in a sick brothel, serving her."

Darjeeling added, "Aye. We all have the madness in some way. Hers didn't wait long before it took her. And it has taken her to some unusual places." He gazed back to the hall and paused, pointing up to the sky. "That bird there. It may have an answer for her. I don't though."

Miller didn't even bother to try to understand him. Sometimes you just had to let Darjeeling say words. Once in a while, something useful emerged from his mouth, but not often enough to be reliable.

Miller continued with his complaints, careful to conceal his statements in rhetorical questions. Even as his emotions toiled within his heart, Miller was well aware that criticizing a master, any master, could quickly result in his own death. "But why? Why does everyone have to be so crazy in this order? Why can't we just learn magic and fight this invisible war against the Takers, whatever that is. Why does everyone go insane in the end?"

"Professional hazard, I guess," Darjeeling began. His voice entering a monotone lecturing cadence. "Every time we pass through and return, we leave a little something behind. Think of it as footprints, bloody footprints perhaps. Unless you leave your shoes behind, well, then it's different."

Miller shook his head in confusion. He couldn't understand everything Darjeeling said when he was in the throws of his madness.

"But why? Why does it have to be that way?"

"You might as well ask why we fall toward the ground instead of away from it. Some things just are."

Miller didn't know what to say to that, so he returned to his previous tactic of sulking. Sulking and drinking.

Darjeeling interrupted the pause after a few long minutes.

"When the madness begins, you never see it coming." He paused, searching for the words that he didn't want to speak. "My ring was young when the madness took me. One day I woke up, and everything was different. It was like the world had changed while I slept."

Interested, Miller motioned him to continue.

"I joined the order a bit later in life. My youth was spent as a merchant, I think. At least that is what I remember right now. I was good at it. I traded horses and made a good living. I remember there as a war. I ended up apprenticed to Master Glue. Odd man that. It took seven years to earn my ring. After I earned it, another four passed before I noticed changes within me. One evening I went to bed. The next morning, I awoke as someone else. I went to sleep a strong man in his prime. I awoke convinced that If I ate enough fruit pie, I could get my cart to fly, just by asking it nicely."

"Seriously?"

"I wish I was joking. It took me three years to get that cart to fly."

"Did you enchant it? A flying cart is impressive."

"No. I paid some fine young men to haul it up to the roof of the largest barn in the county. Then I simply got in and rolled it off the barn."

Miller looked back, confused.

"It only flew for about a second. Then it hit the ground. It took me three weeks to walk again."

He imagined Master Darjeeling, sitting on his cart, launching into the air yelling "Fly! Fly!" He couldn't help but crack a smile.

"That is when I learned that I couldn't trust my instincts like I used to. Everything changes when you get your ring."

"But Aileen. I thought we were close."

"I thought my cart could fly as well. Look how well that worked."

"I just can't believe it. She knows how much I hate Sword. Why her? Why now?"

"The question you are looking for is, why not me?"

Miller tried to deny it. Darjeeling's calming spell, added to three cups of brandy, had removed his ability to lie. He could only nod.

"There it is. She originally took you from Sword because you could enchant. You met her, got along great, and got a little fond of her. Better yet, she was close to your age as far as masters go. So here is the reality. She seemed to like working with you and didn't mind chatting with you about all the small things in life. Ultimately, she decided that Mistress Sword would make a better ally, and thus a better lover. Maybe the whole thing is just that easy? Maybe you shouldn't overreact to losing something that never really existed in the first place."

He nodded. "That isn't the way of it. I mean, we had a

connection. There were real feelings."

"No, you had real feelings. Mistress Aileen just had someone to gossip with and make herself feel more connected to humanity. A common mistake among newly elevated masters, to be sure."

"So why Sword? She knew it would, well, destroy me."

"Please. You don't look very destroyed to me. The move makes more than a little sense. Mistress Aileen is the youngest master in the White Hand. Every day she is fending off treachery from rivals of the conclave, and personal rivals as well. Many of the other masters don't believe she was trained long enough, or hard enough to deserve a ring, whatever that means. Being a student of Easter brings even more jealous enemies. Sword is a good tactical choice when you think about it. She is the strongest spellcaster in Hermagon's coven. Now Sword can't be used to counter our goals. With December out of action, we need some insulation from the politics right now. Even if this relationship only lasted a year, it would be enough to stall our rivals in the order."

"You mean there are political reasons? Come on. I know Aileen. She was a priestess. She has appetites they teach at the temple."

Darjeeling snapped back in anger. "You don't know anything. How old are you? Twenty years at most? Come tell me all of the things you know after you turn two hundred years old. Then maybe I'll listen. Aileen is defending herself every second of the day. By defending herself, she is defending you. Don't you dare besmirch her for doing something that will help the both of you, and maybe even the goddess as well, if Phyllicitus should ever regain her senses."

"Sword is going to ruin my life. Why shouldn't I get upset?"

"Oh, you should get upset. There is no reason to stop you. What you can't do is act like a child. You need to keep your mind about you, or the last problem you will need to worry about is your relationship with Aileen."

Miller felt sadness begin to well up in his heart. He started thinking about all of the things Sword had done to him. How long it took him to open up to Aileen.

That was the sting. Aileen knew of the abuses Sword had heaped upon him. She knew of his shame. She didn't care what all of this meant to him. The thought of her not caring, of becoming just another White Hand master, twisted with madness and disconnected from decency, overwhelmed him. His heart ached in his chest.

"I'm releasing the calming spell. It tends to build up, then it becomes even worse when you leave the enchantment."

He felt his gut begin to wrench like his heart was on fire.

"There is a small chance that the aftereffects can be permanent. Also, you will want to be aware that suicidal thoughts are not unusual. You should be recovered in a few days though, if, well, you don't do anything permanent. And if you decide to take your own life, please do it somewhere we won't have to clean up. Let's be kind to Frantz, shall we?"

Miller felt a jarring sensation in his gut as the channels released. He felt his strength leave him. The world spun and he fell onto the ground. The cup with the floral designs lay discarded at his side. He curled up into a ball on the wet grass, agony cutting into his guts, into his heart. The pain was no longer in his imagination, his heart felt broken, shattered into a million pieces. He couldn't think or talk. He lay there gasping like his life was being forced out of his lungs.

"Well, I think that concludes our conversation. I'll leave Frantz with you to make sure you don't choke to death on your own tongue. Let's reconvene in the hall in, let's say, an hour?"

Frantz walked over, bending down to inspect his face. "He'll be fine. I'll keep watch and make sure he gets back."

"Excellent! I knew I had you around for a reason!"

Darjeeling turned and walked back to the hall, leaving Miller heaving three glasses of brandy onto the ground, and Frantz looking on, smirking.

###

Eventually the pain subsided, and Miller could think again. He had vomited the contents of his stomach a few moments ago, and a few paces away. Since then, he had begun to feel better.

He lay in the tall grass wondering how life had gotten this way. He lay, lost in thought, trying to remember something he had done that would make him deserve this. The concept of 'deserve' had been ingrained in him by his parents since birth. The White Hand dismissed such concepts as childish. He promised himself never to let Darjeeling help him when he was feeling down. He had known better than to drink what Darjeeling had offered.

Deciding that lying in a wet field wasn't going to help him with anything, Miller sat up. Frantz had spread out a canvas to protect his clothes from the wet grass. He sat there with a pitcher of water in his hand, pouring into a clay mug. "Feel better after a good cry?" he said, with a hint of malice.

"Cheeser." All Miller could think of were insults from childhood.

"Yikes. No need to call names." Frantz smiled back and offered Miller the cup of water, holding it just a few feet out of reach. Miller sighed and stood, walking over to take the water.

"Goddess! Your breath stinks."

"Sorry, I've been busy puking. Didn't get a chance to freshen up."

"Well, just make sure it doesn't happen again, especially near my shoes."

Frantz stood and began rolling up his tarp, tying it tight with a small cord. Miller wondered where the tarp had come from. He hadn't seen it earlier. Then he realized that he had no idea how long he had been out here.

The tarp didn't matter though. His entire life had just changed, now it was time to learn what this new life would be. "I guess we should go back."

"Finish the water first."

"Why?"

"Because it can help clean you out and restore your body's natural balances. Water is good for that kind of thing."

"Natural balance? What does Master Darjeeling teach you? I've never even heard of that."

Frantz shrugged. "Master Darjeeling is far-traveled. He has a more nuanced view of the world than you. Drinking water is the least crazy thing he asks us to do, believe me. One day I had to wear cheese on my head from morning to night, then compose a poem about it. It's funny looking back, but at the time, it wasn't. Darjeeling told me that he would kill me if I didn't do a good job of it."

Miller shook his head in disbelief. "Yeah, I heard he's like that."

"Yeah, he is."

"Better than Sword though."

"Yeah, he is. He tries to teach his apprentices, but sometimes he doesn't make much sense."

"I'm guessing that your poem was wonderful?"

"No. It was awful. I'm lucky that he had no taste in poetry. I did learn that if you include the word 'asses' in your poetry, he will always approve."

Miller finished the cup of water. He traded Frantz the cup for the rolled-up canvas and they began walking back to the hall. Cerna opened the door as they approached.

"He's still with us?" Cerna asked as they entered the hall.

"I guess so. I gave it even-odds that he wouldn't be."

Cerna stared at him. "Keep your head in the game, boy. Things have gotten serious for you."

That caught Miller's attention. He didn't know what Cerna meant, but if he was giving a warning then there would be a reason.

He walked past Cerna into the hall. A conversation abruptly stopped. Five masters of the White Hand stood in a circle, turning to face him. Brita stared his way with wide, fearful eyes. Easter walked forward, always the leader.

"If you have quite recovered, there is work to be done."

Aileen said nothing to him, avoiding his gaze.

"Work? What do you need?"

"Start packing. We are moving our base into Home's Hearth," Easter said.

That surprised him. Moving into Home's Hearth was directly counter to the command of the goddess. Phyllicitus would not be pleased.

"And the goddess? How have we factored her into this decision? She won't want us in the town."

"The goddess can get over her little snit. I think we have enough masters with us. We can do whatever we want."

Miller's eyebrows shot up in surprise. Did the masters seek confrontation with a living god?

Aileen finally spoke up. "Phyllicitus will come to us, or at the very least, invite us to her temple. She is very good at being snide and spoiled. She can't force anyone to do anything though. She is weak that way. The Takers have regrouped. This isn't the time to play games and we are not about to start with her little tantrum."

But she was still a goddess, tied to forces beyond the arts of the masters.

Miller remembered how Home's Hearth was before she returned. It was a mess of petty disputes, family clashes, and endemic poverty. Within a week of her return, all of the hopelessness in the town had disappeared. Within a year, farms were blossoming, sickness was gone, and people were genuinely happy again. It was like the sun rose to brighten the entire land. All of that was done by the goddess.

The people would do anything for her. But what would she ask them to do? Miller was suddenly afraid. He was unsure what the goals of the masters were. They could as easily be trying to topple the goddess as trying to help her.

He reached down and felt the hilt of Chamise's knife. Not long ago, the Eisenvard had enforced their vision of Phyllicitus's law. He remembered hundreds of armed men that would scour the roads and countryside, hunting for the White Hand. Masters could return from the Crooked Gate. Apprentices could not. The order had lost many apprentices in those days. She had disbanded the Eisenvard when she returned, angry at their violent and sometimes deadly ways.

People could do bad things while simply imagining what Phyllicitus should want, rather than doing what she actually wanted.

Cerna reached over and tapped him on the head. "Stop thinking, start packing. You'll give your brain a cramp. You aren't good at it."

Easter was scowling at him.

Miller was grateful for something physical to do, something that didn't involve dealing with the new drama here in the hall. "Got it. I'll start packing.

MEETING THE TEAM

Chamise awoke. Memories called to her from long ago. She heard the sounds of laughter and camaraderie coming from outside the Eisenvard keep. Those sounds had long been missing from her life. No matter what the Free Mages said about their family, it wasn't a close one. The Free Mages united because it gave them a common defense, but they never had a common purpose. Here, amongst the ghosts of the Eisenvard, she remembered when a great purpose united them all, even if it was hollow, broken, and doomed to fail.

She lay in a small bundle of blankets, curled up on the stone floor. She remembered years ago when the yard was filled Eisenvard. In those years, they would assemble three times a week for sport before training. Now, years gone by, the yard lay empty. Even the rooms were empty.

But someone was out there. She wondered what they were doing.

Pushing the covers from her tired body, she stood and reached for the woolen breeches. She preferred men's fashions as they were much less burdensome and easier to fight in. She thanked whatever sheep had grown that wool, as the cold had brought on a slight shiver. The chill went through her, reminding her of just how much this place had changed. There were no welcoming fires, no hearty breakfast. There were only blankets that smelled of horse and a half-eaten apple.

Her stomach rumbled. She set to the apple, finishing its husk before the brown could seep deeper into the core of the thing.

She heard the calls of men coming from outside again. They cheered, laughing at some prank. The calls were familiar, they beckoned her from the past. After sitting alone in the dim room for ten minutes, she gave up and went to see what was happening. She dressed, pulling her plain wool gown over her sleeping shift. Then she slipped on her low shoes, quickly brushed her shoulder-length blond hair, and went to investigate. She moved out of the narrow sleeping chamber, into the lesser hall, then through the hall of wisdom. She passed by the carved words of the credo and emerged into the morning sunshine.

It could have been a better welcome.

Schaller sat on the steps in front of the entrance. He had been a respected swordsman, a knight's aid, and an armored juggernaut when the Eisenvard ruled Home's Hearth. A large cup, mostly empty of drink, sat next to him. Years ago, it would have been an insult to relax on the steps of the chapter house. Now, even Schaller treated it as normal.

He turned his head to face Chamise, scowling. He continued to be unsure whether she was truly one of them. She had embraced magic after her mother had been burned. A sense of regret and sadness settled on his mind. Chamise carried enough of a burden, he didn't think he needed to add to it.

"Come to face the morning?" he asked.

"Please, not again. We were up way too late last night. I'm done arguing with you."

They had stayed up well past midnight, debating, then arguing about the order. They discussed histories, its rules, and how the way they dealt with crafters had played its role in the final days. Three full bottles of wine had been devoured as they fought, debated, and aggravated each other until dawn. She couldn't just go to bed, not after he called her a witch. The anger from last night had left her. Somehow it all worked out. At least they weren't enemies, she reflected. Although, that could change.

Chamise walked up to stand beside Schaller on the stairs and looked out to the yard. A group of ten men stood in a crowd. Each man held a small net that was fixed at the end of a three-foot wooden pole. Another man was dragging a tarp out to the side of the field, preparing to set up the goal. He was having a difficult time with it, as one of his arms was missing.

"I know him," she said, pointing at the man. "He sold me apples in the market yesterday."

"That's Otto. He's a good sort. He still likes to be on the team, but he isn't much good, having just one arm."

"So why do you let him play?"

"Nobody's brave enough to stop him. The man fights exceptionally dirty, and he doesn't like it when people remind him of his little scratch."

Chamise nodded back. "I understand." She imagined how it would be, to be maimed and unable to heal. The goddess could heal so many wounds. She thought for a long moment about what it would take for Phyllicitus to turn her back on someone. It would take a lot.

They passed the time in silence. After ten minutes, Schaller stood with his cup and re-entered the building. Chamise watched the teams form. The first team set up the goal tarp using two rickety, man-sized poles to hold up the light cloth. Another was being worked on by the one-armed man.

She grew annoyed with herself. He had given her food and she hadn't even asked his name. She resolved to be friendlier to people, then she looked around at the Eisenvard keep, the place where they had condemned her mother. Somehow, she knew it would be difficult to put on a welcoming face.

"Stop scowling. Here, take this."

Schaller had returned from his trip into the building carrying two large cups. She took one from his hand, smelling the sweet spices of warm cider. Not knowing what to say, she just sipped, trying to forget their long discussion last night of evil, witchcraft, and her mother. He seemed to be trying to make friends. Chamise just wasn't sure why. Oh well, she thought, at least he's not trying to burn me alive. It was hollow progress, but progress nonetheless.

They had burned her mother alive. It wasn't far from here. On silent lonely nights when she slept, she could still hear her mother's screams.

Not for the first time, she wondered why she had come back. Waiting on an apprentice necromancer to keep his word seemed like a useless way to spend her valuable time. Miller wasn't an unknown though. He had been crucial to pushing back the Takers three years ago. She hoped that he could do so again and that he could show her how he did so. There were too many magical arts for anyone to master. The books that the Free Mages kept were half secrets themselves, with words being encoded, or meanings obscured.

Miller would keep his word.

Chamise didn't have anywhere else to go, at least until Miller arrived.

"I know that one-armed man," she said, gesturing with her cup back toward the man fumbling with the tarp. He held a pole between his knees as he stretched, trying to attach a clip to the tarp's edge.

"Red? It doesn't surprise me. He was good friends with your father."

"He is the one who sent me here. I guess he was doing me a favor."

"You guess?"

"Not sure yet." There was no use lying to an Eisenvard, especially one so experienced as Schaller. They were taught how to spot lies and those who speak them. In addition, Chamise didn't really care what Schaller thought of her.

A single player broke off from the scrum and began walking toward them. He was tall and muscular, with short red hair paired with a pointed beard which only grew on his chin, leaving his cheeks baby smooth. As he approached closer, his features began to stand out. He wasn't just handsome, he was beautiful. Chamise began to smile as she took in his presence. There seemed to be a gem in the rough of the Eisenvard after all. Then she recognized him, and her excitement turned to panic.

"Chamise! Remember me?" he said as he approached.

"How could I forget?" she replied, deadpan. "I thought you were dead."

She had hoped that he was dead.

Schaller laughed at her response. "We are all sort of dead, just stuck in this midpoint to the afterlife."

The stranger looked taken aback by her cold response. "I didn't know we were on bad terms, sorry, I would have sent someone else over."

"Don't be a fool. You and I aren't on any terms."

Schaller interrupted their approaching verbal duel. "Take it slow Reegan. She just got here, and no matter what baggage you have left from days past, she is in the family. So state your business and let's not argue."

"I wasn't trying to argue. It's just that Geoff didn't make it on time, again. So now we are one short, again. Someone has to sit out."

Both Reegan and Schaller shook their heads in disappointment.

"Who is out this time?"

"You are, old man. You got the short straw."

"I was looking forward to a match. I can't say I'm happy with Geoff right now."

"It's his job at the smithy. They only let him off when business is slow." Reegan paused before turning to Chamise. "It's been great seeing you again." Then he turned and walked back to the group of men, who were busily passing out wooden sticks topped with small nets.

After Reegan had joined the crowd, Schaller turned to her. "Can I interest you in a game of nets? It will be great to get some exercise and maybe release a little steam."

She shook her head. "I'm not sure that is a good idea. I don't want to be near Reegan. We have a history, didn't you see?"

"I saw. I just thought you might enjoy a fight against team-Reegan today, and perhaps a victory."

She smiled, thinking about knocking that cocky bastard to the ground. It had been years since Reegan and her were together. She remembered her clumsy attempts at seducing him. It turned out to be an easy task. She also remembered how her heart felt when she discovered that a half dozen other women found it easy as well. Then she thought about placing her fist in his face. The thought made her happy.

"Sure, I'm up for a small game of nets."

"I thought you would be."

Chamise walked onto the field, Schaller by her side. He gestured to a group of five men standing to the right of the other group. "Those are your teammates."

"It looks like you've been feeding them well."

One of the men was huge. He towered over Chamise. She stood next to him eye-level with his chest. His belly looked like he hadn't stopped eating since the Eisenvard had disbanded. His friend was a little smaller but could only be described as small when he stood next to him.

"Yes. That's Dex. He's fast enough, but the years working in kitchens haven't been kind to him. Prian is decent enough. I'll introduce you."

The men stopped talking as they approached, turning to see the newcomer. She felt small. Not only were they tall, but half of them were also wide, and not with muscle. "Today is your lucky day, gentlemen. You have someone to fill in for Geoff.

This is Chamise. She will do you all proud." Smiles greeted her. They must not get many new players, she thought.

"Let me make introductions before you start talking her ears off." Schaller guided her up to one of the heavy men she had just been talking about. "This is Prian. He plays raider mostly when he isn't sleeping. He's a good enough shot for this game."

Prian smiled down at her. He stood a foot taller than Chamise. His dark hair and dark skin contrasted with hers, even though it was streaked with gray. His smile was broad and honest.

"How did Schaller talk-a you into this game? You know-a we are all Eisenvard, eh?" Prian asked, his voice spiced with a foreign accent.

She scoffed. "Don't worry about that. So am I." His surprised look was priceless.

His grin didn't fall away. "All right then, glad to have you. Can you play Guard?"

Guard was a good place to put a weaker player. All she needed to do was keep the ball out of the goal. This isn't going to be so bad, she hoped. It had been five years she last played a game of nets though. Chamise smiled back, feigning confidence. "Easy."

"This big guy," Schaller continued while placing his hand on another man's shoulder, "is Dex." He loomed over her, even larger up close. I can't even reach his nose from down here in normal-land.

Dex's voice was deep, and a little frightening. His chest was so large she wouldn't be able to wrap her arms around him. She could tell that Dex had been a giant of a man, but that was long ago. Now he was simply tall and gone to fat. Dex kept his gray curly hair cut short. It made him look like a small dying weed was growing on top of a hill. His skin was pale white, marked only by three burns along his left arm, and a cut that ran the length of his right.

"Hey. Eisenvard, eh? Who did you serve under?"

There was only one answer.

"Silver."

The men grew quiet. She saw that they recognized the name. They remembered what happened. They remembered her mother.

A new man spoke up. "That makes you Silver's girl, right? I didn't think you would ever be back here." He was tall, like Prian, but unlike him, he continued to stay fit. His tan skin testified to his life as a working man. She could see the outlines of muscles beneath his arms.

Chamise tried to put on a friendly face. "It wasn't my first choice. The Goddess and I are trying to work some things out right now, so I needed a place to stay. Are you all right with me being here?"

Go ahead, say no, Chamise thought. I dare you.

Schaller interrupted. "It isn't like that. Ulf just likes it when all the cards are on the table."

Ulf wasn't smiling. His green eyes looked wild, like a dog sizing up its meal. They didn't just stare at her, they stared at everything she did, every motion, every gesture. Chamise judged him to be dangerous. She decided they had better make friends quickly, or just stab him now and get it over with.

"Ulf. Isn't that a foreign name?"

"Sure is. I was born in the lands of The Wolf. My parents never lost their barbaric roots, no matter how hard I tried to guide them out of it."

"Don't they still worship the First Gods there?" She was getting interested in Ulf's history, even if it wasn't a smart hobby.

"Oh yes. The old ways are still alive there. It may be the last place in the world where they live on."

She thought about it for a moment, then decided to give him a reason to at least find her useful. "Maybe not. I have a friend who is well traveled. I'm supposed to meet him in town soon. He told me tales of Bear God worshipers in the north. I could introduce you."

Ulf nodded dismissively as if she had simply agreed to

something he had suggested long ago. She thought about introducing him to an apprentice necromancer. She smiled at the humor of it, expecting that Ulf wouldn't have the slightest idea who he was talking with.

After a moment, she thought better of the idea. The Wolflander people had a reputation. They were a brutal group, one didn't just walk among them.

I had better make sure to introduce them while they are both in Home's Hearth, and the goddess's peace is unbroken.

"Oh, just so you know. I'm the other guard. You and I will be getting to know each other, very well."

She bowed her head in welcome. Now she knew who she would be playing alongside. Wolflanders were famously difficult to team with. They were wild, independent, and didn't like listening to other people's plans. Adding Eisenvard to that mixture only made them more violent.

Schaller continued the introductions. He gestured at the one-armed man.

"You know Red from the market, of course."

The one-armed man stood there, holding a net larger than normal. She wondered if it was oversized because of his wound, to give him some small help. She was surprised. Eisenvard didn't give handicaps in this game. She was glad to see a small change in the Eisenvard at the very least.

She was happy to see Red at the very least. "Thank you for the apples," she said.

"And finally, we have Gable. He plays the center position." The short man walked up and bowed formally. He had an average build, with long straight brown hair flowing down his back. Chamise knew many women who would be jealous of his perfect locks. His voice was high pitched like he was on the verge of panic. She offered a grin as he spoke.

"Welcome. We're always glad to grow the company. Things are, well, so small now. But even now, we grow larger!"

She didn't like the look in his eyes. His gaze lingered on her just a little too long. Chamise calmly evaluated slamming her fist into his crotch. If Gable didn't mind his manners, she decided, she would pummel him into a lump of mush.

The thought made her smile.

Schaller didn't wait to give her time to speak with the others. He just announced it was time to play. "Come on, let's play nets!"

Prian walked over to a stack of equipment, fetching a bundle of nets. Each net consisted of an arm's-length handle connected to a net the size of someone's head. The idea of the game was simple enough. Each team would try to catch a leather ball, then to put it into the other team's goal. Team members could toss the ball back and forth or simply run with it. Running with the ball was an invitation to be hit with sticks. The Eisenvard were using old cloth sheets dyed different colors, blue and green, to represent goals. Goaltenders stood next to the goal within a safe area that the enemy raiders were banned from entering. Guards could enter their own safe areas, but not cross to the enemy's side. The first team to five goals won the match.

He began handing out nets. Chamise took the last net and smiled back at him. "It's been years since I played this game. I'll try not to disappoint the team." Just for the fun of it, she batted her eyes in her best damsel in distress imitation.

"Are you kidding? Just having a new player is a treat. We stopped caring about the whole win-or-lose thing long ago."

"Great. This will be fun then."

"Don't worry. I won't let anything bad happen to you," Gable said, in an attempt at gallantry. Ulf looked at him as if he were the village idiot, shaking his head in disbelief.

They walked over to the other team. Schaller had already told them that Chamise would be playing.

"So here is the enemy team," Schaller said as he introduced his team. "I'm playing raider, along with Jeamers." Jeamers was an impressively muscled man, calloused, bearing a half dozen old scars. He looked like another person devoted to labor, his arms were strong and well defined. She noted their states. They didn't have wealthy trappings. They barely had serviceable clothing. The Eisenvard had obviously fallen socially.

Jeamers gestured at a tall thin man, graying at the temples, then at the man next to him. "Tabor and Reegan are our Guards. Eadric is our center."

"Glad to meet you." She wasn't though. This game of nets was starting to feel like a bad idea. These men either didn't want her here or wanted her here a little too much.

GAME ON

A few minutes later, Chamise was on the field ready to play nets. Memories of her youth went through her mind as she breathed in and out, preparing for the game. Ulf stood thirty feet to the left of her, with the goal between them, twenty feet behind. She hoped that he would be up for the job. If she had to play this game, then she wanted to win. She remembered when Schaller asked her to play. She was hesitant at first, but after laying around her dark room for a few hours, playing a physical game like nets started to appeal to her.

Red picked up the fist-sized leather ball in the same hand as he held the net. He only had one hand, but he didn't act like it would be a problem. With a flick of his wrist, he gently tossed the ball into the air then quickly scooped it up with his goal-keeper net. Chamise walked back a few steps into her position, surprised at how excited she was to play this game. She hadn't played it in five years, but memories of playing nets on the drill grounds didn't bring pain.

Red walked to the edge of the Safe Area. A bold line had

been drawn on the grass with chalk. He screamed, "Game On!" as he launched the ball forward.

The ball leapt into the air, propelled by the arcing motion of his net. It went high, ending its flight just past midfield. Prian and Dex watched it sail overhead.

Chamise cocked an eyebrow. That wasn't the best way to start a game, missing their raiders with the first toss. The ball fell down toward the field, only to be scooped up by Reegan, the opposing center. The raiders needed to get the ball early. They were the goal scorers. If they didn't get the ball, then there wouldn't be many points.

She gripped her net handle tighter. Her heart skipped a beat when she saw Reegan pick the ball out of the air with his net. She didn't feel the same attraction to him now, only a bit of shame from their failed love affair years ago. Thoughts invaded her mind. Oh no. Why did it have to be him? Reegan and she had too much history between them. She felt angry, imagining him laughing at her distress.

Reegan didn't keep the ball. Instead, he pivoted left and lofted the ball toward his team's raider, Jeamers. Dex was caught out of position and couldn't react fast enough to block the ball. Snatching the ball from the air, Jeamers sprinted by him heading directly toward the goal.

Ulf leapt into action. He raced forward and placed his body between Jeamers and the goal. Red didn't know which side of Jeamers to guard, so he guessed left and moved to the side leaving a wide gap on the right.

The other players hadn't left enough room for Chamise to make a play to block. She stood on alert, ready to guard the goal. Edging to the side, she moved in front of the goal, just outside the goalkeeper zone. Team members were not allowed in the goal zone. She anticipated Red's block strategy and put herself in a place to intercept passes. The pass never came.

Ulf crouched as Jeamers moved in toward the goal, preparing for a burst of energy to put the ball into the goal. Five paces from Ulf, Jeamers cut right and whipped his net around, propelling the ball behind him at lightning speed. Reegan was there waiting for it. He used his net to scoop it out of the air.

Dex didn't notice the pass in time. Ulf keyed in on Dex's movement and dashed out of position to block the no-longer-threatening raider from approaching.

Chamise's attention snapped to the other raider. They had done another quick pass. Schaller was between her and the center of the field. His eyes were locked on hers, but he didn't seem like he was ready to make a catch. He was ready to block her, but she didn't see why.

Reegan held the ball in his net less than two seconds before he launched it into the corner of the goal sheet. Red was too far away to stop it as the ball struck the sheet.

Reegan's mocking voice filled the yard. "Goal!"

She couldn't help herself. "You've got to be kidding me. That quick?" was all Chamise could say.

"Hey! Stop looking like you want to murder someone! It's just a game!" Red called out to her. Then he smiled, pointing his net at the back corner.

"Your serve, Chamise!" Red scooped the ball off the ground and sent it slowly spinning toward her in one swing.

Chamise didn't bother with the net. She snatched the ball out of mid-air, then purposefully walked outside of the boundary marker. She grumbled under her breath. "Nice and slow for the girl, eh? We will see about that. You boys are way too out of shape to be playing these kinds of games with me."

"The tears of the unworthy shall show you your throne," Ulf replied, quoting one of the older credo verses that hung emblazoned on the keep walls.

Chamise shot him a look harsh enough to curdle milk.

"Zero! One!" She announced the score as she returned her attention to the field, trying to find her best target.

Prian and Dex were being covered by the opposing Guards. There were no obvious targets. She glanced toward Ulf, but his attention was diverted. Ulf gazed at the outer gate that exposed a rich coach paused in front of the entrance. An elegant blonde-haired woman wearing a jet-black gown stared into the courtyard, enthralled with their sport. Chamise laughed to herself as she recognized Aileen.

Ulf had different priorities right now, he missed the most important player in the game. She stood in the gate watching. Poor Ulf, Chamise thought, always playing the wrong game.

Reegan stood next to Dex to guard him. She could still get the ball to him. After a few seconds of delay, she dropped the ball into her net and took up position. She watched the raiders begin to move, trying to guess her first pass. Dex hadn't moved though, as if he had known all along that he would be the receiver. She fired a quick overhand shot. The ball leapt out of her net, sailing over Ulf's head, leaving his raider, Jeamers, far behind. Dex faked a left turn, pulling Reegan out of position. By the time Reegan understood what was happening, Dex was already in motion, snatching the ball out of the air with his net.

"Come on! Run it!" Chamise screamed. He just needed to get it a little closer.

She was overcome with excitement. "Go! Go! Go!" Chamise chanted as she sprinted across the field line to retake her position.

Reegan moved to cut Dex off. Dex didn't try to stop him. Instead, he passed the ball to Prian. Prian snatched it out of the air and began lumbering toward the opponent's goal.

Chamise could see failure coming. Prian moved slowly compared to Reegan. He trudged down the field, too heavy to be quick but too strong to be easily stopped. "Come on Prian, just pass the ball!" Chamise called out, trying in vain to salvage the play.

Eadric moved to the center of the enemy goal while Reegan sprinted back to guard the left side. Chamise watched as Reegan moved forward to harry Prian. Dex didn't like what he saw. Instead of passing, Prian took a shot at the goal. The net slashed to the side, propelling the ball toward the goal sheet. Reegan sprung out of position and caught the ball in his net.

Chamise was just beginning her cry of "No!" when Reegan

launched the ball. It flew through the air toward her, toward their raiders. Jeamers sprinted forward attempting to net the ball, but Chamise moved to block his path. The ball hit the grass, bouncing past her legs toward the goal.

She didn't want to be embarrassed in front of the others. She wanted to be, no, had to be the one who made goals, not lost them.

She scrambled after the ball, scooping it from the ground with her net. Jeamers moved behind her, only a step away. He pushed her to the right side of the field with his larger body, coming up beside her and slamming his net into hers.

She saw Reegan moving toward the other side of the field into the same position that he had just scored from. Quickly, she ducked and moved around Jeamers, flinging the ball out of her zone toward one of her raiders. Prian caught the ball, surprised by how quickly the play had changed. He turned to take in where the opposing players were located. His moment of indecision allowed Tabor to move into his guard position.

Prian didn't like how the defending guards were moving so quickly. He shot at the goal from straight on, forty paces away. Eadric snatched the ball from the air right in front of the goal, ending Prian's dreams of a quick point.

Eadric didn't hesitate once he had the ball. He snapped it toward the sideline where Tabor had taken up position. Tabor caught the ball, and in the same movement, launched it downfield. It sailed over her raider's heads. Jeamer moved back and caught the ball.

Chamise was only ten steps from him as he spun to attack her goal. She moved to intercept him, but he wasn't heading directly for the goal. Jeamer was barreling down on her at full speed.

His quick movement surprised her. She wondered what he was trying to do. He looked like he was going to pass, but his stick was in the wrong position.

She looked around for Schaller, but that was a bad idea. At full speed, all six feet of Jeamers slammed into Chamise. She flew off her feet, rolling as she struck the ground. Her combat training kicked in as she tucked into a roll, sparing her from a broken arm.

She scrambled up, recovering from the hit. Schaller shot past her. He flicked the ball to the side, directly into Reegan's net. Reegan took two large steps toward the goal and heaved a powerful overhead throw. The ball raced into the corner of the net, where Red didn't have a defending arm. It slammed into the goal cloth.

Chamise growled in frustration. Her arm hurt. It was going to have a bruise tomorrow. Next time I'll wear armor, she thought.

She shook her head in disgust as the opposing team celebrated their goal. It never changes, she thought, the Eisenvard would strive to win at all costs, even when there is nothing at stake. They would never change.

"What is going on?" she yelled loudly, turning her body toward her team. "Can't you even try?"

Anger and frustration boiled over. She walked over to Ulf and grabbed him by the shoulder, spinning his eyes from the gate and toward her. "Can't you keep your mind on the game for a second?"

"Sorry. But, well, something is going on out there."

She glanced toward the gate. A wagon had stopped in front of it, and Aileen was still standing there in the entrance, watching. Chamise wondered how long Aileen would stand there watching.

She saw Ulf staring at Aileen. He looked ready for a fight. "Look. Let's pretend the nice lady is rooting for us. All right?" Chamise said, unwilling to announce the arrival of a White Hand master.

Ulf narrowed his eyes. "I've just got this feeling. I've learned to pay attention to them. Call it an instinct. Something isn't right with that woman."

"Right. A feeling." Chamise tried to dismiss Ulf's concern, or at least give him something else to think about. "Let's finish this game. Then we can all go find the pretty lady. Maybe we can have tea?"

Ulf's response was cold. "You don't have to be an ass."

Chamise shook her head in distaste. "Can we just get organized enough to prevent a single goal?" She asked the team. Her voice rose with passion. "These people are making fools of us!"

Red spoke up. "All right, First," he said, giving her the title normally reserved for lance leaders. "What's your plan. I yield to your experience. Lead on."

"Look," she said, pointing at the sideline. "Whenever Reegan gets over there, he shoots at your soft side. Every time. Let's just try not to give him that shot. Schaller, you are Center, can't you fall back and defend the weak spot?"

Schaller shook his head up and down. "I can do that. But who is going to get the ball to our raiders?"

"We can't keep their ball out of our goal, why should we care about our raiders? Let's just finish the game with some dignity. Do we have to lose by double digits?"

Prian, attempting to help her but somehow failing, added his comment. "Again."

Chamise was inflamed. "Again? Seriously? How many times have you lost to these one-trick ponies?"

"Most of the time," was all Prian could say. Dex stood next to him with a grin on his face, nodding in agreement.

"Yeah. They practice, and stuff."

"And stuff?"

"Yeah. And stuff."

Chamise gave up talking. She moved forward, grabbing her teammates one at a time, and dragging them to their positions. She gave each of them instructions in short terse words. There would be no room for confusion.

Finally, Ulf moved to the serve corner. Red tossed him the ball. Ulf flung it into play, landing short, a bouncing shot that moved at an angle across the field. Reegan moved forward to snatch it up, but Chamise was there before him. He was larger, but she was faster. She dodged left as Schaller scooped up the ball, then tossed it back to Ulf who had just gained the field. Ulf was a sprinter, and he moved quickly. Ulf raced with the speed of a wolf along the sideline. He crossed the centerline before Tabor moved to intercept him. Reegan fell back toward his goal as Ulf passed by, confused about where this new strategy was heading.

Dex and Prian approached the goal, just outside of the safe area. Crossing into the safe area would earn the other team penalty shots. Neither of the raiders wanted that. Tabor came out of his position as Dex got lined up to receive a pass. Ulf cut left and snapped the ball back to Gable. Gable snatched it out of the air, took a step, and shot the ball into the goal. The ball struck Eadric in the forehead, surprising him. It bounced high into the air before it stalled in its arc, and gently flopped back toward Eadric's goal net.

Just before it hit, Chamise slammed into him at full speed. She kept low, where her velocity would compensate for her lightweight frame. She struck him left of the pelvis, just missing his sensitive parts. Eadric spun completely around, falling to the ground. The ball fell, striking his shoulder and rolled into the goal.

Chamise just stood there watching the slowly moving ball score a point. She smiled down at Eadric, then smirked.

"That shot was for Schaller. The score is One Two."

Chamise began walking back to her goal. Red stood there, smiling like it was his birthday.

Ulf's attention was lost to the gate again. He stood near the opponent's server corner, staring across the hundred-foot divide. Chamise could read his body language. He wasn't smitten by anything, he was on alert. His hackles were raised, ready to fight.

Then she glanced back toward the gate. Master Easter stood there, staring back. She recognized him clearly. Aileen stood next to him, her long, elaborate, black dress stretching from her bosom to the ground. Chamise hadn't seen her in years. Now here she was, full mistress of the White Hand, betrayer of Phyllicitus, directly in front of her.

Two White Hand masters. She reached down toward her knife, Master December's own blade. She had killed him for it in that tower. It wasn't there anymore. Miller had it now. All of a sudden, she regretted her decision to give it to Miller.

"I'm telling you, something is wrong with her, and her friend," Ulf continued.

"Ulf, remind me to never doubt you again," Chamise said. Fear began to creep into her spine. Well, she thought, I might as well get this over with. It isn't going to get any easier.

She dropped the net on the ground and began jogging toward the gate. Wherever Aileen was, Miller would be close behind.

COINCIDENCE

The street was noisy. Sounds of workmen shouting, children playing, and the marketers hawking their goods filled the air. The Rat sat across from Hazel, her eyes firmly planted on his, and nibbled on a late lunch. Bright green lettuce contrasted with slender shavings of ham and slices of red tomatoes. The fresh bread covered with sweet cheese served as a lovely dessert. Hazel leisurely spooned her soup into her mouth, enjoying each scoop, its rich aroma drifting across the table toward him.

"Very good. Your table manners have improved these past few days."

Hazel smiled back at him. It wasn't an honest smile. It was a crooked thing, too-long hidden behind a mask. Now that she was one of them, that she was taken, she could let that smile show, if just a little.

"Thank you, Uncle."

She reached forward with her empty hand and touched his. The Rat noted how much she liked to touch him. He'd never met anyone who enjoyed being taken as much as she did. It surprised him that she had been so pliable. She hadn't resisted at all when she discovered what had occurred. Unlike most people, her first words as a taken were not "Why me?"

Hazel's first words after she was taken were "Do we get to kill my family now?"

Now she sat across from him, neatly ladling soup into her face. Happier than she had been in her entire life. The Friends were very pleased with their new family member. Of course, they agreed with her request. The Rat had lost an entire afternoon to that grisly task. After he cleaned the small remote farmhouse, he had to go back to town and fetch supplies, along with a mule and an extra shovel.

Luckily, Hazel's farm upbringing had made her an efficient assistant. The bodies were converted to useful ingredients quick enough. Now he was tired.

The Rat reflected how poorly Hazel behaved in public. Such things were key to fitting in and remaining hidden. He found her mannerisms particularly abhorrent. They continued to be poor, but good enough for what he needed. He hoped that the Friends wouldn't become overly infatuated with her and not allow him to use her as he originally intended.

He gently smiled, and squeezed her hand, allowing the Friends to more easily commune. She would know that he had a purpose for her, but she would not know what it was. Truthfully, she didn't seem as though she even cared what the purpose was. As long as the ruse held, she would be happy in the role of his niece from the country.

He watched as she finished her soup. She had recently gotten into the habit of wiping her face after eating, now she reached for the water bowl, dipping her strong fingers in it, then gently dabbing at the soup on her face. Finally, she wiped her face dry with the clean cloth he had brought with him for just this purpose.

"My dear, you've allowed some filth to accumulate under your nails. Perchance you should soak them for a few minutes? You know what I say, don't you?"

"Yes, Uncle. A clean body is a happy body."

She smiled again, dipping both hands into the bowl. Dried blood had accumulated under her nails. The work at the farmhouse had been a bloody mess. She had raked her father's face, again and again, screaming at him with unleashed rage. She hadn't used words to describe how she felt about her family. The Friends had communicated that well enough. It is good, he reflected, that their history is ended.

Hazel didn't like silence though. She started talking about how much she liked living in the town, how interesting the craft of alchemy was, and how much she wanted to meet others who were... like her.

The Rat allowed her to drone on and on about hopes, fears, and other things that didn't matter anymore. As he finished the last slice of cheese, the Friends began to call out. He watched as Hazel froze, then began snapping her head around, urgently trying to discover what was happening.

Can you be any more obvious? He thought.

"Calm down," the Rat commanded softly. "Give them some time, don't try to force it. The Friends will let you know what you need to know when you need to know it. Don't think too much, just observe."

A serving girl walked up carrying a pitcher of wine. She had seen Hazel's search of the crowd and naturally thought she was looking for service. The Rat held up his hand and spoke to her. "We're finished. Thank you for the wonderful meal."

She beamed at the compliment, and especially at the whole silver coin that he slid across the table toward her.

"Come, niece. I feel the urge to walk and capture some of this afternoon's wonderful sunlight."

"I would love that." Smiles, agreement, docility. If the Rat hadn't seen her murder her own parents three nights ago, he might believe how much of a perfect little girl she was.

"Come along then. I'll show you a treat today."

They walked through the tidy streets of Home's Hearth, the Rat leading her into an area wealthy with old money and grand homes. They paused when they encountered a garden flush with red, white, and pink plants in full bloom. Hazel stared at the exotic plants growing around marble fountains. The empty street allowed her the space to gaze jealously at the mansions that lined the street. He thought to himself, Once the Friends have had a victory or two, I just might own all of them.

He motioned her onward. They turned a corner and moved past the magnificent homes into an area where the stone road curved. The homes were replaced by massive trees. It was as if the town had been carved out of an elder forest.

Hazel became interested. "Aren't we still in town? Why haven't they harvested this wood yet?"

"Because nobody dares. Phyllicitus won't command it, nor will any nobleman permit it. This is the area we call The Gardens. It is as old as the city, and just as storied. Wealthy people come here to take their leisure."

They followed the winding cobblestone road. After the turn, a marble archway stood over the path. A handsome young man with light hair and a colorful yellow tunic stood blocking the path. In his right hand, he held a long red staff with a small red ribbon tied to the end. Iron gates filled the archway, making passage impossible. The gates continued to each side, transforming into an iron fence line that blocked any further passage through the forest.

"Hold," the young man announced. "I don't recognize you. What is your business here?"

Hazel batted her eyes at the young man, trying to be alluring. The Rat knew better. He simply placed his hand on her shoulder, asking the Friends to calm her down.

"My apologies," the Rat began, "my niece has just moved into the town, and I wanted to show her areas she should not go, especially unaccompanied."

"Oh, well, that is probably wise. It's best to be invited in, if you understand."

The Rat scowled back, not angry, but feigning affront. He knew exactly what happened to young women in the walls of

The Garden. "That is the point, isn't it? The invitation is the tricky part, getting out with your honor intact is another."

The young man smirked. "Well said, sir, well said."

The Rat turned to leave, grasping Hazel's arm, pulling her along. Hazel stumbled a bit, intent on taking in the lush gardens beyond.

She gave the young guard a coy wave as they walked around the corner.

"What was that all about?" she asked.

"I just wanted you to see it. It's a den of moral turpitude that the goddess seems to enjoy quite a bit. They also have one of the most complete libraries of magical lore in the city, if not the whole lands. I've heard that if you know the right people, and pay the right fees, then you can gain access. I would dearly like to enter that community of scholars, even considering their many perversions."

"Perversions?" Hazel asked, a hint of interest in her voice.

"Yes. Perversions. You didn't think the Goddess of Love was all about friendship, did you? When she says love, she means all of it."

"So it's part of the temple?"

"No. This society has existed long before the temple, before Phyllicitus originally came here. This place was here when the world followed the First Gods and continues on today."

She shivered. "The First Gods? They should not be trifled with."

"Still a worshiper? Your country roots are showing."

"The First Gods don't need my worship. They don't care about what I think. I might be simple, and from the fields, but I've seen enough of the world to know that. Don't disrespect them."

"That, I shall never do."

He continued leading her away from The Garden. They emerged into the wealthy neighborhoods again. The Rat felt the Friends trying to communicate, telling him to move, to go in a different direction. He turned left, passing by a dozen holly shrubs. Each of these had been carefully manicured into tall rectangular towers of green. They cast shadows on the cobblestones, giving it a striped appearance, like bars in a cage. Hazel stopped to touch the pointed leaves, but the Rat didn't slow. She sprinted to keep up, starting to feel the will of the Friends.

Their street emerged onto a wide boulevard. The entrance of a once-great yard stood open before them, grand stone pillars stood beside an entrance. Low walls sealed off the wealthy landowners from what was once the domain of the Eisenvard. Now the old buildings stood deserted, relegated to duties far below their original purposes. A carriage stood parked along the wall that surrounded the old military drill grounds. An elegantly dressed woman stood observing some kind of sport being carried out in the yard. Another shorter and narrower man stood to the side cleaning his nails with a small knife. The Rat could feel the excitement bubbling up from the Friends. A target perhaps?

Hazel started forward, intent on some dire mischief. The Rat took her by the shoulder and slowed her down.

"Let's see what is happening in this game before we show our cards, shall we?"

She only hissed. The Rat noted her susceptibility to the blood rage. Friends could do that to the undisciplined. He would have to be careful with her.

He looked left and right, noting the clear streets. There were no pedestrians on the street, no horse-drawn wagons except this single one. It was eerie and silent. A large man stood next to their carriage, well away from the pair by the gate. He was some kind of warrior. A thick leather hauberk covered his body, and chain mail links showed between gaps in his clothing. A large handle jutted from a curved scabbard at his side.

The warrior piqued his interest. Only a well-traveled man would have that kind of blade in these lands. This was plainly not a group to trifle with.

The warrior had taken note of their presence, moving

between the man and the Rat. He stared at them as if he expected them to pull blades and attack him in an instant.

The Rat rolled his eyes. It was always the same with these types, and he grew tired of it.

Excited shouts rang out from within the walls. He glanced through the gates. Some form of sport was occurring, trampling the neglected lawn even further into ruin.

Motioning Hazel forward, he walked toward the guard, ignoring the man and woman he was obviously protecting. He approached the man. The warrior stood a hand taller than the Rat. His hair had begun yielding to gray streaks, but his arms were wiry and covered with scars that bore testament to his experience.

"Come on, Hazel, let's make nice. Maybe you can make a friend today." The Rat stressed the words 'make a friend.' She smiled back, a hint of glee in her eyes.

"Good man!" the Rat called out. "Don't you know this place is closed? The goddess has banned any from loitering here."

"Maybe you should tell these heretics? They don't seem to have a problem playing games in a closed yard."

"Well, I think we can assume these people have permission. Who are you? What is your business?"

The tall man's voice grew cold. "Our business is our business, not yours. You had best remember that."

The warrior placed a hand on the sword hilt threateningly.

"Threaten me with violence? In Home's Hearth? The goddess will hear of this!"

Hazel walked forward, placing herself between the warrior and the Rat. "Please, Uncle. I'm sure he is simply doing his duty. Let's not ruin such a nice day." She spun around, facing him, then curtsying low, showing her healthy feminine shape to its best advantage.

"I'm sorry. My Uncle is devoted to rules. My name is Hazel. I'm new here and Uncle is showing me the sights. I didn't expect him to be so rude."

The Rat scowled. "You know the rules."

"Oh bother. The goddess didn't make a rule about watching, I'm sure." Hazel stepped forward, closer to the armed warrior. She tried to adopt some mannerisms she had recently learned, and only succeeded haltingly. "But I would ask your name if you can give it."

The warrior smiled back, sensing some kind of possibility in front of him.

"I'm called Cerna. Cerna of Skyrt."

Hazel stepped closer, smiling, locking her eyes onto his. "Please forgive my uncle. He can be protective. I'm his only niece."

The Rat scowled, much like any elder guardian would in a similar situation.

As she was approaching him, the sound of hooves on the cobblestones began to grow. Cerna stepped forward and took Hazel's hand, pulling her to the side of the street. "Best you make way," he said to the Rat, unaware of just how badly Hazel wanted to get closer, or what her true desires actually were.

Just a little closer, the Rat thought, and they might catch another stray for the Friends and perhaps grow their little family.

Two tall wagons turned the corner. The first one was driven by a young man with long red hair. He wore dark robes, much like a scribe would wear, except for the broadsword that stood out boldly on his sword belt. The next carriage was driven by an older, portly fellow.

Suddenly a woman emerged from the gateway. She was lightly dressed, grass-stained, and covered in sweat. Her blond hair hung just above her shoulders, and her ample bosom was enough to completely catch Cerna's attention. A moment later he had recovered and was drawing his sword. Hazel gasped, stepping behind Cerna, playing the helpless woman, preparing for an opportunity as Cerna moved forward to protect his two charges.

BRITA AND MILLER

"Chamise!"

The cry filled the air as the lead carriage's door swung open. Miller leapt out of it, landing in a half-run, half-scamper. He moved past the Rat, then past Hazel, without a second glance. Aileen turned to glance at Chamise, then placed her attention squarely back on Miller. Easter didn't let his gaze move away from the game field. Instead, he offered a slight wave of the hand. After a second's hesitation, he turned to face her as she approached. He smiled in recognition.

"Lady Chamise, I'm glad to see you in good sorts, if not the best company."

"Well, I couldn't be picky."

Miller sprinted up to her, reaching forward to take her hands.

"Thank the Goddess. I've been worried about you."

"Thanking the Goddess might be a bit premature if you ask me. I didn't get a great welcome. Somehow I don't think you shall either."

Aileen walked up to join the scene, Cerna following closely behind. "You let me worry about the holy tantrum, won't you?

For what it's worth, I'm glad you made it out of the tower."

She didn't sound glad, simply tired.

Chamise gave her a slight bow, not disrespectful, but not a sign of great respect either. "I didn't mean to interrupt, but I saw you across the field. I was hoping to speak with your apprentice."

Miller was almost bouncing with excitement. Aileen looked around, making sure the other two strangers were far enough away. They had retreated to the side of the road where the older man was leading the woman away by the arm. Miller looked over, alarmed. He chastised himself. He should have checked before he leapt. It could have been an ambush. He needed to get more suspicious, especially when surrounded by so many masters.

Miller hadn't worried about being attacked, not with three masters in his company. But there were different kinds of attacks. The couple, uncle and niece, had moved a respectable distance from them. They continued to walk away, engrossed in a private conversation.

"Looks like you've been recognized. I'm guessing the order hasn't grown in popularity here," Cerna said, staring at the retreating pair.

Aileen shook her head, frowning. "It was going to happen in either case. People were going to find out. This just moves things up by a day or two."

Easter walked up, injecting himself into the conversation. "Can you two move this conversation into the carriage. I'm not comfortable speaking out here in the street like this. Let's keep our business private if you please."

Miller took Chamise by the hand, smiling as he led her toward the head coach. It was a large, solid thing. Dark mahogany wood enclosed a locked compartment meant to keep rich merchants safe from banditry. These types of coaches had become rare since Phyllicitus had returned, but now it had been turned to another purpose.

Opening the door, he stepped up, into the dark interior.

Holding out his hand, he gestured for her to join him within.

She teased, "If this was all it was going to take, why didn't you say so earlier?"

The comment generated a confused look on his face.

"Poor boy, you still don't get it, do you?"

"Be serious, and please get in. We are using two wagons for a reason. We don't want people to know which one is just us, and which one, has a different passenger."

"It never ends with you White Hands, does it? Wheels within wheels."

"Something like that."

She closed the door and the wagon lurched forward. They stared at each other until it grew uncomfortable. Chamise didn't know how to start the conversation that she needed to have, so she leapt into it.

"I don't know where to start," she began.

"I'm glad you got out."

"Thanks. I thought you were dead."

"I may have been for a little bit. I'm not sure."

The memory of Miller's bleeding form on the tower floor made her pause.

"I'm sorry. I should have stayed with you."

Miller shook his head. "You couldn't have gone where I was in any case. Don't worry."

"Where you were?"

"Best not to worry about it. It's another one of those White Hand things."

She took in a long breath, exhaling slowly, building up the courage for the next subject. "And December? I killed him. Do you think he'll come back for me? Back from the grave, I mean?"

She didn't want to seem like a coward to him, but she needed to know.

"I would like to tell you not to worry. December is due in front of some sort of trial, or inquisition. I think his list of things to do is overflowing right now. But December, he can be vengeful. It's a good idea to keep your eyes out. Aileen is with us now so she will be able to keep him in check. I hope."

"You hope?"

"Like I said, Master December can be... unreasonable, when it comes to slights."

"Slights? I shoved a dagger through his neck. I thought he had killed you." Her voice transformed into a whisper. "At the very least, it had to hurt him."

"I've seen what happens when they come back from beyond the door. It hurts, I can tell you that."

"So how am I going to survive this? Do I need some kind of magic weapon to kill him again?"

Miller thought about the enchanted Eisenvard knife she had used to slay December. He thought about December's blood pooling on the stone floor. "No. You've already killed him. Now you need to apologize somehow, to make it up to him."

"What?" Chamise exclaimed. "Like I owe him a favor?"

"You did kill him. That's a personal thing among the White Hand. You'll need to make a peace offering. Trust me, you don't want Master December to come up with an idea how this could be done." Miller thought about how Master December had gained his name. Master December had killed every person in his home village. He drained the blood from every family member he had ever had, erasing the past—root and branch.

"I think he's going to kill me, no matter what I say."

Miller didn't sound like he had any idea how to escape this dark fate. "Let's see what December says when he returns. For now, let's talk to Master Easter and Mistress Aileen. If anyone can help, they can."

They traveled in silence for another awkward few minutes. Miller felt every bump and hole in the road. Chamise stared at him. They had started to grow closer on the road. She wondered if that was all behind them now.

"Well, at least I should get some tutoring before December returns. I've still got your promise to teach to enchant like your guild does. Don't I?"

Like the guild? He thought, not hardly. Differently perhaps, but he would not let her drink from that dark well. Miller did not want to expose her to any more of the White Hand than he had to.

"Yes. I won't break my promise to you, ever."

Miller watched the weathered carriage door open. Slim fingers reached in, with only the dark band of a master's ring decorating them.

"Move back. Give me some room. Chamise dear, it's your time to leave."

Chamise nodded. "I understand." She climbed out of the carriage.

"I'll contact you soon!" Miller called out as she walked away.

"You had better."

Miller scrambled back away from the entrance as Mistress Aileen pulled herself up into the carriage. There were no steps or platform, so she was forced to haul herself up like some sort of common laborer, like himself.

"You are going to ruin your new dress if you keep climbing like that." He gestured at the brown streak of dirt that now decorated the front of her elegant black dress.

"What, this?"

He felt magical channels stir as Aileen whispered three words of power. She moved her ring hand across the brown stain. The mud seemed to boil as she touched in, then it cooked away, like boiling water. There wasn't even a wrinkle on the dress now.

"That's new."

"I got it from Easter. You know how much of a stickler he is for appearances."

He hadn't known. Now that he thought about it, Easter always looked well turned out. It made sense.

She continued, "I wanted to talk with you about Mistress Sword." She hesitated, as if unsure how to start, even though she already had.

His mind raced. She had caught him unprepared for this conversation. He immediately retreated into the role of apprentice, unspeaking, and unhelpful.

"First, let me start by thanking you." She reached out and took his hand in hers, pulling it into the space between them. "I want you to know that I truly value you. I appreciate you for more than your crafting skills. Just by being with me, being my apprentice, you have made my first years as a master easier."

Miller panicked, snapping back the only question he could think of.

"You aren't sending me away, are you?"

It was Aileen's turn to look frightened and surprised. "Send you away? Why would I do that?" She squeezed his hand as if clutching for a lifeline that was slipping away.

"Really? Is that how you are going to play this? I sort of expected better from you."

"Better?" Aileen's temper snapped like a whip. "Better than what? Waiting to get permission from my apprentice?" She spit the word apprentice like it was poison. "Face reality. I'm a mistress of the White Hand. I will live thousands of years. You are a young boy, an apprentice even."

"I'm four years younger than you!"

"Right now, but in a mere hundred years, you will be dead. And what good will you have done me? I need alliances right now. December is off the field right now. I need allies at my side. I need Sword because the wolves are circling and the most dangerous come from her coven. I need her spell power. I need to bridge the gap between our cabal and Hermagon's. I'm new to this Master-of-the-White-Hand thing. Believe me, if I can't keep the other masters at arm's reach, they will devour me."

"A hundred years? Seriously? You are only four years older than I am. You haven't been alive a hundred years. You are talking about abstractions. Dreams. I'm here now. You put me in front of Sword, now."

"That's 'Mistress Sword.'"

"Sure. And if I don't get her title right, are you going to help her beat me? Have you picked up a taste for her little perversions?"

Aileen's hand whipped out, slapping his face and sending him reeling back. His head smacked into the wall of the carriage with a resounding thunk.

"Remember where you are. Remember who I am. Don't you dare put me in the position of having to defend what I do, especially to you."

"Especially to me? What did I do? Why are you so angry with me?"

"Why am I so angry with you?" She began to shake. "Don't play the fool. I spoke with Faust. I know what happened between the worlds. Leave it to you, you are oh so much better than everyone, so much purer. You were offered the ring, but somehow you managed to decline. Now we have one less defender as these Takers seep in from between the worlds. You are going to have such a nice little life, by leaving me to defend you. Don't worry about all of the people who will be consumed, don't worry about the families that will be taken, eaten, or worse. You will have your comfortable little life away from the danger because I will be facing it every day."

Miller was stunned into silence. He had never thought about the consequences of his desire. The masters were few in number, and every day they fought against what threatened to seep into the world. A single tear ran down Aileen's cheek. Her voice was choked with emotion. "You are leaving me in the middle of the fight. That fight will last thousands of years, if we are lucky. If we are unlucky, then everything will be dead by next year. But you go ahead and chase your dreams. Do what feels right."

She ended at a whisper. Reaching out, she opened the carriage door and stepped out. Miller reached out toward her.

"Please, wait."

"Wait? Wait for what? You aren't committed enough to earn the master's ring. In the end, that will kill you. The only other part of your story will be those you leave behind."

She slammed the door.

RESOURCES

The establishment had seen better days. There were no patrons today. A dozen square tables stood abandoned. Dirty mugs, chicken bones, and a skittish cat were the only remaining occupants. Cerna looked on, his droopy eyes patiently awaiting what he knew would come next.

Miller walked forward, away from Brita, into the middle of the room. The others were arriving now. Aileen stood by the entrance in quiet conversation with Easter, sharing secrets, plotting, preparing.

He did not see Mistress Sword at the New Pony Inn. Only a few moments ago she had entered this new place and promptly turned around. She left, announcing to all of them that she was off in search of habitable lodging. Somehow that made this place appeal to Miller a little more.

Darjeeling walked into the room and stopped to join the quiet conversation. Frantz trailed behind, carrying a large leather bag over his shoulder. He looked exhausted. Passing by the masters, Frantz stopped in front of Miller.

"I'm supposed to give these to you."

He held out the leather bag. Miller reached out and pulled it out of his hands. It was heavy and cumbersome. The bag was large enough to put three helmets in and heavy enough to have filled it with sand.

Instead of asking, Miller opened the bag and began rummaging through it. A vial stand made from silver and inscribed with cooling runes, another smaller pouch full of chalk dust, a small vial of red ink, and a dozen other alchemical tools filled it.

"This looks like a small potion laboratory. What am I supposed to do with this?"

Frantz smiled back his open, falsely-optimistic grin. "That isn't my task to determine. I was told to give it to you, now you have it. I'm done here. It's in your hands now."

Miller looked at the bag, then at the room filled with furnishings and leftover meals. It was a pretty poor location, especially if there were supposed to be customers about.

"Don't leave. I'm going to get some clarification." Miller put the bag on the floor and walked toward the two masters who were still whispering to each other near the door. He stood at a respectful distance for a short minute before Aileen turned from the conversation. "This better be good. We are kind of busy here."

He gazed at the faces of the masters. They didn't look glad to have been interrupted.

"Master Darjeeling has sent me a collection of alchemy supplies. We still need a place to comfortably house Brita. Are there rooms for this? I'm not sure where to set up."

Aileen didn't give his request much time to sink in. "We have the entire inn. There are eight rooms upstairs, the great room here, a few storage rooms to the side, and a cellar. Assume that you have any authority that you need and get our equipment and volunteer anyone you need to take care of the details. We only have about six hours before the temple sends someone. I'm sure they will try to interrupt us. We need to be ready by then."

She had already turned back to her conversation by the time Miller backed away. Miller returned to the center of the room to stand near Frantz. "We need to clear out all of these tables onto the street, clean them up, and store them somewhere. We also need to clean the floors of this room, this will be where we put the circle."

Frantz gave a quick laugh. "Have fun with that. I don't serve Aileen. I'll be with my master."

"Nice try Frantz. But in six hours, a group of priestesses will be here from the temple. I can only assume they are here to eject us from Home's Hearth. If your laziness causes Easter's plans to fail, well, I'm sure there will be an opportunity to explain yourself both to him, and to Master Darjeeling."

Frantz looked on, horror slowly dawning on his face as he thought about the various fates that could await him. "Alright then. Let's put that guard to work while we start cleaning up."

Cerna just scowled back. His hand went to his sword hilt as he stepped closer to Brita. She had started singing to herself. The song was an old drinking song about a crowded campground and a drunken soldier.

"Cerna has his own task. This one is ours. He needs to be next to Brita until we get the circle drawn."

Cerna nodded back to Miller as Frantz gave up his game. Both Frantz and Miller began moving tables out of the main room and depositing them outside. The new scratches on the floor fit in well with those previously made. After the furniture was moved out, Miller went to the well and pumped water into a pail. He was sweating profusely when he returned to begin cleaning.

The floor was littered with years of food, animal droppings, and dried unidentifiable things. He set to it with a will, scrubbing, mopping, and even sanding the worst of it off. The floor would have shone if he had polished it. Instead of polishing, he began his circle as soon as there was sufficient room.

First, he drew the inner binding core to keep Brita and whatever had taken her contained. Then he inscribed the words of unbinding around the circle in hand-sized letters. He worked quickly, but building the last circle that surrounded this required another hour of labor. He was exhausted by the time he allowed Cerna to lead Brita into the circle. Then he linked the circle to natural essence flows, and Miller felt the channels assert themselves. Flows of magic in the room changed, avoiding the outer circle as though a mystic wind pushed them past.

Just as Brita was sealed off within the circle, she began singing in earnest. The jarring change in her volume caused Miller to pause and pay attention.

"She's active today," Cerna observed.

"But she wasn't very active before we completed the seal, was she?"

"No. She was passive and complacent all day."

Something had happened. Miller walked around the circle, inspecting the runes. This circle was essentially the same as the last one.

He went to the bag of alchemical supplies and selected a small bag of telling-sand. He tried to spill sand over the boundary of the protective circle, but the circle repelled the enchanted telling-sand.

"This sand is the least enchanted thing that can be made. Even with the very small touch of magic, it can't penetrate the circle. If the Takers are using magic, then she has been cut off from it."

Cerna's next question was the obvious one.

"From what? I've never heard of Takers using magic."

Miller shook his head in confusion. "I don't know."

"Any guesses?"

"Just one, but I don't have any proof."

"Sometimes you don't need proof. Sometimes you just need to make a decision."

Cerna's words were those of a warrior, not of a crafter. "No, in this case, proof is the most important thing. We need to figure out how to identify the Taken and we can't do that without some sort of test."

Frantz returned to the main room. Fresh dirt decorated his pants and several new food stains had appeared on his shirt. His previous well-kept attire had been transformed by the cleaning job into a simple mess. Only his luxurious hair remained untarnished.

"What's the problem?"

"They don't like my singing," Brita responded before any of the others could. "They have no taste. If they would just listen, they might pick up the tune!"

"She is trying to tell us something," Miller said.

Cerna responded, "What? It sounds crazy."

Frantz would have none of it. "She has been quite insane for a while. I can't believe you are giving this any weight. I think we should take Master Darjeeling's advice and simply kill her. Then we can resurrect her spirit and simply ask what is going on."

Both Cerna and Miller responded to that. "No."

Miller continued, trying to appease Frantz's ego without giving too much ground. "We already know the problem. Somehow, the things from between the worlds have gotten into her soul, not just her body. If we kill her and bring her spirit back, that is all she will be able to tell us. We need something more."

Cerna wasn't going to let it rest there. "Look, Frantz, or whatever your name is." He paused to allow that hint of disrespect to sink in. "Master Easter has charged me with protecting this young woman against all threats. He explicitly told me that I was allowed—no, encouraged—to put a sword through anyone who attempted to either seize or harm her. Let me be clear. If you touch this girl, I will cut out your heart and deliver it back to your master. Then I'll tell him all about what a stupid apprentice you were. Do you understand?"

Frantz took a step back. His arms came up in a gesture of surrender. "Easy friend, we are all on the same team here."

The look in Cerna's eyes made it clear that he yearned for an excuse to cut Frantz down on the spot. "Then you had better act like it, or we will have problems."

Miller felt the urge to intervene, to make peace between warring parties. Frantz was the apprentice of an insane White Hand master. Cerna was a mercenary under the hire of yet another master. Miller could think of no better way to keep these two in check than the fear of each other.

He remembered serving dinner to Mistress Aileen and Master Easter once. They were discussing politics and the upcoming conclave. Master Easter had given her advice that stuck in his head. He said, "Never interfere with your own victory. Sometimes you need to let events play out."

Miller looked at Cerna and Frantz, so near the tipping point so early in this journey. He decided to let these events play out.

"That took a while. Did you get what you needed from them?"

Chamise ignored Schaller's voice. He kept trying to direct her, to lead her. Right now, he only annoyed her.

"Just a bit. That young man that traveled with him, his name is Miller. He and I have business between us."

"Business?" His voice seemed to fill in the blanks, assuming a torrid affair that had never happened. What he didn't know was just how hard she had tried.

"Sadly, just business. Where is everyone? Did they all leave after the game?"

"No. We waited for you. After a few hours, some of the gang decided that drinking was a better use of their time. They went off to the taverns."

"Not keeping with the old ways?"

"They've mostly given it all up." He sighed in defeat. "It's all gone now. All of the glory, all of the cause. It's just gone."

"Well, good riddance, if you ask me."

Schaller's eyes grew wide in shock. "You can't be serious.

You were here. You remember how we were at our strongest."

"Yes, we were so strong that we ignored the very reason we existed in the first place. If you ask me, the goddess did us all a favor by disbanding the order. Now we get to live like normal people, and maybe understand the world that normal people live in."

His sarcasm was cutting. "Oh yes, the normal world is so joyous. Let's all celebrate."

She got up and walked from him, striding purposefully away, as if to rebuke his sarcasm. He rushed back to join her again as she walked back to the main building. She avoided stretches of the muddy, torn-up lawn that the earlier game had birthed, concentrating on keeping her shoes free of mud. If only she could keep her life free of attitudes like Schaller's.

She could not stay silent. "You know, not everyone thinks that we Eisenvard were so amazing. Most people in the land thought we were just a group of thugs, so close to thieves and murderers that even the goddess could not tell us apart."

Schiller nodded in weak agreement. "Yes, until the necromancers came to take their children, or they were taken and began murdering their own families. Then all of a sudden we became the heroes again."

She bit off her hot retort. She remembered how it was during those dark times and he had a point. People went insane, banding together in mobs, killing, burning.

"I'm not saying that everything we did was wrong. We just got lost. We took those words carved on our wall too seriously. We never tried to apply them to life, only use them to target people. I can't help but wonder if the first Eisenvard did the same thing. What were they like, before the credo, before the oaths? Didn't they do it all better?"

Now it was Schaller's turn to be silent. He seemed to choose his words carefully. "I know you lost a lot."

Before he could continue, Chamise spun on her heel, striding directly at him until she stood chest to chest, looking up into his eyes a hand span above. She almost screamed her reply.

"You murdered my mother! You effectively murdered my father as well! Lost? Everything I have lost was taken by you!" she screamed, as she pounded his chest with an accusing finger. "If anyone in this cursed order understands why we were sent away and knows what made it happen, it is me. You tore out my heart just so you could pretend to be holy. The truth is, you were never holy. But you were always a murderer."

He tried to marshal a defense, but it was weak. "It wasn't me. I didn't burn her."

"You stood by and did nothing! How will you recover your precious honor now? How will you fix this? All of you?"

His head fell, shame crept into his voice. "I can't. I wish that I could, but I can't. There are a lot of things from back then that I would undo. That is not the least. It still haunts me."

"Well, it haunts me every day. And it will the rest of my life. So join the club."

"The Credo says not to give in to despair or hopelessness."

Her response was bitter and subdued. "The Credo also told you to kill my mother. Why should I believe in it now?"

He couldn't answer. He kept walking by her side until they arrived at the main building. She entered the hall, witnessing the scrawled lines of the Credo carved along its length. She remembered passing through this hall every day of her youth, memorizing the passages, believing in them. It had been so hard to blot them out of her life, but here they stood, unforgiving.

"I'm sorry for yelling at you," she began, trying to regain a sliver of his friendship. "I know it wasn't entirely your fault, but please don't pretend that Eisenvard had it right, or that you were an innocent bystander."

"No, I was a bystander. None of us were innocent that day."

She looked back down that hall, feeling anger rising toward those carved words that could never be altered, or humanized. The belief that there was an absolute truth had done more evil than the things they were fighting against.

"Schaller, let's not do this. Let's not become enemies over this."

His gaze softened. "No. I should rather be your friend if you would have me." He reached out an eager hand, but she did not take it.

"Can you do me a favor?"

"What would you have of me? If possible, I will grant it."

"Can you arrange a meeting with the others, all the other Eisenvard left here in Home's Hearth? I have something that I would like to say that may help all of us put the past behind, where it belongs."

He nodded. "I can do that. Is tomorrow night soon enough? Some of the others won't be able to escape their tasks until the sun sets."

"That will be fine." She gave him a weak smile, reaching out to touch his hand reassuringly. "This won't take very long. I just have something I need to say."

He nodded. "Until sunset tomorrow then." He walked down the corridor, turning toward the rooms he sometimes stayed in.

The gentle smile fell from her face as he walked away. Every step she took down the long hall made her face scowl more. She arrived back at her sleeping room nearly enraged. Thoughts of the Credo, her burning mother, and a murderous necromancer hunting her down while she played nets stoked her rage to red hot levels. She pulled up the bag containing all of her belongings and violently spilled them onto the floor, stopping when the item she searched for appeared.

She reached down and picked up the mace. Its two-foot metal shaft bore the scratches of a dozen fights and two full battles. She had recently re-tied the leather cord, working it so it fit comfortably in her hand. Six metal shafts, angled to penetrate armor, jutted out from a poured weight fitted to the end of the killing tool.

Alone, in the darkening room, she planned for tomorrow. She remembered the lessons her father had taught her, how to strike first and hard. He always told her that she was too small to defend, and it would be best just to win quickly rather than prettily. Now she planned for her win. She planned for her killing stroke.

SPEAKING WITH AILEEN

Aileen lagged behind the row of carts.

Easter stood by the road next to his horse, waiting for her. "How did it go?"

"How do you think it went?" Aileen quipped.

"Given that you can still talk to me, I'd say it went pretty well."

Both turned to walk along the cobbled street, the two coaches just ahead of them.

Aileen said, "You know he is going to die, don't you? The rings are tied to our fates. Not accepting one feels like a death sentence."

"I don't know if that is true, but I expect it is. Miller wasn't ready when the ring presented. I talked to Faust about it for a long time. He doesn't have any new insight into how the ring works now that he has passed from life. He saw what he saw. Miller got the option for the ring and turned it down."

"I know I'm new as a master, but I've never even heard of such a thing."

Easter said, "I've only encountered tales of such a thing twice in my life. Neither time ended well for the apprentice." He continued, "So, what will you do? The order, well, we don't let apprentices just leave. It's too late for that. He has entangled his fate with us just by being around. The space between the worlds will come for him eventually. It usually happens while asleep, but there have been other times where the walls between worlds just crack, and an apprentice is simply snatched away."

She shook her head, frowning, trying to come up with some way for Miller to escape that fate, and failing. "All I can do is keep him close, under whatever protection we can give him. At least that way he may have a chance to escape it."

"Let's be clear about this. In the three-thousand-year history of our order, no one has escaped the space between the worlds. The only safety is the ring."

Aileen walked on in silence, her hands toying with her blond hair, nervously twisting them into braided tangles, before falling away. She sighed in resignation. "He has the talent to gain his ring. Maybe the problem is me."

Easter placed his hand reassuringly on her shoulder. "You have been a fantastic mentor for him, much better than Sword had been. Truthfully, there isn't any more you could have given him."

"Yes. That may be the problem." She thought about the other masters, the other apprentices who had gained their rings. "Maybe I've done too much for him. The other masters who have succeeded, they don't give as much. They don't care as much. Perhaps he needs a master who can be a little colder."

"He already had one of those. Remember? Plus, you are already his second master. Who could you get that would take a two-time failure? Yes, Miller has superb enchanting skills that are very useful. But if your intention is to get him a ring, who would be willing to train him? Enchanting won't help with that."

She spoke her next words softly, as if not believing they were escaping her lips. "I could send him back to Sword."

Easter stopped dead in his tracks. "No."

"Look, I'm trying to save his life. I know there are real problems there, but this is his life we are talking about."

"No. It would be better to let him die than do that."

She raised her hands up to her chest, imploring him for a better idea but finding none.

"Listen," he began, "I've been a master for a long while. I've seen this kind of thing before. When someone gets a ring, their bonds to the master can be finished, or continue on. It is up to the pair of them. But if you introduce personal hatred outside of that, if you betray him to Sword, he will carry that grudge for a thousand years. Ask yourself this. Do you really need to train your own blood-enemy?"

"But he's got to learn to survive! He has to get harder and stronger. He needs to be able to face what is between the worlds and come away unscathed."

"And you need to learn to stop engineering everyone's future. Sometimes we need to let people walk their own path."

"Are you seriously telling me that? You've been engineering my future since I was in the temple. If you had left me alone, I would be comfortable at the feet of the goddess every morning. I would be surrounded by peace and sunshine every day."

"And there would be one less master to stop the cracks between the worlds, the Takers, and all the other dark things that seep through. I'm sorry, but the goddess hasn't been doing a good job at that. As you said, she isn't hard enough, nor strong enough."

She walked on, gravel crunching beneath her feet. The sun had risen high in the sky and she was beginning to sweat in the summer heat. "I hesitate to say it, but I wish December was here. I could have made a deal with him. I would hate for Miller to pick up any of his habits, but the man is plenty hard. Miller could learn a thing or two."

"Not a bad idea. That girl, Chamise, she did a clean job when she knifed him. One stab through the neck. December should be back by the end of the month."

"December carries grudges though, especially when he gets killed."

"True. But if the proper amount of bowing and scraping is performed, he can become reasonable about most things."

Aileen looked over at him, her eyes narrowing, not trusting where the conversation was going. "And what kind of bowing and scraping do you suggest, sir?"

The Rat turned toward Hazel. She sat on an empty barrel, set along the side of the street. The criminals in Home's Hearth have really fallen down on the job, he thought. No one came to interrupt them in a perfectly good place to perform a robbery.

"Why are you upset at me?" her eyes said to him, even without her high-pitched voice. The Friends made sure he could sense her inner feelings, her hurts, her fears.

"Did you see the young man running past us?"

She looked back at him, eyes accusing him of something. He wasn't sure what.

"That was a member of the White Hand. Necromancers. If that boy was there, in plain sight, at least one of the others must have been a master. Probably one of those standing by the gate."

She looked back defiantly, sad that she hadn't been able to scratch the warrior before she had been so rudely pushed away.

I had him! I had him! She thought to herself, feeling a chorus of encouragement from the Friends. She wondered how the Rat had been able to ignore it.

Why did he do that? She was puzzled at his behavior. Why did he take me away? They would have been so happy with me!

"Listen to me," he snapped. "Stop pouting like a young little girl. You can't accept everything the Friends tell you as a command. Remember, they only send you suggestions and requests. It is up to you to choose the how and the when of things. These are not trivial details. You need to think of yourself as a partner to them rather than a thrall."

"I would have made them happy." It was all she could say.

"You would have made them dead. A single White Hand master can kill you in a moment. Never forget that. If you ever fight one, be sure the battle is worth your life because that is the price you will pay."

"My life isn't worth much, anyway. Let me spend it where it will accomplish something."

The words came out of her mouth, and out of her heart.

"Dear, you need to slow down, watch what I do. Don't charge off recklessly. Besides, we discovered something today that may be valuable. That simple discovery is more than worth the price of staying alive."

She was close to the edge, where the newly taken decided if they wanted to continue to live or not. Normally he didn't worry about such details, the taken didn't last long anyway. But Hazel had somehow become important to him. He didn't know why yet, but he wanted to.

She said, "Discovered something? Yes. Necromancers have returned to Home's Hearth. But we would have found them out anyway."

"Did you not see the second coach? The one with the older coachman? Did the Friends not sing to you about that?"

She shook her head, surprised.

"You weren't listening then. There was someone in that second coach. One of us."

"One of us?"

"Yes. Now we have a mystery to solve."

"A mystery? Now you are speaking in riddles."

"Indeed I am. You don't have all the facts yet, my dear. Rest your tongue and let me speak."

Hazel looked back, contritely. She didn't want to anger the only lifeline she had, especially given how excited her Friends seemed to be. She could feel her heart leaping with emotion, and she had no idea why.

I'm going to tell you something amazing, and perhaps a little frightening. Walk with me, but act like this is just a normal conversation. I'm heading toward the market to buy a basket of bread and meat for traveling. We will be taking a trip outside the city tomorrow. For right now, your task is to listen, not to question."

They turned and walked toward the noisy crowd. The Rat led her through their midst, dodging around stalls and gaggles of young people standing about while they gossiped. After a few minutes of moving through the crowd, he began speaking softly enough so that only Hazel could hear his voice.

"One of the people we just met was a master necromancer. Do you remember tales them from a few years ago? The Eisenvard were patrolling the roads day and night looking for them."

"I remember. I didn't give it much attention. There was a famine that year."

"That was wise. The White Hand would not have come to a sleepy village like yours unless something was truly amiss. Luckily for you, it wasn't. The necromancers are real though, and they are our sworn enemies."

"Enemies? What had we done to deserve that?"

"My dear, these are necromancers. They play god by digging up graves and binding spirits from the beyond, creating horrors the like that you couldn't imagine. They don't need a reason."

She walked a few more steps before she tried to ask her first question. The Rat anticipated it and interrupted her.

"So how do we fight necromancers? These people, hardly human anymore, can be killed by traditional methods. Swords will cut them, arrows will pierce them. The challenge comes when you face their wizardry in battle. They are dire enemies, wielding the power of darkness, lightning, and fear. Another challenge is that when you do manage to kill one, they don't stay dead. They can raise themselves from whatever terrible fate awaits them on the other side of the last door."

"Sweet Goddess. They can return from the dead?" she asked. The irony of the prayer was not lost on the Rat.

"Oh yes. But it takes them a little time to return. It usually takes a few months before they are seen again. Death is not a one-way trip for Masters of the White Hand. Luckily only the masters have that ability, their servants and soldiers do not."

"So… you're saying I have an enemy who is a wizard, and can't die. Are there any other tidbits of information that I should know?"

"Don't be so alarmed. The Friends have been in conflict with these abominations for centuries. They haven't lost yet."

"Are we leaving town to run from these White Hand people?"

"Oh no. We are simply going to meet up with a few others, like us. I want to tell them what we found face-to-face. Sometimes the Friends can garble the message, and it gets misunderstood. It is important that we all know precisely what is happening, and exactly what to do. We are so very close to our victory, we can't let anything get in the way."

She tried to ask another question, but the Rat held up a single finger to stop her. "It is a waste of time to ask more. It is much easier to simply come along and learn for yourself."

She nodded, continuing their walk through the lovely market district.

Hazel followed the Rat into the inn. Low ceilings and yellow cracked walls displayed with faded attempts at artistry. The delicious smell of roasting vegetables and chicken moved through the room seductively, transforming it from a forgotten error into a comforting shelter. The food smelled good, really good.

The inn was a mere six-hour ride from the gates of Home's Hearth. The weather had been pleasant during their ride. The sky was clear, showing only a bright sun and far off wisps of high clouds. A light breeze cooled the skin, retreating as they entered the inn.

"Please say we get to eat. It's been a long ride from town."

The Rat smiled back at her, expecting that question, and pleased in his predictive skills. "Of course. This place has the finest chicken dinner in the land. I think we've walked enough to deserve a good meal. The others haven't all arrived yet, so we have time."

The Rat gestured toward one of the long tables. It had five empty seats, with only three other people sitting at one end. Their devoured chicken bones and dirty soup bowls lay discarded on the table before them. The Rat led her toward the empty side of the table, gesturing for her to sit before taking his own place. Before he got comfortable, a serving girl appeared at his side.

"Welcome travelers!" she chirped, her young smile betraying her fatigue. It was a tired smile like she had been hard at work for as long as she could remember. Her black hair hung greasily down the thirteen-year-old girl's back. It had not been cleaned in weeks. "We've got chickens! We've got ale!" Her enthusiasm, while welcoming, conflicted with the fatigue on her face.

"It looks like you've been busy today."

"Yes, we have. There are a lot more people than usual today. Some sort of gathering is happening, I think."

"Oh, a gathering, eh? What are they gathering about?"

"Not sure. There's a group of people, farmers, merchants, a few woodsmen, and soldiers. They have some sort of business out in the barn."

"Aren't you curious what they are doing?"

"Sure, but I'm too busy to give them my time. Plus, the innkeeper tells me that I've got chickens to sell and beer mugs to fill, so I'm not allowed to interrupt them. Can I interest you in either?"

Hazel spoke up. "You can interest me in both."

The Rat smiled back. "I would like a cup of the soup, with a small potato. My dear niece seems to want the chicken and small beer for both of us."

The girl spun to leave, but the Rat's hand stopped her, pulling her back by the arm.

"Before you go, just one more thing. I have business with these men that meet in your barn. I would appreciate it if you could keep your ears open and tell me what you overhear passing between them. I want to know what they are up to in your barn before I go meet with them. Can you do that?"

He poured a single silver coin from his purse, watching it spin on the table for a few seconds.

The girl smiled, nodding happily. "Sure. I'll keep an eye on them for you."

She walked away, the thought of a new silver coin giving energy to her steps.

Hazel whispered to him over the table, trying to avoid being overheard. "Who are these men?"

"The most dangerous sort, I'm afraid. They are a group of Taken, one and all. I'm sure they are up to no good."

"Taken? Why did you pay that girl to spy on them?"

"I didn't pay her to spy on them. I paid her to let me know if she could be hired as a spy, and if she would sell her information."

"Why?"

"Because that way, I would know whether we should Take her before we leave."

Hazel grew quiet, then glanced back to him. Her eyes widened in excitement. "Can we? Please?"

He nodded, noting her growing pleasure. She's grown a taste for this, the Rat thought, as I guessed she would.

"After dinner, of course. You don't want to ruin your meal. Believe me, it will be worth the trip getting here."

The young serving girl reappeared within moments. She carried a tray with a roasted half chicken displayed on it. The chicken had been covered with local herbs and savory spices. Three small potatoes were displayed alongside the chicken, along with some fresh green lettuce. After placing the tray in front of Hazel, she sped off toward the kitchen only to quickly return with two mugs of beer and a large bowl of soup.

The meal turned out wonderful. Hazel's eyes rolled up in pleasure at her first bite. The Rat spoke about the local area and the travels he had made, taking the time to appear normal. Hazel listened intently, enraptured in the moment. Just before the meal was finished, the young girl returned to the table.

"I've got something for you. Those men you told me to watch, they are going to be gathering in the barn soon. I think they are going to be setting some sort of plan. They've been waiting for someone important to get here, but it looks like those men have arrived. It won't be long now."

"Excellent job."

"And excellent chicken," Hazel complimented, her gaze becoming hungrier, even though she had just eaten. It must be the Takers, she thought, they've gotten a strong grip on her already.

The Rat pulled out the silver coin. Placing it on the worn table, he slid it toward her. "I will need to conduct business with these men. I do have another task though. Would you be able to help me again?" he asked sweetly, pulling his hand away to show the coin. The girl snatched it up quickly, a genuine smile shone on her face. "Yes. What to do you need?"

"I'll need to conduct my business first. When I am finished, you and I should talk privately. I will tell you what I need taken care of."

"Aye! I will be waiting!"

"And so will I."

He laid a half-silver coin on the table as well. "For the meal."

Then the Rat stood, holding out a hand for Hazel to take as she pulled herself up. "We will talk soon. Soon we will be like sisters," she whispered, unheard by the serving girl.

HURRIET

Hurriet was tired. She had been out of her home for two days. The supplies that she had so quickly scavenged from her kitchen ran out yesterday. She had been surviving off the burned ends of bread she had begged for on Baker's street. Her stomach continued to grumble as she sat on a bench normally reserved for the customers of a cobbler family. The merchant had taken a small bit of pity on her and left her alone while she tried to come up with a plan.

The more she thought about the alchemist and Gar's death, the more defeated she felt. She didn't know what to do about any of it. One thing was sure though, she could not go home until this mess was resolved. She had slept in a woodshed last night. Luckily it was summer, and it hadn't rained. She needed a plan.

Rising from the bench, she started walking down the street. It was afternoon and the enticing aromas of ovens had given way to the smell of horse manure cooking in the middle of the street. The sun bore down on her. She tried to keep to the shady side of the street and out of its direct glare but had little success.

She thought about going home, about the room that was waiting for her. She might be wrong about the alchemist. He might be harmless.

But she might be right. She considered her discomfort, then remembered Gar's dead body lying in the middle of the street. It was too early to give up yet. She needed to give things more time, at least that was what her intuition told her.

Sleeping on the cold ground didn't seem appealing though. Home's Hearth was filled with inns. The people of the town had been kind to her so far, tolerant of her being underfoot. A thought occurred to her, perhaps she could appeal to one of the less populated inns. Sleeping on an inn floor was far better than cold dirt.

The walk from Baker's street to the market took fifteen minutes. She passed three inns, each was populated with visitors. The nearby market made those inns popular. Something farther out would suit her better. She came to the grand statue of the goddess. It stood tall, three times her height, with a narrow base carved from sandstone. It had four sides and sloped upward at an angle. A carved symbol, the Star of Phyllicitus, stood engraved on each of the four surfaces. The statue marked where the commerce district began. She would be in the market soon. That wasn't where she wanted to go.

She turned left and began walking along Bridge Street. Soon enough, as to its name, she was walking across a series of bridges. Each of them crossed a man-made stream that supplied fresh water to the city. If she walked long and far enough, she would come to the walls of Home's Hearth, then to a series of streams and wells that generated life-giving water for the city. As she was walking toward the final bridge, she came across a well-paved street. A sign, carved into the shape of a loaf of bread, hung outside a dark green building.

She recognized where she was, Baker's street. Remembering a small inn farther down the street where her father took her once last year, she turned right. The sun had begun to wane in the sky. Businesses had begun to close. Workmen began to crowd the street as they headed home for the night. Hurriet kept walking, gazing from side to side, hoping to find some sign of the New Pony Inn.

None of the buildings seemed familiar. It had been years since she had visited here. With no other idea, she kept walking, exploring the streets. Some time later, with aching legs, she saw the inn. A single horse stood untethered in front of the place. She remembered it being full of light, with song and merriment pouring out. Tonight, it was quiet. Dark Curtains blocked the windows so only slivers of light shone out. It felt cold. She didn't like walking up to it, but she had no other plan.

Gar always said to have a plan. She shrugged and stepped toward the inn.

Surprisingly, the horse trotted up to her.

"Hello, you," she greeted the horse. "You're a friendly one."

The horse nodded its head up and down. Its brown fur was clean and well brushed. The horse was a mare. It wore no bit or bridle, only its natural beauty. She could tell this horse was valuable. She particularly liked the white diamond-shaped spot on its forehead. She reached up to stroke the horse's cheek, spending a moment in the pleasure of its company. It was docile, looking down at her with deep brown eyes. She felt something, some kind of emotion from it. Her intuition told her that the horse was a good thing, and spending time with it would be a good idea.

But darkness gathered as the sun began to set. She looked at the empty inn. They should have room enough for her tonight, even if only on the floor. She patted the horse one more time.

"Good night. Time to find a bed."

Hurriet stepped around the horse to head into the inn. The horse stepped in front of her.

She scowled at the horse, annoyed at it.

"Where are your owners? Do they know you are out here?"

The horse continued to block her from entering the inn.

She set her hand on the horse's chest. Gently stroking it, she walked around to its side until she had an unimpeded path toward the door. The horse seemed to sense her motive. It moved between her and the inn, blocking her path yet again.

"You're blocking me on purpose," she stated, annoyed with the horse. "Why are you being like this?" Her father would use reins to pull a horse out of his way, especially when it was being difficult, but there were none here. She didn't understand why this horse was impeding her.

She tried to walk around it again. It stepped into her way, blocking her path yet again. The horse stood tall. If she stood on her tiptoes, she could not reach the top of its head. Its speed and bulk made it impassable. Worse yet, it seemed to enjoy this game.

"Oh well, I guess you win." She couldn't think of a plan to avoid the horse. If she spent enough time out here, someone would be along for it. Again, she gave in to her intuition and simply stood in the street, petting the horse and chatting with it. Surprisingly, the horse never answered back. Somehow, she expected that it could.

A few straggling workmen came by, but none stopped to talk. A woman with graying brown hair, wearing an apron spotted with flour, walked up to inquire how she was, and if she needed help with her horse. Hurriet chuckled at that, explaining the tricks the horse was up to.

"I'll bet the owner is in that inn. I'll go fetch them."

Hurriet watched as the horse let her pass by. She slowed as she neared the front stairs. Putting her foot on one stair, she began the climb.

"Kind of spooky, isn't it?" the woman said, fear beginning to creep into her voice.

Something was wrong here, she thought.

Hurriet asked the horse, "Is there something bad in there?" unsure of what was happening here. This was Home's Hearth, with the goddess in residence. Bad things weren't supposed to happen here. But something bad had happened to Gar.

The woman didn't open the inn door. She tepidly knocked on it, as if it were a residence instead of an inn.

After a few moments, the sound of footsteps came through the door. It opened revealing a young man. He wore the kind of robe that a scribe normally wears, black and somber, with only a single silver ring decorating his fingers. He wore a confused look beneath a disheveled mop of brown hair.

"What are you doing with my horse?"

"Your horse?"

"Yes, my horse."

The man cocked a grin at her as if he were playing. He seemed friendly and open, the kind of man this horse might tolerate.

"She isn't tied up. I found her walking around in the street."

"Yeah. Tying her up doesn't do much good. It's just better to let her have her own way. Was she bothering you?"

"Sort of," Hurriet said, smiling back. "She won't let me go into the inn."

The man's eyes grew narrow. A look of suspicion grew on his face. "Why do you want to come in?"

"I'm looking for a place to sleep tonight. My father knows the innkeeper." That last part was a bit of a stretch, but she needed to be convincing.

"How about it? You don't want this little girl to come in?"

As if it understood what the man had said, the horse shook its head from side to side.

"Huh. I guess I should take a look at you."

He walked down the steps and over toward her. She took a step back, suspicious of the newcomer.

"Not so close, stranger," she warned.

The man put his hands up in surrender. "I don't need to get very close. I just want to get a good look at you. My name is Miller. What's yours?"

It seemed an innocent enough question. "Hurriet."

Miller squatted down so his face was almost level with hers. "And what are you doing over here, eh?"

She thought about telling him about Gar, and about the alchemist. It all seemed too flimsy. Running away was something a ten-year-old girl would do, not a grown up.

"As I said, I want to go inside."

"And you aren't afraid? Doesn't that door look, I don't know, a little frightening to you?"

She peered at the door. There was something there, something that wasn't there before. It made the hair on the back of her arms stand up. Her intuition told her that the door was harmless though, and she trusted it.

"No. It's just a stupid door."

Miller began moving his hands in small gestures. Passing his crossed fingers in front of his eyes, he uttered a few incomprehensible words.

"What are you doing?"

Miller went on for a few more symbols, then stopped.

"I was just checking you."

"For what?"

He peered back at the door to the inn. The steps were empty. He lowered his voice, acting as if he had a great secret to share.

"You should be at the temple. They would know what to do with you there."

"What to do with me?" Hurriet replied. "My mother warned me about them. They would keep me inside forever."

He shook his head. "No, they would teach you. You're special."

"I'm not a priestess. I know what they get up to in those hallways. Mother told me. She said that they make little girls into whores."

His eyebrows shot up in surprise. "I've never heard it put that way before. Plus, this is Home's Hearth. There aren't many of those here."

"Mother isn't from Home's Hearth. She says that her people's ways are better than what they got here and that I've got to per-serv myself, whatever that is. She says that the temple is full of them."

The mare moved, nudging Miller to the side. Miller had found the conversation with the little girl interesting. He turned toward the mare, then saw the man standing in the open door of the inn. Master Darjeeling looked down at him, a broad smile stretched across his face.

The mare nudged Miller again, impatient with him, urging him toward some kind of action.

"Can we go for a walk? There are some things that you need to know before you decide to go into the New Pony. Things have changed, and maybe not for the better."

Hurriet didn't know what Miller was talking about. She nodded, again trusting in her instincts. A fat man had walked out of the inn. He stood grinning down at them. Hurriet grew frightened. This man should not be trusted. Then she saw another. This man came from behind and whispered into the fat man's ear. She recognized him immediately. The long red hair was a giveaway. It was the stranger the alchemist had set them to follow, the man that killed Gar.

She began to shake with fear. Miller glanced down at her, then back toward the door.

"Do you want to get out of here?" Miller asked.

She nodded up and down, never taking her eyes from the inn door.

Miller reached down and took her hand. He gently lead Hurriet to the right. She stumbled but recovered before she fell. Miller held her hand tighter and felt the quivers.

"Keep walking. We'll be out of sight soon enough."

Hurriet's eyes had grown wide. Her gaze darted side to side, then behind them as he led her away. The mare followed a few paces behind.

They traveled four blocks before Hurriet spoke again.

"I know that man," she whispered.

A sense of foreboding descended on Miller. "The old one?"

"No, the younger one with the red hair. I think he killed my brother."

It took Miller a little time to process what the girl had told him. He wondered what Frantz had been up to. Had Frantz murdered someone in Home's Hearth?

"You said that your brother was murdered."

"Yeah. I think."

"You think? You don't know?"

She gave Miller an angry look. "I sort of know. I got a feeling. Gar was only a year older than me. He just laid down in the street and died. Something tells me that the red-haired man had something to do with it."

"Something tells you? Like a gut feeling?"

"Something like that. Ma always told me that I've got good feelings when it comes to things like that. Grandma did too, I guess. Most likely I'm right."

Miller looked down at the girl. She had some crafting talent, that was for sure. He wasn't sure how much, but it would be enough to attract the attention of the order. The White Hand loved to recruit children. A small girl, her brother recently deceased, would make a prime target for the master's recruitment efforts. She had already attracted the attention of Master Darjeeling. It might be too late to keep her isolated from danger.

"That red-haired man is named Frantz. I know him."

She didn't respond with words, but the look on her face told Miller all he needed to know.

"You're right to be suspicious. Frantz, and me too, I guess, serve a bunch of wizards. They aren't nice people."

"Why would he kill Gar?"

That one simple question took the wind out of him.

"I have no clue. I'm willing to look into it though. I'm not on the best of terms with Frantz, but I can ask him what happened with your brother."

She scowled back. "It probably doesn't matter. This Frantz guy won't tell the truth anyway."

"You're probably right."

They walked on a few more minutes before Hurriet changed the subject. "Where did you get this weird horse anyway? It's super smart, and kind of annoying, like it enjoys toying with me."

"Yes, the mare is like that. You get used to her, and she's great to have around. She saved my life at least twice."

"And where did you get her?"

"Sorry. I bought her from a farmer up north. We were renting an inn, and Mistress Aileen sent me out to buy a horse. Somehow I got lucky and bought her."

"What's her name?"

"I don't know."

Hurriet's suspicious look returned. "What do you mean, you don't know? You bought her, didn't you? Why don't you name her?"

Miller smiled, glad to have something other than a murdered brother to talk about. "Horses like this are special. Up north, they're called Great Horses. The locals believe there are special horses, and they are somehow connected to the Horse God. It's best to wait until the horse tells you its name, rather than to make up something the horse would get insulted by."

"Horse God? Like from back in the days of the First Gods? My ma told me stories of them. They bring winter, and war, and bad stuff."

He shook his head. "Your mother only told you half of the story. There was once a war in Home's Hearth, back when the goddess wasn't living here." He paused to craft his story. He doubted getting into the subject of where Phyllicitus had been would help this young girl.

"There was a Stag God back then. Something happened to upset it. The Stag God came here to make war. He brought his shaman, and they raised an army of creatures. It wasn't good."

"Why? I mean, what good did it do? I still remember parts of that. There was a lot of screaming and people got hurt."

Miller remembered as well. He had been in the service of Mistress Sword when the worst of the fighting broke out. Some in the Order fought to bring down the temple, believing it too weak to stop the Stag God and his shaman. To make matters even more dire, the Takers returned and brought chaos across the land. Aileen had created a reputation as a warrior priestess, fighting both wizards in the Order and the forces of the Stag God.

Somehow it had all stopped. Master Easter had managed to pull victory from the jaws of defeat. He convinced Aileen that the real threat was from the Takers, not the Stag God. They joined forces to purge the city. Somehow they had triumphed when the Eisenvard rose up in rebellion. Phyllicitus had returned at exactly the right time. All of these events interconnected. He didn't know how to explain it to such a young girl.

"No one really knows. I suspect that the Stag God was drawn here because it didn't like the Taker infestation."

"Takers?" Her voice turned fearful. She knew what Takers were.

"That's what Master Easter thinks anyway. Other masters, er, wizards I mean, disagree. It's all over now, thank the Goddess."

"Except you haven't told me why you don't name your horse."

"Yes, I did. You just don't listen. I don't name the horse because she already has a name. She will tell me, I am sure. I just need to be patient, as do you."

The horse snorted from behind them. It seemed to be enjoying Hurriet's confusion.

"Yeah, laugh it up, four-legs," Miller shot back, playfully.

Curiosity filled Hurriet's mind. For the first time in days, she felt wonder at life. Somehow, even with Gar's death, she knew that she could go on.

"So what am I supposed to do about this Frantz wizard then?"

"I think we find you a place to hide out for a few days. I'll talk to him, find out what really happened."

"He'll just lie."

"Then I'll have Aileen talk to him. He can't lie to her, no one can."

A thought occurred to Miller. He needed somewhere to put a young girl, one who most probably had a small bit of crafting power. The order would take her in without question. Given that Frantz may have killed her brother Gar, that wasn't going to work out well. He needed someone knowledgeable, dependable, and discreet. Someone who would not cave in when facing off with the masters.

He knew the perfect woman for the job.

THE UNHOLY PLOT

"My Companions! My Fellow Travelers! I am returned!" the Rat announced loudly as he marched into the barn.

The barn was crowded, with fifty men and twelve women within. It was large enough to fit a dozen horses if they had built the stalls to hold them. Now the barn was empty besides the four hay piles the men had pushed aside to make room. He felt the Friends call out, connecting each of them to their brethren. For a moment, he was one with each of the other taken men and women. He spread his arms, welcoming their fellowship. His heart danced with joy. Soon, he knew, the world would feel like this. Everyone would be part of their family.

He believed in them. The Friends could end war, end crime, end strife. The world of men and women killing each other in a mad scramble for survival would soon be at an end. He would be the one who made a true world of peace. There were precious few who could see the truth of it. He knew how lucky he was to be at this crossroads of history.

Almost as one, the crowd called back. "Welcome! Welcome!"

A few people moved forward to touch him, allowing the Friends to share information in a quicker and deeper way. In the space of a few moments, the Rat collected the experiences of long-range scouts, the logistical knowledge of barge masters, and a detailed description of the food supply from the local farmers.

"It has been too long since we met! I've brought a new member of our family!" Gesturing at Hazel, the Rat gave her a quick bow, presenting her to the assembled company.

Again, they called out their welcome.

"I have news, the kind that is best spoken face to face." He paused for the drama to take hold. "I will start with the good news. A few days ago, I completed one of my critical tasks. I believe that I have discovered how we might best our enemies, the dreaded necromancers, and end this battle. I have divined a new magic, one that will not only interrupt a necromancer's journey back from the lands of the dead but will also remove all magical talents they possess." The Rat bowed in mock victory. "That will make it oh-so much easier to end them and remove them permanently from this world."

The Friends knew of his most recent discovery. After dozens of trials, he had finally come up with an idea. He simply had to fuse the necromancer's inner aura, what could be labeled as a soul, with something that would resist any effort to change. It had to be something more powerful than a dark crafter's spells, and more permanent than a thousand-year lifespan. He only wished that he could have fully tested it. The magic was right, the theory was right, the implementation was possible. Now it was time to discover if he could demonstrate it.

Bending down, he motioned to Hazel. When she stepped forward, the Rat gave her a small pouch of silver and whispered instructions. She left on her errand and he began speaking to the crowd again. He went through the crowd and talked to each of them individually, laying out detailed schedules and actions for his fellow Taken to perform.

After filling them in on their roles, he began to discuss the complication.

"There is one problem, and I hope you can help me with this as well. Yesterday, Hazel and I were on a walk through Home's Hearth. What should we discover? None other than a necromancer. Even though the goddess has banned them, they still dare to intrude on her domain. I asked myself, how did they know to come here? What is their mission in our Home's Hearth? Do they know how close we are to building the weapon that will destroy them?"

The crowd grew silent. There had been enough battles with the necromancers. They had learned caution through hard lessons.

He continued. "I tell you this to prepare you. There may be a hard battle coming soon. I have just begun answering those questions. Soon we will know what they suspect, and we will counter them. For right now, stay hidden in the shadows. We will avoid meetings like these for the next month until we are ready to strike. The Friends will let you know where and when to gather."

The crowd murmured their assent. One man, a large burly laborer, scarred arms bulging with muscle, spoke up. "The Friends, they tell me there is more to do. Something here, among us."

The Rat had felt it too, the call of action. Soon the crowd would be energized into some cause that the Friends would provide. Hazel entered the barn, pulling the young serving girl along by hand. She looked nervous as she scanned the crowd.

"Ah, you made it!" the Rat called out happily. One of the last tests was about to begin.

The girl responded nervously, "At your service. What will you be needing?"

She hadn't expected to be the focus of the meeting.

"A simple task." The Rat produced two metal vials from his jacket pocket. Each appeared to be a burnished metal, their smooth surfaces caught the light, highlighting their seals. One was covered in red wax, the other in black.

"I have two recipes that we wish you to try. One of these will surely take your breath away with its flavor. Just a sip will do."

The serving girl began trying to back out. She tried to speak loudly, but it came out a panicked whisper. "I'd rather not, sir." Hazel reached out quickly, grabbing the serving girl's arm. The girl jerked backward, but she was unable to escape Hazel's grip. The crowd went into action as the Friends communicated their needs. An old man whose best years were behind him moved forward. Bending down, he grabbed her legs, holding her in place. A woman with long brown hair stepped up and grabbed the serving girl by her hair, pulling her head back. The girl opened her mouth to scream but quickly shut it as the Rat moved forward with an unsealed metal vial, red wax dried on the side of it.

The girl shook her head back and forth violently, refusing to open her mouth. More of the Taken grabbed her, holding her with their firm grips. She grunted as loudly as she could, trying to alert her parents in the other building. Her call was hidden below the calls of the Taken. Cheering, they set to holding her until she could move no more.

"I don't think you understand my dear. You and I had a deal. I paid my share, now it's your turn."

The girl tried to shake her head, but two of the Taken had her in their grasp. All she could do was squirm to no effect.

"But I see you don't intend to cooperate. A pity. I was so enjoying your company."

The Rat felt the Friends reach to someone in the crowd. A man from the crowd stepped forward. He wasn't tall, standing only as high as the Rat's jaw. Muscles testifying to hard labor stood out from his arms as he approached. He was bald and wore huntsman leather. The Rat could smell the scents of blood and the deep wood still upon him.

The Rat held out the two vials toward the woodsman and he took them. The Rat then drew a knife. The razor-sharp blade was longer than his hand.

The girl's eyes went wide as he thrust it into her upper right arm. He thrust it again and again. She screamed as the knife cut into her. Blood began to flow rapidly from the wound. Finally, he stopped jabbing and twisted the knife. The girl opened her mouth and screamed in pain. As she screamed, the huntsman stepped forward and poured the fluid into her mouth. She spit it out, covering the face of the huntsman. The Rat began stabbing her left arm now, creating another stream of blood and pain. The Taken moved forward, grabbing her, forcing her to the ground. They held her down while the red vial began its work.

After a few moments, the girl's resistance began to weaken. Her eyes became glassy and unfocused as she continued to protest. Mumbling, disjointed words emerged to both curse them and beg for her life.

The Rat took the black vial from the woodsman. He unstopped the vial, preparing it for use. Hazel felt the call of the Friends. She grabbed the girls mouth, forcing it open as others held her bleeding arms apart. The Rat spoke to her in a sing-song voice as he slowly poured the dark liquid into her mouth.

"It's all right. What you are doing here is going to help us a lot. You should be proud." Hazel tried to calm her but it only made her more terrified.

The girl tried to spit it out, but the taken woodsman held her mouth closed. She merely caused a small bit of it to dribble down her cheeks. The girl continued to resist, losing more of the precious fluid.

"The hard way today? I guess so. I wouldn't have chosen that if I were in your shoes." Indeed, he had been in her shoes just three short years ago, and he had chosen to cooperate instead of resist. A choice he had yet to regret.

The Rat pulled up his travel bag and removed a silver tube. It was hollow, like a pipe. One side of the tube had a rounded cap with small holes drilled in it. The other held a large boiled leather cap laced on the end.

He moved toward the serving girl, motioning the others to move her head back and open her mouth. She tried to resist as the woodsman shoved his fingers into her mouth. She tossed her head side to side and bit down tightly, blocking the way to her throat.

The woodsman drew a long bone-handled knife. It was a hunter's blade, broad and pointed, perfect for skinning a deer or a man. He put the blade against her face.

"Open your mouth or I'll cut a hole in your face."

The girl's eyes went wide in shock. The woodsman pushed the knife in. She tried to move out of its way but it cut into her cheek.

"Alright!" she screamed, panicking at the sight of her own blood. She opened her mouth.

The Rat shoved the rounded end in, carefully aligning it with her throat. Two other taken pushed her down to the floor, holding her in place. The Rat gazed down at the pipe jutting from her mouth. Without hesitation, he savagely kicked the padded end of the tube, thrusting it down her throat. She tried to move, but the others held her in place. The Rat removed the large leather cap, exposing a gap in the side of the pipe. He grabbed the last vial and unsealed its black wax cover. He set it next to the finger-long hole in the pipe. Slowly, carefully, he poured its contents into the gap. He watched as it slid down the tube into the girl's stomach.

"If it is any consolation," the Rat began as the alchemy began to take hold of her, "you are contributing to a great future. Your sacrifice will bring in an age of peace and tranquility. You will help end war, savagery, and suffering. Rest easy. Your life had a purpose and you have fulfilled it." He waited a moment, then added, "Your parents would be proud."

She realized that she was doomed. The girl began to struggle. She tried to free herself but the Taken held her down. She began to grow weak. Her movements slowed as the potion asserted itself.

He waited a few moments while she became still, then pulled the silver pipe from her stomach. It came free easily. It trailed an arm's length of mucus and a small helping of this morning's breakfast behind it. He began undressing the girl, exposing her milky-white flesh to the barn's air. There were no goosebumps. She didn't resist. The potion had taken its full effect.

Then he set to work. Drawing a short narrow knife, he coated it with more potion from the black-sealed vial, then began to carve into her chest, arms, and face. The cuts formed a chaotic sequence of lines and connections. They were not runes. These were much older things, left over from an ancient time. Most of the old arts were a mystery to him. This array of cuts was just one of four ancient carvings that he had found in his travels. One was enough for their purpose. The carvings somehow kept her spirit whole while she approached the final door. Coupled with the vials, it calmed the flows of magic that surrounded her and kept her in stasis, aware but unmoving.

He felt the Friends call out. The others in the barn felt it too. They all stepped forward, coming closer to him, closer to the girl's immobile form.

"Now is the test!" the Rat called out.

He kicked over his travel bag, spilling two dozen wicked cutting knives on the barn floor. "Now we eat! Eat of this girl! Eat! We will take her essence into ourselves and grow on her power!"

The taken were slow to advance. A large burly man stepped up first, picking up a knife before cutting into the girl's already bleeding arm and slicing a finger's length of meat from her. His bloody hand took up the meat and slid it into his mouth where he swallowed without so much as chewing. Red blood stained his face as others approached. The girl looked on in horror as the crowd set to devouring her. Each of the Taken sliced a single piece of flesh away, then consumed it. As they feasted, the Rat prepared his test supplies. He pulled three flasks from his bag, each covered in leather and sealed tightly. Uncorking the end, he walked to the Taken after they finished their meat and offered them a sip. He observed the reaction to the mixture then moved to the next.

When the Taken were finished, the girl had been reduced to a bloody mess of bone and leftover hunks of flesh. Most of her skin had been cut away. Her muscles were cut to shreds. Most of her organs had been consumed as well. The Rat felt pity for the girl. It was unfortunate that she had to be alive to perform the test. She got to feel all the pain, all the cutting. Her soul lived in her mangled body, even now. He didn't consider himself to be overly cruel, so he did one final favor to the poor girl. He reached down to grasp her head. Then he pulled up quickly, snapping her twelve-year-old neck, releasing her to travel through the final door.

Hazel stood to the side. Her eyes were wide in excitement. Blood coated her mouth and face where she had eaten heartily, completely surrendering to the call of the Friends. Her voice quavered as she asked him a question.

"What did we just do?"

"We did a critical test, my dear. Weren't you paying attention?"

"But we ate her."

"Yes. By eating her, you took in part of ancient power. I've confirmed it with my alchemy. Don't you understand what that means?"

"It means that we are cannibals."

"No. You are taken. You are far above common people now. You are wolves. They are sheep. You merely ate as is your right to." He paused before continuing. "Just think about what you took in! Ancient power! Flows of magic and might!"

The Rat called out to the room, commanding their attention. The Friends hummed their approval throughout the crowd, eager in their anticipation.

"These are the things that the gods are made of. I say to you, if you eat of this magic, you will become the magic. And now, soon, we will share the greatest feast of all! We shall take the goddess herself! We will take her power! We will eat her, and we will become a legion of gods!"

###

Chamise looked at Miller, partly annoyed, partly happy to see him. It had been a while since they got a chance to talk, really talk. She missed their conversations when they used to travel together. She admitted that she felt closer to him since the trip from Ingalls to the tower. Then the battle happened. Everything changed.

"Who's your friend?" Chamise said, gesturing at the young girl beside him. She looked dirty, skinny, and as nervous as a child could be.

"That's Hurriet. I met her yesterday."

Chamise grinned. "Taking in strays?"

"I'm not a stray! I live here. You're the stray!" Hurriet snapped back.

Chamise held her hands up defensively. "Easy girl. I'm not criticizing. I just know this moron. He's apt to take in the worst sort."

"Yeah, like you."

A broad grin broke out across Chamise's face. Miller began to laugh.

After a moment, Hurriet spoke up. "Wait a minute. You two are teasing." A scowl appeared on her face as she crossed her arms.

"Don't worry. Chamise is actually friendly most of the time, despite outward appearances."

After a few chuckles, Chamise finally asked, "So Hurriet, why did my friend bring you here? Looking to learn how to play nets?"

Hurriet scowled back. Miller spoke up. "No. She needs a safe place to stay for a bit. A few days perhaps?"

Hurriet nodded her head in agreement.

"She's got some talent and got noticed by Darjeeling. I was hoping to hide her with you until he forgets. In any case, it will allow me to assess her talents. Who knows? Maybe she can learn something from you in the process."

Chamise shook her head in disagreement. "I've never taught anyone magic. I don't think I'm a good teacher."

"You're good enough at spellcraft though."

Hurriet broke in, her voice filled with excitement. "You're a wizard too? And you can teach me to be a wizard?"

"Slow down, it doesn't work like that."

Questions began to pour out of Hurriet. "How does it work then? Is there a book or something? I heard a tale that a magic snake needs to bite you. Do I need to sacrifice animals under the full moon?"

Holding his hand up, palm outward, Miller tried to interject. "Slow down. None of what you said makes any sense. Stop and listen for a moment, will you?"

The pout returned to her face. Chamise chuckled, offering a broad smile.

Miller continued, "First of all, we will need to observe you for a few days. Some folks have a lot of talent and are worth training, others only have a little. Then we need to have a discussion about what living in the world of crafters means. Chamise is a Free Mage, crafters that owe no allegiance to anyone. There are other magical guilds out there. Some are darker than others."

Hurriet knew what he alluded to.

"The White Hand," she whispered, as if afraid that some invisible horror would overhear.

Both Chamise and Miller spoke at the same time. "Exactly."

"I can't teach her crafting, at least not here. I would have to return to Ingalls." She gave Miller a piercing look. "I have my own magical studies to do here in Home's Hearth, as you well know. I'm not in the market for an apprentice either."

Miller nodded. "I suspected as much. I'm just asking that you give her a place to lay her head until I can speak with Aileen. She will have some ideas."

Chamise spit back a response. "I know what her response will be. She will scoop this poor girl up faster than you can say boo."

"You don't give her enough credit. Her heart still has feelings, even after the ring."

Chamise narrowed her eyes. "Oh, dear Miller, you are so naive. Every day that goes by with that ring on her finger steals a little bit of her heart. Soon enough, it will be gone."

"That is in the future. Right now, I want to keep Hurriet away from Master Darjeeling and his apprentice Frantz. Let's solve the immediate danger first, shall we?"

"Don't I get a say in this?" Hurriet asked.

"Sure. I would prefer that you made informed decisions though."

Hurriet paused to inventory her feelings. She spent a long moment trying to find her intuition and discover a path forward. Finally, she came to a conclusion.

"I'll stay here for a few days, but I'd like to keep the horse."

"The horse?" Chamise asked, surprised by the request.

"Yes. Something tells me that I'll need her."

Miller nodded his head up and down, unsurprised. "That sounds like a good idea. You will need her if Darjeeling finds you. I'll have to ask her first though."

Chamise knew the mare was special, but her eyes shot up when Miller mentioned consulting the horse.

"Sure. Ask the horse. It's probably smarter than you anyway."

Miller smiled back. "I already knew that. Let's find Hurriet a place to clean up and get some sleep, she looks like she needs it."

WAYWARD DAUGHTER

Aileen paced around the edge of the protective circle. Its fresh white inscriptions stood out against the old stained floor. Miller sat on a three-legged stool, fatigued and out of energy. It had been a long day.

He had spent the entire day seeing that Brita had what she needed. She no longer had to suffer living in the open. A bright yellow and blue tent stood in the center of the protective circle. Master Darjeeling somehow managed to have a tent gaudy enough to belong to a spice merchant or a theater troop. Oddly, he had it packed and at the ready.

Miller had no idea why he would travel the lands with such a thing. Darjeeling told him that he acquired it in a dice game with the Gypsy King. Miller had never even heard of a Gypsy King. The bright tent stood planted in the center of the gloomy inn. It was large enough to hold six people comfortably, and Miller had enough room to stand while he assembled it. A few nails in the place of stakes, and there it was, jutting from the floorboards like a circus had moved in.

Brita squealed in pleasure when she saw the tent under construction. She smiled and danced, especially when she saw the bed of pillows within. Again, Miller had no idea how Darjeeling had managed to pack fourteen pillows and carry them along, but he had stopped asking questions long before the pillows came out. Even Frantz was mystified.

He watched Brita's shadow move across the tent walls. A lantern inside the tent projected a very alluring image on those walls. The sound of bathwater and giggling filled the air. It made him both happy that she had found some small comfort, and sad knowing that it would not last.

Aileen continued her pacing. She circled the tent like a hawk intent on its prey. On the first two rotations she had stopped to check his circle glyphs. Now she didn't even bother to pretend interest. Just in case this was a sign of impending disaster, and most things with Aileen were, he pulled himself out of the chair to intercept her.

She slowed as she approached, ruining the vigorous pace of her circling.

"Mistress, can I be of use? You appear, well, uncomfortable."

Aileen returned a kind smile. Her eyes seemed sad, but her hands shook. Nerves? Anger?

"Nothing that you can help with, I'm afraid." She continued her walk, circling the tent, circling Brita, lost in her own thoughts.

"May I walk with you? Perhaps some simple company?"

"I would like that. It's been too long since we walked together."

They walked another circle, her eyes no longer focused on Brita, but on some other issue, far away. "I know that Sword and I are distressing. I never wanted to hurt you," she began.

"Please, let's set all that aside. I don't feel ready for another spirited discussion." He tried to put humor into his voice. It seemed to work as Aileen gave him a small smile.

She signed in resignation. "In truth, something is weighing heavily on my mind. I moved us into Home's Hearth hoping that it would bring Phyllicitus to her senses. The opposite seems to have happened."

She produced a crumpled paper that had been hidden in her hands. "She is sending Sister Fidelity, along with seven other temple sisters. They will be evicting us."

"Fidelity? I met her today. She doesn't seem to be high ranking enough for that kind of task."

"I know. It's an insult and an eviction, all in one."

"Do we have to obey? I know it's her city and all, but can't we quote one of her own rulings? I remember a few years ago, we had a lot of freedoms granted to us. I don't remember them ever being rescinded."

"Sure, we could use legal maneuvers to delay a few days. We don't want this to become a contest, but I'm afraid I've set that in motion."

They continued walking.

Miller said, "If only Phyllicitus would send for me. If only she would come herself. I know that I could talk some sense into her."

"Can you go to her?"

"In the temple? Surrounded by priestesses? That would provoke an incident, wouldn't it?"

The thought made her smile. "There is the crux of it. Now that I've put us in direct conflict with the temple, how do we come out of it holding a peace branch?"

He said, "So go see her when she isn't at the temple. Isn't there another place she visits? She can't hide every minute of every day. I think that you may be making more of this than it warrants. The reason she is upset is that she misses you. If you can just see her, she will probably give in."

"You are probably right. She doesn't mind giving in. Surrender is almost her first name."

"Well, she isn't the Goddess of War, is she?"

"No. She is not, even when people she loves need her to be."

"Do you mean, even when you need her to be?"

Aileen stopped—a quirky grin on her face. "You've been

learning lessons from Easter, haven't you? Nice try, but you aren't manipulative enough yet. Give it time."

"Thought I'd try. Someone has to end this stalemate."

Aileen reached out and took his hand, pulling it close. She pushed her arm in the crook of his elbow. The walk continued for another minute in silence as she considered how to solve the dilemma with Phyllicitus.

She thought, perhaps it was just an emotional issue. Perhaps she could simply visit Phyllicitus and everything would be back the way it was. She considered what might come of such a meeting. In the worst case, Phyllicitus would insist that she return to the temple. The thought oddly comforted her.

But she was too far gone now. The order had their hooks into her deeply. Then Aileen stopped, annoyed with herself. Miller was right, she was over-thinking the problem. Phyllicitus had a long relationship with Easter. She knew the order better than most. She had been trying to turn Easter away from the White Hand for centuries. She wondered if Phyllicitus had a longer agenda than simply being piqued at her for joining the White Hand.

She said, "Alright, you've convinced me. There is no way I'm going to get out of this gently so I might as well go down fighting. Phyllicitus, if she stays with her habit, will be visiting The Gardens at least once per week. Next time she goes, we go too. I'll corner her there and work something out."

"And Sister Fidelity? She doesn't seem like she embraces patience. I'm guessing that we will see her soon."

This time, Aileen's smile was crafty and mirthful. "You and I will go drink a bottle of wine. If Fidelity decides to show up, we will let Easter handle her."

"That sounds like a good idea to me," Miller said, cheerily.

"I'm going to get changed. Why don't you check on our lovely guest? Make sure she is comfortable. Tomorrow will be hard on her. Darjeeling has an entire course of potions, poisons, and other concoctions to feed her. You might want to ensure that she gets a good meal tonight as well."

"Consider it done. I've been meaning to talk to her anyway. Today, on the road, she said a few odd things that I've been meaning to follow up on."

Aileen released his arm and walked away, gesturing for him to be off to his duties. "Give me an hour, I'll be ready."

Brita pulled herself up from the portable wooden tub. Its smooth wood was covered in water. Her feet splashed through small puddles scattered across the floor. She felt happy and clean for the first time since the Friends had taken her.

The Friends had started giving her urges again. They wanted to know what caused her captors to change location. She didn't really care though. Miller had given her a little tent and a tub of hot water to clean up in. Sometimes she simply appreciated what she had.

Something seemed off with the Friends though. They still communicated with her, but she couldn't feel any of the other Taken. Normally they would all share the feeling of being linked, of being part of something bigger than themselves. Since Miller had put her within the duel circle, those connections had faded away.

She heard Miller's voice from outside the tent. "Need any more towels?"

"You wish. Keep your distance or I'll call for help."

She couldn't call anyone. Nor, it occurred to her as she thought about it, would she want to. They had found a way to give her some privacy and brought her to Home's Hearth. Surely the temple could help her, she hoped.

"I didn't mean while you were naked," he replied.

"How disappointing."

"So get dressed then. I've got to talk to you before the Priestesses get here."

She felt the jolt of interest from the Friends. "Priestesses? Why are they coming?"

"My guess is that they are coming for you, and to eject us from town."

"Why?"

"Maybe they are jealous of your pretty face? Or it could be that you are the only one of the new Taken that we've managed to collect, and they want to see you."

"I hate the way that you say 'collect.' It makes me feel like some sort of harvested plant."

"More like a flower, really."

She smiled at the compliment. Sweet words always kept her calm and cooperative. She liked the way he had become more attentive as of late. Plus, she thought, Miller was sweet on her. She had seen the way he looked at her. It was obvious.

She walked out of the tent. Her long dark hair was still wet. It was lovely, hanging past her shoulder almost covering her ample bosom. She had picked out a faded red dress that complemented her curvy figure. It showed her off well.

Miller walked over to a lone table abandoned on the edge of the dining hall. It screeched as he pulled it closer to the circle's edge. Then he fetched the ledger, ink, quill, and a small stool.

"Not more questions. I bore of questions."

"I'm trying to discover how they took you. Don't you want to know as well?"

"Well, I did before. Now I'm wondering what good it will do. It's not like I can un-take myself."

"We don't know that, do we? We really don't know a lot. I think it's best if we continue our word games, at least for the next week."

Miller thought about other avenues of investigation that were suggested. Darjeeling suggested simply killing her in cold blood, then summoning her spirit to converse with. Easter and Aileen had almost agreed until Miller brought up the fact that the same tactic had been tried on the first generation of Takers to no avail.

He opened the book to a blank page and began preparing the quill. "Just humor me, alright? It will at least pass the time.

Remember, I was able to fight them off last time they came."

She felt flirtatious and bored. "Only if you kiss me."

Miller shook his head, smiling. "Sorry. You will have to wait for the Takers to leave you before you get a kiss from me."

"You're no fun."

"Yes, well, think of it as an occupational hazard for wizards."

"Necromancers you mean."

"No, I mean wizards. You need to raise the dead to be a necromancer. I've never done that, so I'm not a necromancer."

"Technicality."

"Truth."

The conversation was going nowhere. He decided to change the subject.

"Let's talk about the carriage ride, can we?"

"Fine." Her lower lip stuck out in a pout.

"You seemed to get talkative when we stopped in front of the old Eisenvard barracks. What did you sense?"

He carefully used the word 'sense' instead of 'see'. Questions had to be asked carefully.

"Lots of people. Eisenvard playing games. People playing at sport."

"Sport? That's all?"

She paused, trying to think how to respond. She didn't want the Friends to interfere with her ability to answer.

"It's all a game of hide-and-seek, isn't it?"

Miller scrawled a note in his book. "Hide-and-seek?"

"Yes, the game, like children play." She carried on in a lecherous voice, "Do you want to play hide-and-seek with me? I have this lovely tent now."

Miller shook his head in confusion. "I didn't see anyone playing hide-and-seek. What did they look like?"

"There were two of them."

She started feeling early signs from the Friends. They were growing uncomfortable with this conversation. Miller continued scrawling in his book, unaware of her changing expression. She didn't know how to tell him about the couple, the other

Friends. Words failed her.

Abruptly, she stomped forward toward the edge of the circle. "I saw your Mistress Aileen walking with you. Are you sweet on her? Oh, you walked so closely together."

Miller snapped his head up, annoyed. "No. It isn't like that."

"Oh? What is it like then? A parent and child perhaps? Or maybe a cousin that you secretly want to kiss?" She put her arms out as if she were in a dance. She gracefully danced along the inner edge of the protective circle mocking his denial. "Oh Mother, please sleep with me tonight! It's so cold. Please keep me warm."

Miller felt anger rising in his heart. "Why do you have to be so evil?"

She stopped dancing, hurt at his remark.

"I'm not evil. I'm just trying to talk to you. Why won't you listen to what I am saying?"

He shook his head in confusion. "I don't understand what you are trying to say. It all sounds disjointed, crazy."

Her response was drawn out. It sounded like she knew what she wanted to say but could not find the right words.

"Crazy? Like Ebber?"

"Who?"

"Exactly. Can't you just listen to meanings, or intentions, instead of these pesky words?" She exhaled in frustration. "Listen to what I'm trying to mean."

Miller's response was acidic. He was tired of the games. "Isn't that what we use words for?"

"That is what you use words for. I use words to get you pointed toward the right star. You never listen though, so caught up in your words and all."

He was caught flat-footed. The idea dawned upon him. She had been trying to communicate for weeks, but for some reason, she hasn't been able to.

"Let me ask a question."

"No. We are never alone."

"Never alone? Even now?"

"Never."

The truth slowly dawned on him. Brita was trying to talk to him, to let him know what was happening to her. She couldn't. The things that 'took' her would not allow it. Brita was trying to cooperate with him but couldn't.

He pulled his book up, scribbling madly in the margins of the last doodle he had made.

"Can you play a game with me then?"

"A game?" Her laughter was delightful. "What kind of game?"

"A word game. I'll say a word. You say the first word that pops into your head."

She paused in thought, her lips pouting for just a moment.

"It doesn't sound fun."

"Better than just sitting here staring at each other."

She smiled, leaning down to expose her luscious curves. "We could do other things."

His face turned red. "So, no. We've talked about that before." After he recovered from his shyness, he continued.

"I'm going to say words. You just reply with one word."

She tried to respond, but he interjected the first word before she could.

"Secrets."

She smiled before she responded.

"Heart."

"Dogs."

Her eyes grew wide before she responded.

"Master."

Miller jotted down notes in his book before he continued.

"Choices."

"None."

He stopped writing.

"None?"

"None."

He was stumped. Was she completely under their control? If so, how did she communicate with him at all? Why wasn't she like the Taken before?

He tried another word.

"Defense"

She snapped back the answer. "Hide."

Things started falling into place. A thought struck him. Reaching down to the book, he turned a page, then ripped a blank one out. Then he ripped that page in two. On one page, he wrote, "They have me under their control." On the other page, he continued his thought, "I can make some decisions, but not all."

He placed both papers in front of her.

"Look at these papers, please. Read them, then close your eyes."

She smiled back at him.

"If I do, will you spend some time with me? In here? In my tent?"

He looked back at her, meeting her eyes.

"Yes. I swear it. Now point at the paper that is most true. Don't look, just point."

She closed her eyes and pointed at one of the slips.

"Don't open your eyes. Pull your hand back. You don't get to see what you pointed at."

She brought her hand back to her side.

Miller exhaled. He was afraid the experiment would not work. Maybe it still didn't. She had selected "I can make decisions, but not all." That left the door open. There may be a way to move forward.

He ripped out another page. He wrote again, scribbling quickly. "Can they read?"

Holding the paper up so it was easily visible, he gave her the next command. "When I tell you to open your eyes, you will see a question. Answer it as quickly as you can. Are you ready?"

"Yes."

"Excellent. Open your eyes."

As soon as she saw the words, she felt the Friends exert their power over her. She didn't want to answer the question. She didn't want to be here talking to Miller. She could feel fear, as if Miller would kill her if she answered the question. There was no right answer. She was doomed.

She cried out in pain.

Miller set down the paper. Brita could not find any words to answer with. She frantically tried to think of a way to tell him, but it would not come. Moments passed as she thought.

Miller didn't interrupt. He let Brita have the time she needed. After five minutes had passed, she abandoned the effort. She needed to tell Miller what was happening.

She tried something different, instead of using her own words, she grabbed onto someone else's words that were buried in her memories. The words emerged from her throat as a beautiful cheery tune. She sang her response using a refrain from a children's song. "Anything I can do, they can do better. Tee da da, da da!"

He put the quill down. Using writing to communicate would be a dead end. What had she said? He needed to pay attention to meaning rather than words? It was like a puzzle. Each piece unlike the other.

He felt a sliver of hope. Somehow Brita was still trying to help him. He would need time to think about how to converse with her.

Slowly he stood up, gathering his focus.

"Back up toward the tent, will you?"

"Why?"

"I promised to come in. So I'm keeping my promise."

He stepped up to the circle. He spoke the words of release, unbinding the circle, then he reached out toward Brita. Her smile shone as she walked forward, quivering in anticipation.

He opened up his heart channeling and sent restful aspects and thoughts toward her. She pulled in a deep breath and sank to her knees. A moment later, she was sound asleep on the floor. While she was unconscious, Miller walked into the tent and collected the six sensing runes he had left there.

He had found a small clue today. Would it be enough to

point the way forward? He didn't know.

THE VISIT

The door swung open, whipping around on its iron hinges and smashing into the wall. Powdery mortar sprinkled down onto the clean wooden floor. Sister Fidelity erupted into the room with nine other priestesses following her.

She paused as she entered the room, staring at the tent pitched in the middle of what was once the main serving hall. A huge circle lay drawn on the floor, inscribed in mystical symbols of power. The walls had been stripped bare of their previous decorations. Freshly painted symbols of power replaced them, standing out against the dirty tan of the walls. Banners, a few paintings, and an old musty stag's head lay discarded in the back of the inn.

Master Easter walked out from behind the tent, its garish blue and red walls looked oddly at home within the cascade of painted symbols.

Easter gestured an apology. "I'm sorry. The inn is closed now."

Sister Fidelity didn't accept any of it. "Who are you? What

are you doing here? Where are the others?" She fired the questions off, not waiting for answers.

"Others? Oh, I guess they are about the town somewhere. Is there anyone, in particular, you want to talk to?"

Fidelity motioned to the priestesses. They began to spread out across the room, grabbing the one table, chairs, and travel gear to move them out of the inn.

"I would be careful with all of that. These symbols, they are a bit of a protective spell. You could start a very large fire. You could burn the whole inn down around us."

Sister Fidelity scowled at Easter, calling his bluff.

A strange scent began to fill the room. It smelled of pine mixed with burning sap. Easter smiled at what was about to occur.

"Well," Easter continued, "you could be burned up. The fire would be death-fire, so I would be fine. Those who don't know the secret of it would have a hard time though." Easter smiled, motioning toward the symbols covering the walls, floor, and some of the ceiling.

Sister Fidelity stomped forward, not intimidated by Easter. "You cursed little man. I have no time for your little games. I'm on the business of Goddess Phyllicitus herself."

"Er, so am I."

Suddenly, a loud snapping sound filled the room for only a few seconds. Easter held up his hands. "Everyone stop! Now!"

The priestesses paused to see what the commotion was about, but Sister Fidelity motioned them on. A young blond priestess returned to her task, lifting the heavy book from a table. A tower of flame sprung up around her. She screamed, filling the room with her horror. The inferno cooked her alive, transforming into a woman-sized swirling tornado of flame. It lasted only for a few seconds, then it sputtered away. Only a pile of ash and a discarded book were left behind.

"Janine!" Sister Fidelity called out the name of the unfortunate priestess. Then she pointed an accusing finger at Easter. "What have you done?"

"Me? No, that was you. When Phyllicitus asks me about it, I'll be sure to give her all the details. I warned you. I begged for you to stop. Now you have placed the lives of all these servants of Phyllicitus in dire peril. The shock. The horror."

Her eyes grew wide, now understanding what kind of danger they were in. "It's a trap!"

"No, it's a safety precaution. Do you see that tent?" Easter pointed into the circle where the tent stood.

Sister Fidelity was hardly listening. Instead, she concentrated on trying to figure a way out of this mess.

He waited a few moments for her to speak, then gave up, continuing his previous thread. "That tent contains someone who has been infected by the Takers. If they come into contact with anyone in this town, there is a chance they can spread the infestation. No, I'm sorry, these runes are protective, and you just endangered all of Home's Hearth by charging in here with no idea what was going on."

"You can't do that."

"I can, and I did. If you are worried about that, then think about this. What do you think will happen to this entire city if the Taken escapes? Think about it."

It didn't take her long to find the worst-case scenario. "Fire. Cleansing by fire."

"Now we understand each other."

She motioned for the sisters to stop what they were doing. One by one, they gently set down what they were carrying and carefully walked out the door onto the lawn.

"Phyllicitus kept you out of Home's Hearth for a reason. Why did you disregard her wishes? Why bring your death-powers here?"

"As you said, I'm a necromancer. Her wishes aren't my concern. Last time the Takers came, we had an alliance and it worked. We can do it again if Phyllicitus doesn't wreck it. The Takers are back. We need to discover how to stop them again." He gestured at the pile of smoking ash. "None of this matters compared to the doom facing us if we fail."

She took in her breath, then pointed at the pile of ash. "But Janine, what of her?"

Easter held up a hand to stop her from going on. "Necromancers, remember? Janine will be fine. I'll have her up and walking around in no time."

The response flew from her mouth. It was filled with spite. "I doubt she will appreciate your dark talents, sir."

"I doubt she will appreciate you getting her burned alive, ma'am." Easter shot back.

Sister Fidelity could only return an angry stare. She had no idea how to proceed, so she did the only thing she could. She spun on her heel and stomped from the inn, leaving behind some final words. "I'm going to inform the goddess. Let's see how you deal with that."

Easter flicked his wrist at the door, sending a small channel of entropy forward, closing the door behind her.

"You can come out."

Darjeeling stepped out from inside the tent, a brass lamp burning wildly in his hand. Brita looked out from the tent folds. Her eyes were red, aggravated by the burning concoction.

"I think that went lovely," Darjeeling said.

Easter smiled back. "Could have been worse."

"Indeed." Darjeeling walked across the room to stare at the pile of ash.

"Not a bad job, if I do say so myself."

"Oh, it was well done. There is no doubt. But can you fix her?"

"Sure. She isn't badly off. I was going to keep her like this for a few days, just so the priestesses don't start believing that raising the dead is so easy."

"She isn't dead though."

"No. Raising the dead always leaves scars. I simply covered her with the glamour. It's an easy trick if you have enough distractions going on. A fire tornado and a White Hand master in the same room did the trick, ey?"

He cracked a smile back toward Darjeeling. "As long as we

put her right before Phyllicitus summons us, it's all fine."

"You think she will then? You think Aileen's plan will pull her out of the temple?"

"Oh, I think it's already working. It's a nice plan, using Phyllicitus's own anger against her. It makes Phyllicitus think this is all her own idea. I like it."

Darjeeling didn't respond, only continued to stare down at the pile of ash that should have been a priestess. A few more moments drifted by. Easter walked beside Darjeeling and stared down at the pile.

"What is the matter?"

He gestured downward. "That priestess, the enchantment was too easy."

"Too easy?"

"She was a priestess of Phyllicitus, in her home city, with her temple within walking distance. There should have been more resistance. I felt her trying to resist, but it was muffled somehow. I'm not sure what is going on here."

"What do you suspect?"

"Suspect? I suspect everything. I suspect nothing. I know that this woman could not defend herself from a simple glamour. I know that it should have taken a lot more channeling for me to succeed with that trick. It was actually a bit of a disappointment. I didn't get a feeling of victory, nothing."

"Maybe she was just weak?"

"That sister, Fidelity, didn't detect it either. I wonder if our enemies between the worlds have been here already. Perhaps they have already begun preparing the battlefield."

Easter turned to look at the doors, the dented walls, then back to the tent. He shook his head in resignation.

"If it were easy, we would have beaten them a millennium ago."

"And this is the Garden."

Miller nodded his head up and down approvingly. "Nice." He had seen it before, but sometimes it was best to let Aileen play the guide.

The White Hand mistress stood by his side, outwardly calm but churning with worry on the inside. Miller watched her wring her hands, then unconsciously fiddle with her shoulder-length blond hair.

"I'm just glad they let me in."

"I thought that you were some sort of member."

"I was a member a few years ago, but that was before."

She held up her master's ring, letting Miller know how unsure she was. She had no idea how they would receive a Master of the White Hand.

He didn't know what to say, so he opted to walk beside her. Sometimes she could be comforted simply by the presence of another human being. How Easter had talked her into becoming a White Hand remained a mystery. He couldn't imagine Aileen closeted away in dark cabals for the next thousand years. She just wasn't built that way.

They reached the end of the cobbled path. A circle of flat stones was arranged in the middle of a grass lawn. Statues of nude people, plucked from different times in antiquity, lay arranged across the lawn. They stood as if in some sort of dance or celebration. Aileen walked forward, reached out, and gently touched a bearded man carved exquisitely from stone. He carried a great shield in one hand and a drinking horn in the other.

"They got a new statue." She gazed at it, lost in its depths. Lines of muscle stood out from its arms. Waves had been carved into the short beard giving the illusion of movement.

"You've been gone a few years."

"Yes." She shook her head, almost in disbelief. Miller could almost see the ghosts and memories of her times here coming back, haunting her.

"Follow me. I want to show you something."

Miller fell in behind her, following as she threaded her way past the statues to a small trail that cut into thick bushes. They surrounded the garden on three sides. The trail had been hidden behind their leaves.

Aileen knew right where it would be. Her feet were sure as she walked the length of the faint path. She followed the trail past the bushes, emerging in another garden area. This garden was smaller, less than twenty paces across, and filled with red, yellow, and pink flowers. Their broad petals filled the air with a beautiful aroma.

The light was softer here. Dusk was preparing to arrive. The surrounding bushes kept the final beams of sunlight at bay. Four torch holders, each taller than Miller, stood in the garden surrounding a single statue of an old man wearing scholarly robes. He held a book in one hand, propped against his stomach. The other arm was raised, holding a chisel over his head, much like it was a sword.

"This is Stevenson."

A pang of fear passed over him. Did she kill him too? Like Madam K?

"Should I know him?"

"You probably should, but you don't. He was the founder of The Gardens. He created the club and gifted the magical libraries held in the basement. He was visionary, kind, and the head priest of Phyllicitus in the early years."

"Wait, the head priest of Phyllicitus founded a magical library, outside of the temple? One that lets any member use it?"

"Yes. He was unconventional, to say the least. Back then, the priests had a lot more freedom for their own pet projects, at least he had freedom. He also believed in the magical arts. He wrote that true understanding of the world would not come from what the eyes saw alone. He was right."

"So why all this? Why the beautiful gardens? Why the perfectly manicured lawns and cobblestone paths?"

"Why? Because it is beautiful, of course. It needs to exist because it needs to exist."

Miller squinted back, confused. "You're talking like a priestess again."

"Sorry. Home's Hearth does that to me. Plus, I think I'm going to need to talk a lot more like that in the very near future."

She didn't respond to his puzzled look.

"I just wanted you to see the statue and hear the name. He was more than a priest, you see. He founded the study of magic within the walls of the temple as well. He was a prolific writer, documenting almost all of the spellcraft that he knew. Sadly, you can't find his works anymore. The Garden is the only place left where they were safely preserved."

"Why?"

"The Eisenvard destroyed them when they were hunting witches. Like most of the things they did. They thought they were in the right, but it turned out quite the opposite."

Miller grew excited. "Can I see his books?"

"Sorry. You have to be a member. That costs some gold."

"Gold?" A gold coin was a lot of wealth, something Barons traded in. It wasn't something for a mere apprentice no matter what the guild.

"Yes. The last tally I paid used every coin I had. One hundred and forty gold coins for one year. I got distracted by the Takers a few years ago and I never managed to come up to date with my payments."

"You could buy a castle with that," he replied in appreciation.

She laughed. "No, you can't. Not a good one anyway. A manor, sure, but not a castle."

"You owe the Garden three Manors? Seems like a steep price to be in a club."

"I don't know. We are about to see though. I guess if they insist, I will have to find a way to pay. Otherwise, I'll be sending an apprentice over for a year of slave labor to enchant things for them."

He looked at the statue. "How bad is it?"

She chuckled, amused that Miller believed she would do that. "Not bad at all. In fact, it's pretty nice."

"Darn," he said sarcastically.

She reached out and snapped his arm playfully. "Don't get excited. I won't send you over until you get the new Takers sorted out."

She began walking back down the path, back toward the last garden. When she arrived, she continued walking until she arrived at another trail. This one was wide enough to walk side by side. It twisted through the brush. The trail led into a copse of trees, towering above them, blocking out the last of the evening's light.

Ahead, Miller saw two lights, torches being carried toward them.

"Just in time. It's getting dark in here. Do you think they will allow us entrance?" Miller said, pointing at the two figures approaching. They were dressed in the colors of Garden servants.

"Oh, don't worry. The Garden will take care of you as long as you are a guest."

"But what if we aren't guests?"

"Then we would not be here. The Garden knows when someone isn't welcome."

"Like necromancers?"

She scowled back, plainly finished with his wordplay. "Enough comments from the apprentice. Watch and learn."

Two people came into view. Each carried a torch in their left hand. Miller stopped, staring at them. They were beautiful, perfect specimens of humanity. The woman on the left wore a slight undertunic covering her ample bosom and a short skirt. The man next to her was handsome, lean, and wore only a loincloth that was covered in elaborate stitchwork.

The man gazed at both of them, then his attention was drawn to Aileen. Recognition dawned.

"Aileen? It's been a few years. I had heard that you weren't coming back."

Aileen's voice rose in surprise. "And who said that?"

"Phyllicitus."

"Well, we'll see about that. Is she here yet?"

"She's been here for hours. Watch out though. She seemed rather testy today."

"She's about to get testier. I need to go settle my account, then I need to talk to her."

A hint of worry injected into his questioning voice. "Shouldn't you do this at the temple?"

"No. She's being difficult. Now is the time. Here is the place. There's too much at stake for it to be any other way. Plus, she's always so much more relaxed when she stays at The Gardens. I think she enjoys escaping from the temple as often as she can."

He nodded in agreement, unwilling to directly comment on the habits of a deity, especially one in such close proximity.

The woman stepped up, taking Miller's hand. He didn't know what to do. This woman was gorgeous. Her beauty overwhelmed any notion of resistance he might have had. She held his hand warmly but firmly, pulling him forward. The man grinned back at Aileen. "First time?"

She grinned back. "First time."

He smiled as the woman led him down the trail, back the way she had come from. The torches broke up the darkness as the bushes became darker, more cave-like. He didn't feel nervous though. The woman hadn't said a word to him, but he absolutely trusted her.

Miller's thoughts began to spin. He was an apprentice to the White Hand. He was always in fear. Fear was a constant in his life. Somehow it had dissipated, if just for this short walk.

They were on their way to see the goddess though, and she wasn't happy with them.

SEWERS

Brother Quiet held a vinegar-soaked rag in front of his face.
The dank rotten smell was overwhelming. A large candle stood
on a pewter candlestick gripped in his left hand. A half dozen
runes coated the burning candle. While the flame burned above,
the magic tied to the runes regrew the wick and renewed the
candle itself. It would never stop burning as long as there was
magic and enough air. It was a useful instrument here in the
sewers.

He peered forward through the dim light. Thanks to his
work, the sewer tunnels were clear of refuse. He had been
clearing, repairing, and re-enforcing the old sewers since before
the goddess returned. He knew his way through the sewer
tunnels like it was his home, mostly because it was. But he
didn't know this new place he found himself in.

"Why did I go down here?"

His voice echoed down the stone tunnel. The night watch
had come to him near dusk. A few townsfolk had reported
some odd noises coming from below. The noises sounded like

screams. They were worried that animals had gotten into the sewers. The watchmen were worried about keeping their uniforms clean, so they called on him to do it.

He swore in disgust. "Always the schite-jobs." That was the motto of the city engineers. As a young priest, he had been drafted into their midst almost a decade ago. Removing rats, sealing burst pipes, and keeping sicknesses at bay had become his life. He was good at it and took pride in the work he did. He kept the system running smoothly so people wouldn't need to worry about it.

That was why he was so surprised to find a hole in the side of the sewer tunnel. It was large enough to walk through. The bricks had collapsed into some sort of gap. The mortar holding them together had weakened and aged until it came down under its own weight.

Odd, he thought, the other walls didn't look the same age. The rest of it seemed solid to him. He walked through this tunnel before and never noted the rot. He would have repaired it otherwise.

The brother walked through the hole and turned. It became its own tunnel. This passage was older, less maintained, but still in good condition. Walking farther, he kicked one of the wall stones. It didn't move. It was solid.

He stopped. It sounded like something was moving ahead. He wondered if a large cat had gotten down here, or a pack of rats. He wasn't sure, so he gripped his candlestick tighter and moved farther in. The enchantment on the candlestick caused the light to become brighter when he gripped it harder, shining illumination into all shadows, cracks, and crevices.

He could see twenty paces further ahead. More bricks lay scattered on the floor, their broken mortar decorating the tunnel floor.

"Ah. Here we go. I think we've found something." He hoped that talking aloud would give whatever animal was in there an opportunity to flee. He didn't want to fight rats or feral cats down here, late night or not.

Walking farther along the open passageway, he came to a corner. Before he completed the turn, he heard voices from farther along the tunnel. He was surprised that someone would be down here this late at night, and in all this stench. He turned the corner, ready to chastise whoever he discovered.

The turn led into a passageway only three steps deep. A large room lay at the end of the passageway. His magically enhanced candle lit up the room in bright light as he gripped hard. It showed wet stone, dripping slime, and a group of occupants.

Seven people stood in the room. It was twenty paces deep with a sunken center. A black ooze filled the center of the room. Brother Quiet couldn't see where it was leaking from. Two people dropped small fish into the pool from a bucket. Three of them were hauling on short ropes, maneuvering a barrel into the center of the dark pool. The barrel floated buoyantly. For some reason, part of the barrel had been cut away to form some sort of boat.

Odd, he thought, what's going on here?

"What do we have here?" a woman's voice called out from their midst.

Brother Quiet stood frozen as well. He took in the people. They worked in absolute darkness. How did they see? Was there a spellcrafter down here?

Then he recognized the tall man. It was one of the alchemists that lived in the crafters quarter. Brother Quiet had purchased ease-weed from him once before. The alchemist stood away from the pool, closer to the woman who had just spoken.

"Ryley? What is happening here?" Brother Quiet asked.

Ryley responded with a short laugh. "What is happening? You've just stumbled on a dark conspiracy, that's what is happening. Can't you tell?"

Brother Quiet was confused, then he thought better of it. He felt panic rise in his guts. There was no reason for them to be down here if they were good men. He had assumed that nothing bad could happen now that Goddess Phyllicitus had returned. He was wrong.

He spun on one heel and began sprinting down the tunnel. Splashing and rushed footsteps chased behind him. He didn't look back.

Turning the corner, he ran faster. His breath pounded in his lungs. It was at least another three minutes to the exit, even at this hazardous pace. He turned again racing to where the gap in the tunnel's side was. He felt pulled to the side.

His face smashed into the sewer wall. One of the men from the dark pool had caught up and grabbed him by the shirt. He hung on to the man's arm tightly, screaming for help. The man picked him up and slammed him against the tunnel wall. Brother Quiet let go, then tried to scrabble away. He screamed at the top of his lungs. In a moment, two other men were upon him.

They grabbed his arms and held him down. One of the men, the one with a single blinded eye, pried the candlestick from his fingers. After a quick glance at the burning flame, he extinguished it by turning it upside down and pressing the burning wick against the stone floor.

Brother Quiet continued screaming as they began punching him. They slammed fists into his body, his face, his arms, his jaw. He felt a tooth pop out and blood pouring down his cheek.

"Please, no!" He tried to beg. "Please don't kill me! I'm a priest!"

Then he felt the constraints on his leg. He felt a belt or a rope wrapping around them. He kicked and writhed, trying to escape, but he was held firmly. The absolute darkness of the tunnel made him blind. Somehow, his attackers were not. He tried to calm down and understand what was happening. Ryley could have given them some sort of potion, but why would he do that? Brother Quiet didn't know Ryley personally, but he knew how Ryley sold alchemical drafts to the temple. It didn't make sense.

He felt himself being dragged back through the gap in the tunnel, toward that room. Then he was falling, splashing into some cold liquid. He felt it seeping into his clothes. It was sticky like some kind of syrup. He struggled for a moment. Someone set their hand against his chest and pushed down. Others held his hands by his wrists. He couldn't see.

Panic set in. In a frenzy, he struggled to escape. His struggles didn't matter. He kept his breath in, hoping against reason that the goddess could save him somehow.

Then he felt the sting. Something had jabbed into his arm. Then he felt a second sting on his leg. Snakes had bitten into him.

He knew this was the end.

The Rat watched as the man's life ended. He hadn't died, but what was once a promising member of Phyllicitus's temple was now his latest experiment. The Rat thought about what was going to happen to the man. He smiled.

It was lucky, really, that the priest had stumbled upon them. It saved the Rat some time and effort trying to find another member. He had refined his technique of turning priests and hoped for a successful trial.

The Rat gave orders to the others. "Enough, pull him up."

The men silently obeyed, dragging the wet and stained body out of the basin. One of his snakes released its hold and slithered back into the depths. The other followed suit just a few moments later.

Snakes were such useful creatures, he considered. It was easy to get them to do what you wanted, and they never asked for anything in return. Snakes and alchemists had a long history together. They knew each other well.

"So here is the crux of our solution." The Rat produced a leather flask from beneath his short cloak. Uncorking it, he gently bent down and poured its contents into Brother Quiet's limp mouth. He didn't allow any of the contents of the flask spill. He took his time making sure the perfect measurement was made. In less than a minute, his precision was rewarded.

Brother Quiet sucked in air. The sound of gurgling came first, then he turned his head to the side and vomited. He whimpered as he continued to vomit. The contents floated atop the dark pool, mixing brown and green streaks into the black surface.

The Rat stared down at the young priest. He could feel the Friends trying to connect, trying to bring this young acolyte into their family.

His snakes had been living in a solution of drugged waters and infected blood for weeks. He had finally discovered how to get the Takers into the snakes. He took a little pride in how useful the snakes had become. It was yet another new weapon for him to wield.

The goddess had strong magic in the city. She didn't wield it like a crafter, a wizard, a necromancer, or even an alchemist. The goddess was magic, at her essence. She could no more cast a spell by reciting magic words that he could. But magic simply acted in her interest, especially this near her physical body.

The Rat was counting on it. He had tried everything to break her spells and nothing worked. The problem was, he guessed, there wasn't any normal spellcraft. Instead, her priests simply used Phyllicitus's magic in their daily life without consciously focusing it. It acted like luck or fate. There was no way to surely tell.

With only a slight push toward life, and without explicitly intending it, Phyllicitus's power had nudged this poor fool back from the final door. Now he sat there, alive by her power, but filled with Takers. The Rat only had to wait to see what her power would do. Would it simply allow the newly taken to expire? Would it allow him to live, even if infected? He wondered if something else would happen entirely.

He couldn't wait to see. His curiosity was aroused. The Rat thought about all the potion crafting he had done in his life. He thought about the six priests that had met terrible fates at the hands of his experimentation. All of the labor, toil, and ingratitude was about to be worth it.

Alchemy was giving him clues into the nature of the Takers. It was showing him hints of godhood itself. Someday, if the fates allowed, he would combine them. He would become the god of men and the god of Takers.

"You may be my finest work," he said to the young brother, not caring if anyone heard his words.

A few minutes later, the Rat began to worry. The priest had not stopped vomiting. Now he was heaving at the side of the pool but with an empty stomach. Soon there would be blood, then death.

He grinned. "Oh no you don't. You don't get away that easily." Reaching back beneath his cloak, he produced a metal vial. He split the wax seal and pulled the cork from its opening. He held the vial above his mouth, but Brother Quiet could not stop heaving. The Rat didn't even try to pour it.

Instead, he signaled to Hazel. She walked forward, a long knife in hand.

"Just like I told you. Remember, a steady hand is the most important."

"Yes, I remember."

She smiled as she set her hand upon Brother Quiet's shoulder. "Don't worry dear. It will be finished soon."

She set the knife against the front of his throat, near the top of his ribcage, and thrust. Only a finger's length of blade went into him. She quickly pulled it out, and with her bare fingers, pushed open the skin so a hole formed.

The Rat bent down and carefully poured the contents of the vial into the new opening. Dark green bubbles emerged, roiling over the entrance wound in cadence with his breathing. Lines of green liquid streamed down the side of his throat. The Rat tried to use his fingers to constrain the liquid, to force more of it into the new hole. He was only partially successful.

The wound began to close as the potion took effect. He could feel elation as the Takers assaulted Brother Quiet's weakened body. After four long breaths, the Takers had become ensconced in his life force.

"We have him."

The feeling of a celebration came from his fellow taken. "Yes."

"Wonderful."

"We're in."

Hazel looked up at him. "So we have him. What does this mean?"

"It means that we can put our new family member into the temple. It means we have a spy. He can report their plans. He can find new priests to take. There is no end to the plans we can make with him."

"Won't the goddess detect this?"

The Rat smiled back at her. She was sharp, and her question brought a moment of pleasure to his heart. "Oh yes, but that is why we must move quickly. We can't wait for her to find us. We need to go to her. Thanks to the young brother here, we will have a way to get inside.

MEETING A GODDESS

Miller and Aileen walked down the path that led through the Garden, side by side with their two guides. The leaves from ancient trees blocked the starlight from reaching them. Bright spots of torchlight lay ahead. As they moved further along the trail, a three-story white house came into view.

The house was more than a manor, it was a palace. Miller stared in wonder. He had seen it before, but every time it seemed to grow more grand. It stretched a hundred paces from one side to the other. Balconies stood out, jutting from the third floor. The sloped roof had an unusual construction, looking more like clay tiles had been used to block the rain, instead of more traditional wood. Life-sized statues of nude humans danced along the edge of the roof in an illusion of celebration, or maybe something more intimate.

Lanterns hung on poles along the length of the house. They illuminated the house while casting shadows on the perfect lawn surrounding it. The top floor had eleven balconies stretching down its length. Windows stretched from the bottom floor into the second, giving the sense of vast interior space. Servants walked about, lighting dozens of torches, setting up tables, and readying for an event.

"Something smells pretty good."

Aileen glanced over. "Yes, the cooking is excellent. Let's hope we get to stay for dinner."

Miller pulled in the aromas through his nose. "Duck, I think. Mushrooms? Something I don't recognize."

"I'm sure there will be a lot of things you don't recognize. Just don't embarrass me. Whatever you see, don't make a big issue of it. No matter what. Got it?"

"Sure." He was excited. He hadn't been allowed into the great house last time he was in Home's Hearth. It seemed like a rite of passage.

She turned back to their two guides. "Lead on."

"Yes. Please follow us."

They continued on toward the house. The closer Miller came to it, the more details he could make out. He had originally thought that the torches highlighted its wonderful features, its windows, and doorways. But as he came close enough, he began to see what lay in its shadows. The detail work was exquisite. Miller was enraptured. The attention to detail and the design artistry combined to make the building itself a work of art.

The window ledges were decorated with ornate scrollwork. The paving stones were laid in a mosaic pattern, forming a winding trail. The stones in the mosaic were shaped in the image of an open book. It was like he was walking on the tail of a long snake. As he neared the main door he saw a fountain. It tossed water into the air, catching the lantern light at just the right angle so that it seemed to shimmer. The sound of musicians tuning instruments and preparing for their show grew as he approached.

The main doors of the house stood open. A young boy, almost into manhood, stood at the door's side, holding it open so they could pass easily within. The interior was lit by iron lamps that hung from the ceiling. Servants were busily attending to them as well, moving from lamp to lamp with long rods, each rod with a burning cloth tied to its end. The wonderful aroma of a roasting duck filled the air.

They walked in, leaving their two guides behind.

Miller smiled as he walked next to Aileen. This place was wondrous. A servant walked by carrying a bowl of wine. It looked like it was solid gold, but if it were, the servant would struggle beneath its weight. It had to be something else, perhaps only layered with gold. His mind explored the process of fixing gold to a bowl, calculated the weights of gold that would be required, and nodded in appreciation at the cost of such a thing.

He wondered what he was supposed to be worried about. This place was filled with the best craftsmanship, the best servants even. Why wouldn't Aileen want to come here? Why would she be afraid to take him?

Dogs barked on the other side of the room. Miller turned his head, then stopped cold. A woman dressed in nothing but a fur cape strode through the hall. She held a leash with six white dogs and a single naked man at the end of it. Aileen glanced over at him, a smirk forming on her face. "See something interesting?"

"What?"

"Remember what I said? Don't embarrass me. Keep up and stop taking eyeball liberties."

Miller jerked forward, trying to keep up and not fall on his own face. "Did you see that?"

"That's what they call normal around here."

"But there was a man on that leash."

"I'm sure he paid for that little indulgence. Rest easy, that isn't the oddest thing you will see here tonight. It's time to practice keeping your composure."

Aileen turned into another room. The walls of this room were painted deep red. Geometric shapes, diamonds, triangles, stood against the wall painted in gold. A servant added wood to a grand fireplace on the opposite side of the room, putting some sort of pot over the fire, trying to get it to boil.

The servant was completely dressed in hard leathers, much like a soldier might wear, but painted with golden shapes that mirrored those on the wall. He was muscular, strong beyond reason. He had the body of a soldier, yet no scars, no evidence of battle. The man bowed deeply as Aileen passed him by, turning down another hallway. They passed by a corridor on the left side whose walls were formed completely of mirrors. The cost of such a thing left Miller aghast. A hallway to the right showed a rounded staircase that originated somewhere below and continued to the upper floors above. Aileen walked onto the staircase and began to climb the steps.

They arrived at the next floor in a narrower space. A long hallway passed by the circular stairs, leading to a row of doors along both sides of the hall.

"Private rooms, no doubt," Miller said, impressed with the size of the house. Just keeping this many rooms clean would require a staff of at least thirty people.

"Brilliant observation. We're not here for that sort of visit."

"What?"

"Keep moving."

She turned right and moved down the hall with a purpose. After less than fifty steps, she turned left, entering yet another corridor. At the end of it, two white doors stood closed, blocking their path. The symbol of Phyllicitus hung from a banner along the walls on either side. Two people, one a middle-aged man, the other a young red-headed woman, stood in front of the doors. They were dressed in temple vestments. The man held a staff of office.

Miller slowed his walking. The woman wore symbols of power on her robe. A spellcrafter of the temple. He had worked with these priestesses on his last trip to Home's Hearth. He found them to be competent magical casters and enchanters. He didn't relish a confrontation here, whatever this place was.

"Aileen. We were expecting you," the man spoke as he offered a slight bow. Miller tensed as the woman stepped to the side. Presumably, she stepped out of their way, but she also assumed a very good position to ambush them as they passed by.

"Were you, now? Last I checked, Sister Fidelity was coming to my inn. Was she not informed of our appointment?"

"Sister Fidelity will take care of your necromancer friends, you aren't needed there. You are needed here. This appointment is for you alone. Your little boy can stay here in the hallway with us," he said, gesturing at Miller.

Miller offered a weak grin. He shrugged his shoulders as if to offer tacit agreement.

"No. Miller is my apprentice, he comes with me." She stuck out her long finger like a dagger. "He has been here before, been with Phyllicitus before. By the Bear God, you may even recognize him yourself."

The man's eyes grew wide at the mention of the First God. Such comments were generally frowned upon anywhere near Phyllicitus. This was The Garden and the rules were different here. The priest gazed at Miller, taking in all of his features. His eyes relaxed in recognition. "Yes. This was the lad who helped last time. Wasn't it you that came up with the way to find the Takers? Farm spells if I recall. That was nice work."

Miller bowed humbly. "Only with the help of this temple. Sadly, the Takers have returned. Once again, I need your help."

"And Aileen's masters? Don't the necromancers have any capability here?"

Aileen snapped back. "Their capability is to ally with the temple once more, and beat back this threat."

"Yes, we all want to defeat the Takers and protect the people. But the temple doesn't want to do it at the expense of a soul. How has your soul fared in the service of your new order?"

Aileen's anger snapped into place, offended at her spiteful remark. "You dare question my cause? You who stand by in the lap of luxury, who face no dangers more dire than boredom, question my fealty? I didn't see you out there fighting the fight. My apprentice held off two hundred of the Taken in a pitched battle, not two weeks from here. Where were you? Busily tending to our goddess? Fluffing her pillows perhaps?"

Aileen hissed her next words. "Out there, the cracks in the world bring horrors. Every day they take more and more of the common folk. The commoners call it cowardice when their leaders sit in this place far from the site of the battle, and so do I. Soon enough the battle will come here, to you. By then, it may be too late."

"Now look here," The man began to stammer. Aileen shouldered him aside, reached out and grabbed the door handle. Its bronze length felt cool and luxurious in her hand. She didn't care. She was in no mood for luxuries today.

Pulling the door open, Aileen motioned for Miller to follow her as she stepped into the room.

Miller hesitated before he walked into the enormous room. The door led to a multi-room apartment. A long sofa stood in the center of the room, matched with a mahogany table. Five sitting chairs were scattered about as if leftover from a long night of drinking. The room was large enough to fit twenty people without too much discomfort. Two doors leading to other rooms stood against the left wall, a single door decorated the right.

Shining red brocade wall coverings stood out in stark relief to ivory accents and statues of horsemen that reached to his waist. A grand marble fireplace embossed in gold dominated a corner, and an open door led out to one of the balconies. Lush carpet lay on the floor, inviting all into the room. One of the doors to the left opened. A young woman walked into the entrance. She appeared surprised at their rushed entry. The other door slowly closed. Miller didn't see who was behind it.

The young woman spoke first. She wore a light red dress that both showed off her voluptuous figure and was practical enough for everyday use. She had brown hair brushed straight down her back, with a fabric cord tying the long hair into a braid. Miller tried to look past her beauty and determine who she was. She wasn't a priestess given her clothing. Miller considered the cost of such dress. Whoever this maid was, she was close to Phyllicitus.

"Hold on there. This is Phyllicitus's private apartments. Let's use some manners, shall we?" She shook her long brown hair in anger.

Aileen sneered back. "We don't have time for manners. All of our spare time has been devoted to her games. It's all used up."

"Too bad for you. When you become the goddess, you'll get your way. Until then, behave."

Miller stared back, surprised. Aileen didn't hesitate. "Really? The goddess has done everything short of sending me a personal note ordering me to come and grovel before her. I'm here now, ready for my groveling. Do you need to make some kind of witty point? Don't let your new position get to your head. Remember, I used to have your rank, title, and duties. So far, I'm not impressed with what I'm seeing."

Miller rethought. Perhaps she was a priestess, but of some kind he hadn't seen before.

The woman let a few moments go by, then made up her mind. "Well, some sort of meeting needs to happen in any case. You might as well storm in there. Have your conversation, but don't let your anger get control of your tongue." She paused again. "I know how you can get."

Aileen gave her a slight grin, bowing slightly at the waist. "Much appreciated. I didn't want this to get ugly."

"Oh, it got ugly a year ago. You're just seeing it now. It might have been a good idea to come by and visit now and again."

Aileen ignored the comment and walked past her, Miller in her wake. He gave the guardian sister an apologetic look as he passed by.

Aileen grasped the handle of the other door and pulled.

There was a short hallway inside painted yellow like daffodils in the springtime. The air was heavy with perfume. It was warmer in here, a bit more humid. Quiet notes of a harp stood out, filling the space with calm.

There was a room at the far end of the hall. Its floors were of carved marble. White walls stood decorated with scenes of palm leaves.

A bath stood in the room at the end of the hall. As he approached, Miller saw that the marble floor was made up of tiles, each decorated with painted scenes of fish at play. The tub was large enough for three people. Right now, two nude women and a nude man stood outside of the tub, ready with towels to dry their bathing goddess within.

Before he could look away, the Goddess Phyllicitus stood up from the tub. He felt the air being pulled from his lungs. She was so beautiful, so enticing, he couldn't even think of why he was there. He wanted to go to his knees, to beg forgiveness, to serve her. Right there, at that place, all of his doubts had vanished. The White Hand didn't matter. Aileen didn't matter. He went to his knees, hoping that Phyllicitus would just notice him.

Aileen paused, turned around, and slapped him hard across the face. He jerked sideways, almost falling onto his side.

Aileen pointed her angry finger down at him. "Don't embarrass me. That's all I asked. Now stop acting like a peasant and get up."

Phyllicitus's laugh rang out like a song.

Miller rubbed his sore jaw as he stood again. He didn't know what happened. All he could do was stammer.

"Sorry."

Aileen said, "It happens to all the young men. No way to avoid it. Just keep control of yourself, all right?"

"It didn't happen last time I saw her."

"How old were you?"

"Old enough. This is just a little more up close and personal than last time."

Miller nodded as Aileen turned her attention to Phyllicitus, Goddess of Love, who was stepping out of the bath in all of her glory. Servants moved forward to dry her, apply scented oils, then offered her a long, elaborate, snow-white dressing gown.

Miller felt drawn to her as she covered herself. The covering didn't have any real effect on his emotions though. Beauty radiated from her, touching everyone in the room. He felt it in his heart, in his soul. He had met Phyllicitus before in one of Aileen's other meetings years ago. She had never affected him like this.

He wondered if the goddess was doing this intentionally, or if it was simply in her nature. Somehow Phyllicitus was reminding Aileen of who she once served. The power was like magic, but he could not feel any of the flows that would associate themselves to such power. Instead, Phyllicitus simply was that power. No external magics were needed.

And that magic could touch his soul, his inner core where his true self lived.

She stepped toward Aileen. Aileen began to tremble, stammering out odd words that made little sense. She tried to keep her anger, to take strength from it. She failed.

"The enemy. Between us, no worlds. Takers are returning. Must help." Aileen had entered the room focused on demanding attention from a goddess. Now she had it, all of it.

Phyllicitus held up a single finger in front of her full, ruby red lips, and hushed Aileen like a child. She came closer to Aileen and reached out gently, stroking her cheek. The goddess's hair flowed down like a golden waterfall, hints of red mixed with the blond to create a beautiful color that was both common, yet more.

Miller watched in disbelief as Aileen collapsed to the floor. She sobbed, crying out, reaching for the feet of her goddess.

She had lost the ability to communicate with speech. Miller could feel pain, loss, despair, and loneliness pulled out of Aileen. He could feel it like he could feel music in the presence of a master bard. It was a dark song, a broken song.

The goddess let her cry. Aileen cried and cried until her breath stopped working. She sucked at the air, trying to pull it in, then fought off vomiting.

Miller tried to help. He opened all of his channels and felt for the source of her anguish. This wasn't something Phyllicitus had done to Aileen. It was something Aileen had done to herself. He didn't know what to do. He stood mere feet away from a goddess, the Goddess. How could he fight this? His spells were useless.

He couldn't just stand here and watch. Aileen began crying out as if her guts were on fire. Using the disciplines Aileen had taught him, and trusting in dumb luck, he cleared his emotions and stepped forward.

"Please, Goddess, please. We need her alive and unbroken. Please let her go."

She looked at Miller. Her baby-blue eyes bore into his soul. "Miller. It's been a few years. You've grown." If Aileen's song was a broken horror, Phyllicitus's song promised joy, love, and a warm hearth at the end of a long day.

The shock of being recognized should have shaken his resolve, but it didn't. Miller looked back into Phyllicitus's eyes, opening his heart to her. He thought about how he felt about Aileen and hoped that Phyllicitus could feel it. Aileen had saved him from madness, from perversion, from self-hatred. She had made him a friend and he wouldn't desert her now, whatever the cost.

The goddess looked deeper into him, nodded, then smiled. "Don't worry, this needed to happen. Her heart has been dirtied. It just wants to be clean again."

"It looks like pain to me."

"Oh, it is pain. She has been hurting for a long, long time. That's why I've been so distraught. I wanted her to come back now and again. I could have eased some of this."

Aileen was breathing heavy now, but no longer screaming in anguish. She would be of no use as a negotiator. Someone had to ask for help, and he was the only one there who could.

"Goddess, both Aileen I need your help. The Takers are rising again. I have evidence that they have returned. It's going to take a lot of work and a lot of luck to find another weakness."

She smiled back at him. "Do you think that I don't know that?"

"Then why are we going through this?"

She reached out, touching Miller on his arm. Suddenly, his disciplines cracked. The charms he had laid about his psyche came unraveled.

"Because I love her."

Miller looked back, confused.

"Listen to me, with all of your heart. Every time you can win a battle with love, it will stay won. With hate, victory will rot away."

"You put Aileen's happiness above the lives of everyone in the world?"

She smiled back at him, like a teacher who had finally gotten their lesson across. "Of course. What kind of world would it be if everyone was sad?" She gestured down at Aileen, who had stopped gasping, and started breathing normally, still too shocked to speak.

Phyllicitus continued, "Aileen likes to save the world. She lives to fight the good fight and stand against the Takers. I fear that she wants to die that way, in some kind of final battle. I've always loved that about her, the drive, the relentless spirit. But right now, her relentless spirit is hurting. She needs to be set right."

Miller nodded. He watched, surprised as Aileen crawled over to Phyllicitus's feet, kissing them, and curling up into a ball.

"I don't mean to disagree, Goddess. Right now, we are trying to save a girl who has been taken. We need Aileen to help us with that, at the very least."

"Oh, she will be fine. Tomorrow she will be right as rain, and the next day I'll let her go back to her little cabals if she insists. She needs some help right now, some time to heal."

Phyllicitus looked into his eyes. There was no question in Miller's mind, she was devoted to Aileen and wanted to save her from the madness she had embraced. "I am declaring that she stays here for at least two days. Once her heart is healed enough, I'll send her back."

"And I? What would you have of me?"

"Of you? You will be welcome to stay here, in my apartments, if you wish. Or you can go back. I'm sure this girl could use your help. It's your decision."

Miller thought about it for a few moments. "I'd like to go back and check on Brita. She may need my help, and I don't entirely trust some of the others. I can fetch back some things that Aileen may need."

"Need? I think that I can get her anything she needs."

"No. You can't get her a solution to these Takers. Right now, that is my job."

Phyllicitus grew cold. "Aileen has taught you well, I see. No, if I could have solved this curse, I would have done so long ago."

"Yet we had done so before."

"And now it's back."

Miller paused before offering his final, and most risky point.

"This time, we will use love."

Phyllicitus turned her glare into a grin. "Yes! We will use love."

He bowed to her. Reaching down, he touched Aileen on the shoulder. She turned upward to look at him. Tears had streaked on her face. She looked embarrassed, yet somewhat healthier, as if she had needed a good cry for a long time.

"I'm going back to get my notes. It will give you something to talk to Phyllicitus about. Can I leave you here, or do you want to go back with me?"

"Oh, Miller," she choked out. "I love you."

"What?" He didn't know what to say. In the presence of Phyllicitus, it was easy to love anyone, let alone a young boy. His heart began to hammer. Could this be true?

Aileen reached out and took his hand tenderly. "Thanks for bringing me. I think I needed this, so very badly."

"Let me know when you want to go back. I'll fetch you. Otherwise, I will be back late tonight."

THE PATTERN ROOM

After a long goodbye to Aileen, and five minutes of uncomfortable conversation with Phyllicitus, Miller left the apartments. He found himself abandoned and left to his own devices. A guide would have been helpful, but he was the servant, not Aileen. He felt confident in his ability to find his way out of the house.

He explored the long hallways, each paneled with luxurious hardwoods. The shine of polished wood mixed with fragrances of flowers and perfumes. Passing by small doors that most probably led to sleeping rooms and embarrassing situations, he tried to follow any large or double-doors that he found, hoping to find the main corridor and eventually an exit.

Wandering through the massive house, he stumbled into a room filled with light. Twelve man-sized mirrors stood scattered around the room. They caught the light from copper lanterns that had been set up just to shine onto the mirrors. Each lantern stood atop a tray that held alchemical materials. A fire burned in the lantern, but no smoke was released. Miller held his hand close to one of the lanterns and found no heat either.

The ensemble of mirrors and lamps gave the illusion of daylight. The light was focused not only on the center of the room, where a dark-skinned woman with jet black hair lounged nude on a raised dais, but also illuminated the six people surrounding her.

Six easels stood ready. Three of the surrounding people were painting her exquisite form on canvas, patiently trying to reproduce the curves of her legs, her bosom. One of the painters, an older woman with wrinkled hands, had produced an image that was almost magical in its likeness. Three men stood in a small group busily talking with each other, ignoring the beauty in their midst.

Miller could see no clear way to bypass the room. He eased in hoping that he would not be noticed, keeping close to the outer wall. He circled around the artists, aiming to escape through a door on the opposite wall. It was difficult to move through the room quickly as it overflowed with distractions. He kept his eyes away from the nude model and was immediately attracted to the walls.

Each wall was painted a dull light orange. As he moved closer, fine details of yellow-gold began to emerge. The walls were entirely covered with thin scrollwork designs. The lines danced and played together in an infinite tangle of decorative knots. They shifted as he walked around the edge of the room, his point of view changing to new angles. Miller nodded in appreciation. He had always been fascinated by illusions like this. Up close, he saw the fine work of the artisan, the details, the care. He loved it.

"Impressive, isn't it?"

One of the painters had moved up behind him while he was lost in his thoughts. Miller turned is head to peer over his left shoulder. A short balding man stood three paces left and behind him. Miller wondered how long he had been standing here.

The short painter recognized the confused look on his face. "Oh, don't worry about it. Everyone stares at the wall piece when they first come here. After a few more visits you will be acclimated."

Turning his head back to the illustrated walls, he responded. "Acclimated?"

"Sure. The painting influences the viewer. Its influence will change over time. Initially, it fascinates the mind, entraps the eyes. Eventually, it just brings on a sense of peace, of mental quiet. As you can see, we use it for artistic purposes. It helps our painting. In a way, we cheat."

"Cheat? Is it even possible to cheat at art?"

A soft laugh erupted from the man. Miller could not see his face as his attention was captured by the scrollwork on the wall, but he imagined the smooth-faced older gentleman would be smiling at his unfamiliarity with this room.

"Oh, indeed you can. This work here was Bronson's gift to the garden. He lived almost three hundred years ago. He learned his art from Stevenson, the finest of the fine. The goddess keeps Stevenson's great work in the temple library to inspire her priests and priestesses. I could say that every magical crafter in this temple cheats even more than I do."

Miller was enjoying the small talk. But he knew that he had errands to run. He had to fetch things for Aileen and to check on Brita, but he preferred to stay here for now. This place appealed to every part of him.

Then he sensed the man walking closer. His hand gently grasped his shoulder, sending goosebumps up his spine. It slowly descended down to the small of his back.

"You know, I am a wealthy man." The artist paused for a moment, preparing himself for the next sentence. "I'm always looking for young men to sponsor. We could become good friends if you had an interest, in art."

The message was clear, and not to Miller's liking.

Miller spun his entire body around. He remembered how Mistress Sword would use that same voice with him, trying to entice. He stared down at the man, old enough to be his father. The man's skin and complexion were soft and completely free of blemishes. This wasn't a man that worked hard to live. Miller's eyes narrowed as he stepped forward, ready for a fight. It caught the artist off guard, forcing him to take a step back. Miller didn't want trouble in this place, but he wasn't going to tolerate this kind of thing.

"Like what you see, eh?" He let his hand drop to his side and began caressing the pommel of the long thin dagger he had kept for Chamise. He imagined how Master December sounded and tried to mimic it. His voice grew sharp, gravely, and hateful.

"If you touch me again, I will take your spleen and feed it to the dogs."

He let his apprentice ring stand out, drawing the man's attention with the danger Miller was trying. It worked.

"No, no, I meant no offense." He backed away from Miller like his life depended on it. He had recognized either the apprentice ring or simply had a healthy respect for the dagger. It didn't matter which.

The other artists stopped painting. All eyes were now on him. The conversations had ceased, the other artists stared with wide eyes. The lovely nude model had begun to stand, most likely to flee, until Miller met her eyes and froze her in place with fear. All she could do was quiver in terror. Miller didn't like himself right then. He turned and finished walking across the room, leaving them to their art.

Miller strode out of the art hall, his temper slowly ebbing. Perhaps demonstrating his anger had not been the best of plans, but it got him away from that stranger. The man's touch made his back crawl with disgust. Yet this was not Miller's place, it was his. He was the invader here.

The hallway ended, forcing Miller to choose directions in yet another hallway. He was growing frustrated with the maze-like layout of the house. The glitz and beauty of the place were beginning to wear on his patience. It seemed like a huge display of wealth without any reason behind it. The left hallway led toward a set of stairs descending to the lower level. The right led toward a painting of a fat man wearing a white sleeping shirt and nothing else. It stood next to a set of white doors with brass plates on their surfaces.

Doors had begun to annoy him as well. He headed left toward the stairs. The sounds of people talking and the smell of cooking met him before he was halfway down them. Emerging into the lower level, he came into a large hall filled with six long tables, each could hold up to thirty people, but right now, only one of the tables was full. People sat with each other eating what looked like lamb and some sort of grain he was unfamiliar with. The smell of alien spices tickled his nose like ghosts of flavors from far away.

Before he reached the floor, a servant boy walked up to meet him. The boy wore a red tunic with the marks of two musical notes stitched in with thread of gold. He bowed low, avoiding Miller's eyes.

"Welcome, sir. Will you be dining on meat or fish tonight?"

His stomach grumbled, but not from hunger. His nerves were raw after his last encounter. He wanted to go somewhere private and simply calm down. He thought of his smithy, back in the north. It was starting to look pretty good to him.

"I'm sorry," Miller started, "I didn't come here to eat. I was hoping to find somewhere quiet. I'd like to do some thinking, and everything keeps distracting me."

The boy looked up, gazing into his eyes for a few moments. "I'm sorry. I don't know you, sir. Are you a member?"

Miller was perplexed for a moment. He didn't know anything about memberships. He had assumed that this place functioned like an inn. He guessed this was a very private inn. He went to his next plan, name-dropping.

"I'm here with Goddess Phyllicitus, if that is allowed."

The boy's eyes grew even wider. Sky blue eyes shone up at him, taking Miller in with a new sense of respect.

"Oh, of course, sir. I know a good place to do some thinking if that is what you are looking for. Some of the sisters have used it for meditation before."

"That should be fine. Can you point me to it?"

"Oh no. This place can be a labyrinth to new visitors. Let me walk you there so you won't get lost."

Miller gestured for the boy to lead the way. He moved around the back of the stairs, through an oak door with images of sea creatures carved in them. Miller had never seen their like, multi-armed things that floated in the oceans. He had read about squid and octopus but had never seen them.

The door opened into a hallway wide enough for three people to stand side by side. Every ten paces, a statue stood proudly, showing off its form to any who traveled the hall. Miller passed six statues before he turned to go up a flight of black marble stairs. At the top, another wide hallway led into a set of double doors that had been painted red. The hallway was enormously tall, almost four times Miller's height, and the doors were only slightly smaller. Their red surface was painted with words. The boy took him forward, passing through to the interior as he tried to get a glimpse of the foreign language.

He entered a library. Bookshelf after bookshelf towered high overhead. Hundreds, no, more likely thousands, of books stared down at him. The boy paid this treasure no mind. Instead, he led Miller past them. Miller tried to slow down, to at least read the titles, but the boy kept his steady pace.

After a few minutes they arrived at another door. This one was painted brown and left undecorated. The boy opened it, motioning him forward into the room.

Miller stopped at the entrance, his breath sucking into his lungs. A white floor of the purest marble lay before him. The room was ten paces across, and fifteen wide. Four marble benches stood against each wall so someone could sit here comfortably. The walls were covered in a different type of marble, one with brown and silver swirls dancing along each of the walls. A sunken pit dropping an arm's length lay in the middle of the room, taking up most of the floor area leaving only enough room to walk between the pit and the benches. The pit was built from the same pure white marble that the floor was composed of, only the floor of it was covered with drawings.

The surface of the floor was a chaotic symphony of random designs, brush strokes, chalk marks, lines, and swirly trails drawn or painted on. Taken piece by piece, it made no sense. But the whole of it was overpowering. As he looked at it, he felt his eyes drawn to the marks like bees to honey. It was hypnotizing, it pulled him in and his curiosity didn't want to let him go. It reminded him of the golden scrollwork he had found earlier, but much more powerful. He could feel no magic, no channels, no flows. Yet it had power over him.

The boy stepped back. "I'll return to escort you back after the dinner guests have finished. I think that should be in two hours or so. Is that all right?"

Miller barely understood what the boy was saying. His attention was on the design, the pattern. He didn't know what the pattern meant, nor how it worked. He knew the feeling though. It felt like the arrowhead had felt between the worlds. This wasn't a magical artifact. It was magic itself.

"Hold for a moment if you please." Miller tried to form words, but it was difficult. "What is this place?"

"We just call it The Well. It was built a long time ago by one of the temple High Priests. If you stare at it a while, it will clear your thoughts and help you think better."

He had tried to solve the puzzle of the arrowhead while he was between the worlds. He tried to discover how it could do magic, yet not use magic. This Well was that same power on a massive scale.

"Is this like the art room?"

"Art room? Do you mean where the easels were set up today? We do art in every room here."

"Yes. The red room with the golden scrollwork."

"Yes and no, I guess. I'm not sure how any of it works. That room has a lesser effect. This well was created by a man named

Stevenson a long time ago. I gather he was interested in the First Gods and tried to learn their magic. This is one of the last pieces he crafted."

"What happened to him?"

"Happened? That was three hundred years ago. He's long dead."

He marveled at the thought that someone had gained the secrets of the First Gods, of the core of magic itself. Miller gazed in astonishment at the art. He could see the flow of power in the work like a map laid out in front of him. He could feel no channels, no sinks or flows emanating from it. If he were a master necromancer then he could call Stevenson back just to talk. He had never been so strongly tempted in his life.

"Is that all, sir?" The boy took a hesitant step away and be about his business.

"Yes. Thank you. Please don't forget to fetch me in two hours."

Miller never let his gaze leave the well. What was it? What powered it? How did it work? The questions came endlessly, but they didn't overpower him. He had confidence that if he simply looked at the right thing, in the right way, all of its secrets would be revealed.

A soft noise woke her. It sounded like something was sliding across her floor. Hurriet's eyes sprang open. For some reason she bolted awake, her fight-or-flight instincts kicking in, telling her she was in danger. She tossed off the single woolen blanket and scrambled up, glancing left and right around the dim room, trying in vain to find what was making the noise. A single window less than an arm span in length, stood embedded in the wall. Thin curtains, spotted with holes, blocked a small portion of the quarter moon that shone this late at night. Darkness dominated the room except for a small sliver of moonlight that shone upon her bed.

A rasping voice came from the far, dark corner. The darkness was thicker there, and it was as if Hurriet was looking into a void.

"What are you doing here, Hur?"

Her heart skipped a beat. She recognized the voice. It wasn't possible, shouldn't be possible, but she knew the voice well.

"Gar?"

"Who else?"

The outline of a young boy began to emerge from the corner. It looked like Gar, but she wasn't certain. She knew that sometimes dreams would lie to people. This had to be a dream.

"How? I thought you were dead," she choked out. She wondered why she wasn't feeling happiness at being reunited. Instead, all she felt was fear.

"We don't have time for this now," Gar's voice rasped. "We need to get you out of here. This isn't a good place for you. You need to leave. You need to come with me."

She protested, "No. I'm safe here. I've got friends now. I've got to hide from the red-haired man. He can't get me here."

Gar didn't listen. A creak emerged and the outer door opened to the hallway. The hallway had a single candle illuminating it, but it wasn't close. She saw Gar's shadow leave the darkened corner, then exit the room.

"Come along. Follow me. I need your help," Gar's voice whispered from the hallway.

Fear paralyzed her. She couldn't rise out of the bed. She began to shake in fear. None of this felt right.

Five heartbeats passed. Another whisper came from beyond the open door, deserted now. "Hur, I need your help. Please help me. Please. It hurts so much."

The voice faded away, swallowed up in the hallway. His voice was rushed, fearful, pleading. She didn't doubt that Gar needed help. She did doubt that any help she gave would be useful. She rolled onto her belly, then used her legs to crawl forward until she found the wall. Pushing against the wall, she stood. Her legs shook as terror bore into her heart. Somehow Gar needed her.

She could not leave him.

Hurriet walked out of the room into the hallway. She saw the candle burning as it sat in the wall sconce. It seemed unusual, as it was past midnight and only the tip of the candle was burned. The rest of its wax shaft seemed unused. The hallway was cold tonight, unusual in the summer. So cold that she could see her own breath.

"Gar?" She called out in a quavering voice. Glancing left and right, she saw a hallway decorated with dark angles and shadows. She tried to understand the odd feeling of the place. It didn't feel right.

Gar's muffled voice came from the left, beyond a solid wooden door that led away from the main hallway. That main thoroughfare was decorated with artwork and testimonies from Eisenvard, their Credo. It was well lit and led to Chamise's rooms. She didn't know where the other door went.

"Come on. Hurry," Gar's whisper demanded. The voice seemed to come from every direction, but her instincts told her where to go. She turned left and walked down the hall, passing three doors before she arrived at the final door. This door was different than the others. A single bar stood disheveled, hanging loosely by a brass hinge. She slowly pushed. The door creaked loudly as it opened.

The door led into a courtyard, with only a single exit point ten paces away. Four brick steps led down to a cobbled entryway. A thin fog had come in during the night when the warm day gave way to the night's chill. The quarter moon could barely be seen through the fog above.

She stepped out.

The voice came again, this time from beyond the exit. A brick arch stood over the walkway, casting a curved shadow onto the cobbled stonework below. A slight squeak of fear came from her throat. None of this felt right. She wanted to scream, knew that she should, but could not.

The voice came again. "Please help me. Please."

She remembered the dozens of stories her mother had told

her. Dark spirits would trick little children, taking them away to their terrible realms and feasting on their souls. She had always thought those stories were made up. Now, here in the darkness and fog, she started to believe them.

A thought struck her. Perhaps Gar had been taken by those spirits. Souls could be captured and returned from death. Everyone who lived in Home's Hearth knew that. Necromancers had come here three years ago. There were many witnesses that still spoke of it.

She turned to look back. The door had vanished. In its place stood a brick wall, completely like the surrounding walls. She peered side to side. Even the windows had been replaced with bricks.

Her eyes narrowed, gazing at the brickwork in disbelief. This wasn't natural. It felt too real to call it a dream. Darkness, fog in the summer, disappearing doors and windows, it all felt like a grim children's tale. Her fear began to fade away, replaced with a sharp spike of annoyance. She knew that someone was toying with her. They had led her out of her safe room. She didn't know if Gar was an illusion or a spirit, but right now she doubted that it mattered. Someone wanted her outside and was willing to use sorcery to do it. She thought for a minute, considering her options.

"Well, there's nothing for it, I guess," Hurriet said to the dark night as she stepped forward to follow the voice. It called to her, drifting farther away, calling out to pull her along. She turned to see the fog-shrouded yard. An open gate that led toward the main road invited her to pass through. She could see the dim outline of Gar standing just beyond it.

She stopped to consider what to do. She didn't want to go out there alone. She knew there must be some kind of clue out there telling her why all this was happening. A feeling crept on her. If she went out there alone, she would never return.

"What are you waiting for?"

Gar's broken voice carried over the yard. It was gravelly, low, yet crystal clear. Somehow Gar's spirit had returned to haunt her, and Hurriet didn't have any idea why. She wanted to rush forward, to hold Gar, to embrace him. She knew that it would be impossible, even with his shadow standing less than a hundred paces away. Glancing up, she tried to estimate what time it was by the position of the moon. The fog had begun to break up. The night felt slightly warmer.

Then she heard the sound of hooves walking across cobblestones. She was surprised to hear someone out and about at this time of night. A horse walked out, emerging onto the yard from around the corner of the Eisenvard keep. The fog did not obscure it. Moonlight shone on the brown fur of the strange horse she had met just a few nights ago. She had put it in the barn earlier in the evening. Now it walked free.

"Huh," Hurriet said in surprise. Part of her wasn't stunned though. The horse didn't seem to obey the rules of normal horses. She grinned as she thought of it unlocking its stable door and sneaking out of the barn, all without being seen. She glanced back toward Gar, who continued to call for her. The fog near the entrance had thickened, but here, in the yard, it had thinned.

More magic, she thought. She shook her head in annoyance, then held her hand out toward the mare. It understood the invitation and walked to her side.

"I've got to see what he wants. Can you come with me?"

The horse gave no sign it had understood. She knew it had. It didn't try to stop her, so she began walking. The horse followed just a few steps behind. She walked until she came to the outer gate, stopping just before her feet crossed out of its boundaries.

The Gar-shadow moved back toward the deserted street. The trees were casting shadows in the moonlight, obscuring her vision. She decided to go no further.

"Gar, I'm not coming out. If you want to talk to me, then come here. Otherwise, I'm going back to bed."

She felt like she was having another one of her sibling fights with Gar, only now the stakes were higher. Gar's shadow moved off the main road down a side street. She waited for a long moment, impatiently counting while she waited. By the time she arrived at twenty-seven, Gar's shadow returned.

"Gar. Come here and talk to me."

The shadow moved closer. She could see features now, even as the fog danced about Gar's form, obscuring it. She reached out to touch the mare. Surprisingly, her vision improved. Details began to emerge as the fog seemed to thin. Parts of Gar were transparent. She could see through him now. He had returned to earth as a spirit.

"Gar!" she called out. "Are you a ghost?"

The sound of laughter came from farther along the street. A new form disconnected itself from the shadow of a mansion. She knew who it was before she could see him. As he moved closer, Hurriet saw the details. A large handsome frame, long red hair. It was the man who killed Gar.

"You're perceptive, aren't you?" he called out, toying with her.

She kept her hand on the mare's brown coat, unwilling to give up her improved vision. She suspected that the fog was still there, but somehow it was just easier to see through when the horse was near her.

"What?! You've got my attention."

"Oh, I think I do." Frantz walked closer. A broad smile decorated his face. Most people would call it friendly and welcoming. Hurriet didn't trust it a bit. She could tell there was a dark streak in this man's soul. She would never trust him.

"I'm here to talk to you about the future, your future to be precise."

She scowled back at him. "And?"

"Well, not to belabor the point, but I'm sure you know who I am."

"No, I actually have no idea."

He paused, seemingly surprised at her answer. "You've met apprentice Miller, haven't you?"

"Yes. He didn't tell me anything about you."

"He's like that, keeps all the juicy bits to himself. In any case, I'm here as a friend. I serve a small collection of wizards, and as part of my task, I am charged with finding new apprentices who have a chance at mastering wizardry. You are such a person. Rejoice! I've come with a future for you, an escape from all of this…" Frantz spread his arms, indicating the surrounding homes and Eisenvard keep, "…drudgery."

It all made sense now. Miller had pushed her away from the New Pony Inn to avoid this kind of complication. She didn't trust this man.

"I'll have to talk to others before I make such a commitment. Momma always told me to ask advice from my elders."

"Don't be a fool. Here's the way it's going to work. You will come with me, and we will teach you the art of magic. In return, we'll make sure that your parents don't have any tragic accidents."

There it was, the threat. Chamise had told her this was going to happen. Luckily, she had been prepared.

"Really? Doesn't that mean that I get to choose my master? And if I choose someone else that hates your guts, then they would train me to become your enemy?"

She felt the mare shift as she described a classic White Hand political conundrum. Miller taught her this trick before he returned last night.

Frantz took a moment to think his next words through. She could hear footsteps coming from behind her, nail-studded boots marching across the hard cobbled surface.

"Now look here. You don't know what you are dealing with," Frantz began, before he was interrupted by a voice behind her.

Chamise called out, clear and loud.

"She knows exactly what she is dealing with."

Frantz offered a sharp, derisive laugh. "Off with you, little Free Mage. You're not ready for this bout."

Chamise walked into the entrance to stand next to Hurriet, carrying a crossbow in her hands. Its aged wood had turned black. Iron bands decorated the curved lathe, its power ready to be awakened at the touch of a trigger. Frantz took a step back instinctively.

"You see, you're the one who isn't ready."

"You can't be serious. My magic can turn a quarrel in mid-flight. Don't be a fool."

"I'm willing to bet that an apprentice like you won't be quick enough to turn my quarrel. I know Miller wasn't. I've seen what happens to necromancers when the hand-spans of quarrel goes through them. It isn't pretty."

Frantz seemed at a loss for words. All he could utter was, "You dare?"

"It's sad we need to meet like this. You could have set up a meeting. Miller could have done all the legwork. If you had just showed up, made your proposal, then left, all of us would have been happier. Who knows? Maybe the girl would have taken you seriously."

"You understand that I'm not here on my own accord." The unspoken threat was crystal clear to Chamise. If she denied Frantz then she would have to face his master, Darjeeling. She had faced down worse White Hand masters in the past. Chamise knew exactly how much power they had. She hoped that Miller had enough influence with other masters to keep Darjeeling at bay.

"Yes. I'm sure your master sent you on this mission. I sort of feel bad denying you your goal. Oh wait, let me consider... no I don't. So here's your choice. You can walk away right now to report back to your master, or I can put this bolt through your chest and have your carcass dumped in front of the New Pony Inn. You can report back to your master using whatever dark arts they choose. Who knows? Maybe they'll bring you back as a zombie apprentice. That might make you better looking."

Frantz stared back, eying the crossbow and its deadly quarrel. After a few moments, he shrugged, seemingly unconcerned.

"Fine then. Remember that I offered a good way forward. Whatever happens with this girl," he gestured at Hurriet, "is now your fault." He spun on his heel and walked away.

Hurreit let out her breath.

"I can't believe that."

Chamise set a reassuring hand on her shoulder. "Believe it. Good idea bringing the horse, by the way."

She hadn't brought the horse. It had brought itself. She had no idea what to say to that, so just kept her mouth shut as they walked back toward the Eisenvard keep.

BROTHER QUIET'S RETURN

Brother Quiet sat uncomfortably. His seat had the most luxurious padding—supple leather tacked down with shining brass-headed nails. A scene of trees and wildflowers had been sewn into the fabric chair back. A single stag, resplendent with a great set of antlers, was embroidered in the center of the piece. He wondered if there was some symbolism there, left over from the days when the Stag God and the Winter demons came to Home's Hearth.

He shook his head, chiding himself for having impure thoughts. The Takers had him now. There was no use resisting. No matter how nice the furnishings were, he would always be ugly inside, until the day he died.

A young priestess walked from an open door. Her steps were unhurried as she approached. She had no idea of the danger she was in. Brother Quiet reflected on her. She could not be any more than twenty years old. Her long dark red hair was well kept. Curls near the end gave her an aura of elegance. He rubbed his own balding skull, contrasting his fifty-year-old baldness with her young lush mane.

"Brother? Sister Fidelity will see you now."

He grunted as if this were a surprise. "Sister Fidelity? I didn't ask to see Sister Fidelity. I asked to see Goddess Phyllicitus."

"I'm so sorry." She looked like she truly was sorry, even if she was simply sorry to be so uncomfortable. "The goddess has instructed that Sister Fidelity manage the temple while she is away. I'm sure that she will see you on her return. We all know of you and the work that you have so nobly toiled at for the past decade."

He looked back with a frown. "It doesn't feel like gratitude."

She took a step forward, placing her hand on his shoulder. "It's just that we weren't expecting you. Last time you came to the temple, well, you told everyone that you intended to stay in the sewers for the rest of your days. I am happy to see that you changed your mind."

He grunted again. Standing, he brushed down his perfectly clean temple robes out of sheer habit. "Let's go see her then. Might as well get it over with."

She smiled back. "Indeed. I think you will like Sister Fidelity. She shares your fondness for order."

He didn't respond.

After a few moments of uncomfortable silence, the young sister motioned him forward. "Follow me, then."

She led him through the open door that she had emerged from. They walked down a long hallway decorated with rare blue-marble walls and a white oaken floor that was polished daily. A large door stood at the end of the hall, with a smaller one on the wall to the left. She led him to the left door, opened it, and walked through.

"Please come in."

He had to duck his head to avoid hitting the overhead door frame. He was taller than most men and towered over every woman he had ever met. Staring across the room at Sister Fidelity, he could tell that this woman would not be easily manipulated or intimidated. He would have preferred to see

Phyllicitus in person instead of this woman.

"Sister Fidelity," his guide called out, "this is Brother Quiet, returned from the sewers. He is here for his next tasking."

"Oh, what a surprise." Sister Fidelity stood and walked over to face him. She stood within an arm's reach. The Takers in his blood became agitated, cautious, fearful. This woman had command of strong magics, and had experience fighting Takers during the last incursion. She might detect them.

"My apologies, sister. I had intended to speak with Goddess Phyllicitus herself. I know she normally likes to talk to people when they transition positions. I didn't mean to take you away from your duties." He bowed low, like the humble priest he was just a few short days ago. Now he didn't know what he was.

"Apologize to me? The legendary Brother Quiet? I would say not. I've been eager to meet you for years. I must say that I'm surprised to see you leaving the sewers, but I'm glad it was to come here. The work you have done, especially when Phyllicitus was gone, should be celebrated. If you wouldn't have kept the sewers open and functioning, we would have been ravaged by diseases and sickness over the years. I know what it takes to keep a city clean and healthy. It all starts with the sanitation and the water supply. Thanks to you, we have never had a problem with either."

"You are too kind. It needed to be done. There wasn't any nobility to the task."

"Yet you were born noble, weren't you? A lower fief lord's son? And yet you chose to spend a decade in the sewers to safeguard the lowest of the city's peasants. If that isn't noble, what is?"

He offered another bow, this time shorter. "As you say, Priestess. But now my time in the sewers is finished. After Phyllicitus returned, the need for me to be down there has been growing less and less every year. People don't throw the trash in the gutters that they once did. They don't pass sickness amongst each other as they once did. The water runs cleanly without any further effort on my part. I fear that Phyllicitus in her grace has put me out of a job. Now I must ask for another one."

Sister Fidelity smiled warmly at him. He was older than her by a decade, but muscular and fit. His towering frame would make him popular with almost all of the ladies and some of the men as well.

"Surely you deserve some respite after such a long time down there. Why don't you take your leisure for a few months at least? Study? Travel? It has been a long time."

"I must ask again, I fear. At my core, I am a man who loves to work. If I have no work, then I have no purpose. My purpose should be to serve Phyllicitus, so I must work for her cause."

She nodded, then turned away walking back to her desk.

"I understand. We both share a love of labor, especially in her cause."

The desk was a simple broad table mostly hidden under stacks of ledgers and scrolls. She picked up one of the scrolls, glanced at the first section, then rolled it back up and set it down again. She repeated this with four different scrolls until she found the one she was looking for.

"I have a list of tasks that need someone. Some of these are easier than others. Out of recognition for your service to the city and to Phyllicitus, choose whichever you want. If you are unhappy with it later, you can always choose another."

She held out the scroll. Brother Quiet took it from her hands and unrolled it. It took some time to read it as he hadn't used his reading skills since taking to the sewers. Reading was difficult since the Takers were breaking his concentration with their nervous whispering. After a few moments, he said "This will do. It works well with my skills."

Sister Fidelity walked around to glance down at the scroll where Brother Quiet was pointing.

"Oh my. That is a good position for you. Keeper of the baths is an excellent position. You will have a staff of five initiates to keep all of the baths in the temple clean and stocked with necessities. You will be expected to be awake early for the cleaning. Also, this position includes cleaning the personal bath of Goddess Phyllicitus. At the very least, you will be noticed by her."

He grinned. A piece of luck had finally found him. Surely the goddess will see the Takers and help him escape from this curse. Part of him was elated at the idea of help, of freedom. Another part had grown to enjoy the new presence. They gave him purpose, a reason to do what he did. It was closer, more intimate than serving Phyllicitus. Their presence was a much more personal thing now and part of him didn't want to lose them.

"That sounds perfect. Thank you."

"No, Brother Quiet. Phyllicitus and the temple thank you."

"You'll do fine." The Rat bent down to adjust a few flowers in Hazel's wide basket. The yellow petals gave a sense of happiness that neither of them felt.

Hazel wasn't confident in her ability to do what he had asked of her. The Rat wanted her to do something that the bad kind of girls did. She never thought of herself like that. Yet here she was.

"I've never done anything like this before. Men don't want me. And truthfully, I'm not that interested in them either." She shook her head in denial. "I can't be a whore for you." She stressed the word 'whore' like it was the worst fate that could be imagined, worse even than being taken. The Rat could still be surprised on occasion, and this did the trick.

"I'm not asking you to be a whore. I'm asking you to be nice, smile, and pretend that you are interested in big strong men."

"But I'm not."

The Rat exhaled in exhaustion. "I said that I needed you to pretend that you liked him, didn't I? I didn't ask you to rut with him right here in the street."

Her face flushed red. Yet again, the Rat was surprised. He had seen Hazel murder people in cold blood, smiling all the time. Intimacy seemed to be a step too far though.

"Yes, but he is a mercenary. He will think that I want to rut right here in the street."

"So what of it? By the final door, woman, you would think that you had never had a friend that was a man before."

"I haven't. Well, I have you." Her voice softened at that pronouncement.

The Rat started to get an uneasy feeling about this talk.

"You have had lovers in the past, haven't you?"

She shook her head. "I told you, I wasn't a whore."

"I didn't ask if you got paid for it. Perhaps you met someone in your village? Someone special?"

"No. It was father and me. It's always been just father and me until you came along." The Rat remembered how she killed her family, screaming in delight as she plunged her knife into their hearts. There were more people living in that farmhouse than just a father. Mother died fairly there as well.

"Well, you need to do this one thing. That inn has one of us within its walls. The guard steps out every two hours to check the street. You need to be there looking sweet and innocent. Strike up a conversation. Talk about the weather, whatever. It doesn't matter how, you just need to meet him."

She rolled her eyes. "Don't think I don't know what you are about. You want me to seduce the guard to get us in there, right? I'm not a fool."

"Perhaps you aren't a fool, but you are in the Takers' power. Let's not pretend this will go well if you refuse their wishes."

"Their wishes, or your wishes?"

He shook his head. His wishes had nothing to do with it. There was a taken person inside those walls. What little investigation he did set his fears alight. A group of foreigners had hired out the entire inn for themselves. They took no customers, yet there were less than a dozen people staying there. Whoever they were, they had resources, and they had one of his own. Part of him wanted to burn the place down tonight and just put an end to it, but he needed to know what was going on. He needed to know if their plans were in danger.

The Rat continued on. "It isn't about me, and it isn't about you. It's about making a connection right now, and then getting information from them in the future. Can you believe that it's that simple?"

"No. Nothing is that simple with men."

Hazel was being unusually obstinate. She was normally so eager to serve his wishes. He wondered what had changed. He needed to know what she was feeling if he was going to convince her of anything.

"Hazel, come here if you please," he asked softly.

She took three tentative steps toward him. They were in arm's reach. The Rat reached out with his hand and touched her face. Her eyes went wide but she did not push his touch away. Closing his eyes, he used his emotions to call out to the Friends within both of them. He wanted to see her feelings, to experience them, to know them. The Friends responded to his wishes quickly. A torrent of strong emotions overwhelmed him. Care, concern, fear, jealousy, and self-doubt poured over his consciousness like a waterfall. It was no wonder Hazel was misbehaving today. If he experienced this kind of emotional storm, he would probably lose his mind as well.

"Look into my eyes."

Hazel stepped even closer. Their faces were a mere hand span apart. She began to shake with a slight tremor. The Rat felt it. She yearned for his touch, for his attention, for his words. Something had happened inside her. He wondered if this was the work of the Friends or if she was just susceptible to this sort of emotional bonfire. He could see into her emotions, into her heart. She had been betrayed earlier in life, and she was terrified by it now.

The Rat decided to take this on right now.

"Hazel, do you think I am sending you away?"

Her grip tightened on his hand.

"No."

The tumult of emotions gave her lie away. She was terrified of anything that might split her from his presence. It was part parental, part submissive, and part sick.

"I'm not going to leave you," the Rat began. "You have become important to me. I need you to help me with this one thing. If the Friends need our help, then we help them no matter the cost. But you will finish up, come back to me, and all will be well. This first step will only be a short one, an hour at most. The second step will be harder, then the third, hardest yet."

"I don't want any steps."

"I know what you want. Don't worry. I'm not going to leave you to the wolves."

The Rat tried to think of pleasureful things, of feelings, of sex. His thoughts were imperfect, as it had been years since he had felt the joy of a woman's embrace, but the Friends knew what to do. She sighed as those feelings rushed into her. Drawing a sharp breath, she pulled her shawl about her bosom in an excited yet embarrassed motion.

"I don't care what you have to do. You and I will always be special no matter what. You are in my life now. I won't let you go. The Friends ask for our service. If that means rutting with the man to gain his secrets, then so be it. Either way, it will be you and I forever. Once we win this battle, there will be no need for these kinds of games. Until then, we play all the games that our Friends tell us to.

She nodded, feeling the truth from the Takers as strongly as he did.

Bending down, he gave her a small kiss on the forehead.

"You can do this. Be someone that the Friends value. Be someone that I value even more. Can you do it for me?"

Nodding, she stepped back. Taking a few minutes, she composed herself, straightened her clothing, and adjusted her basket of flowers. It was almost time for the first act. A single tear welled up in her left eye as she turned away, walking to the street to pass by the inn as she had done a dozen times before. She was looking for a warrior who was at least a decade older than her, and a likely servant of her enemies. She hated all of it, but there wasn't anything she wouldn't do for the Rat and the Takers she served.

BACK TO THE INN

Chamise washed her face in the bowl of chilled water. It had been sitting out next to her makeshift sleeping pallet all night. The room had cooled during the night, so the wash was refreshing. She used an old shirt to dry her face, struggled into a worn leather dress she had found discarded in a pile, then set off toward her goal. She hadn't seen Miller in two days. It was time for their lessons to begin. If he wasn't going to pick a day, then she would do it for him.

She pulled on a pair of loose doe-skin slippers that she had recently won in a card game with Gable and Ulf. They were too small for Gable, but they fit her feet just fine. She got up, pulled up her small bag full of useful things, and walked from the room.

Glaring down the hall, she avoided looking at the codex phrases carved along its length. The words made her angry. She remembered how her father had been inspired by them. She, daughter of the most devoted Eisenvard knight to ever walk the earth, held them in disdain.

Someday, she thought, this building would be gone, and the words with it. She hoped it wouldn't be too long until that day arrived. The thought of the Eisenvard keep burning to the ground gave her a smile.

She turned the corner to exit the building. Schaller stood there with his back to the entrance, staring across the field, at nothing. She saw steam rising from a cup in his hand. The life of a custrel was hard to leave behind for him. It was a life filled with being almost good enough. A custrel wasn't a knight, yet fought next to one. It wasn't a page, yet it served nonetheless.

Schaller had long years of waking in the morning, long before the knight he served, even before the pages. He was always ready, armed before anyone. Now there was no one else, yet here he stood, prepared for the day before the sun rose into the sky.

She walked past him, almost nudging him on the way by. "You could pick a better place to stare from."

He started after her. "You could stop and be social for once."

"What? Did you want to chat? Maybe talk about our feelings?"

That remark caused him to offer a wry smile. "Oh Goddess, no. Let's not get too friendly. We can't give the others a reason to gossip."

She slowed her walk, allowing Schaller's tea a few moments to calm down and stop sloshing over his hand. The tea was hot, yet he never complained. He simply accepted the pain as if it was his reward. He was such a perfect Eisenvard, and totally lost in this new world.

"Well, I've got better things for them to gossip about, being a witch and all."

She had tried to joke with him, but her tone gave away her anger. The remark he had made just a few short days ago continued to sting. Schaller didn't know what to say. Chamise wondered if he felt sorry for that remark, or if he even cared how she felt about it. Chamise had no idea why he was following her this morning, and she didn't have the patience to play games.

"Did you want to talk about something? We've got a little time before we get to my destination."

"I think so, but I'm having a hard time coming up with a good way to start."

"You could start the traditional way. Try calling me a witch and getting a mob to burn me. Would that do the trick?"

"Now you're being something other than a witch, but it sounds similar."

"Bite me."

They took ten more steps in silence before he continued on. "You've been here four days. You don't look like you are making any moves to go anywhere else. As much as you love our company, don't you have a plan to move on?"

Her voice snapped into an angry retort. "Are you trying to run me off?"

"On the contrary. I think I've grown to like you, just a little." Schaller held his thumb and forefinger just a tad bit apart. "You're a pretty good nets player. I was hoping to talk to you about your plans, at least for the next few months. Perhaps I could help you somehow. Or maybe, we could help each other, if that makes any sense."

"A little. Tell me more." She didn't trust him, but talking wouldn't hurt.

They walked through the open gate onto the cobbled road. The homes that lay across the street could rightfully be called mansions in any other city. Here, they were simply called homes, even though the wealth held in a single one could equal or surpass any country knight's.

He said, "The order, well, what's left of it, just isn't what it used to be. I was hoping to collect some stragglers and then to start putting a few things back together again."

She stopped. Turning to face him, she told him the honest truth. "No thanks. I'd rather die in a fire. Being burned as a witch would be more honorable than the farce that the

Eisenvard was."

Schaller kept walking, as he tried to keep his face calm. The Eisenvard was everything to him. It played a huge part in her life as well, just not for good.

He continued, "I understand what you are saying. I don't think that you understand what I'm saying though. So please, just hear me out."

"You have fifteen minutes until we arrive at my destination."

"Alright, just listen, then. I'm not talking about trying to restore the order to how it was before Phyllicitus returned. Even I have to admit that we had grown too zealous for all the wrong reasons. Our fear of spellcrafters had colored everything we looked at. But the original Eisenvard weren't like that, were they?"

"I don't know. I wasn't there. All I have to go by is the credo."

"But the credo has been added to a little bit at a time, since the founding of the Order. What if we could go back in time? What if we could return the Eisenvard to what it was originally? A group of knights who guarded the roads against rouge spellcasters and raiders. How would that be bad?"

"I can think of a few reasons involving a lot of history, burning innocent peasants at the side of the road, and arrogance out of proportion from deeds. Besides, what makes you think that you could get Phyllicitus to agree to such a thing?"

He said, "For most of our history, we were not servants to Phyllicitus. Our origins lie far to the north."

"So do the bodies of most of the Order now that the Jarl betrayed them. Do you really want to go back to that?"

"No. What I want is a purpose."

She continued walking, turning left onto the weaver's lane for a few blocks before turning into an alley that jutted off the road at an angle. The buildings grew closer together and the construction began to feel older, more permanent, if that was possible. Three children played in the alley ahead, but they moved to the side, allowing both of them to pass.

Schaller tried to start the conversation again. She had hoped that she would have reached her goal first. Sadly, she hadn't.

"I was up last night pretty late thinking about this. What we need, those of us who were once Eisenvard, is some sort of grand purpose. We need to give our lives meaning, a cause, a crusade, something. I don't think it matters what that purpose is as long as we have one. Without purpose, it feels like the world is simply waiting for us to die. It doesn't feel like there is any reason to do anything."

She knew the feeling very well. She had lived with it every day since they had burned her mother. That one day took her mother, the love for her father, and the companionship of her once-friends in the Eisenvard.

The idea gave her pause though. She thought about the remains of the Eisenvard trying to hunt down the Taken. They had done it before. They even had disciplines to protect against sorcery and mind glamours. Then she shook her head. She thought about the power that Miller and his masters were bringing to bear. She doubted that the remains of the Eisenvard compared to that.

"I admit, part of me likes the idea. But it's just an idea. Our numbers are gone. Our strength is spent. Our time is done. And well, we're still us. That's the problem, not the name of 'Eisenvard' as much as the people in it."

"Perhaps. Perhaps it was time for the Eisenvard to die. All I'm saying is that mayhap a new thing could be born, something that the people need, something that we could do."

She walked past the corner of a building into an intersection of two broad streets. A statue of a woman holding a lantern stood at the center of the intersection. The inn that she had come to visit stood three doors down. Outside of the inn, a tall man that she had seen before, Cerna was his name, stood leaning against the wall chatting with a young woman with straight brown hair that hung just past her shoulders. The woman was fit with pronounced strength in her arms and legs, and somewhat pretty to look upon as well.

"This is where I am bound. We part ways here."

"To an inn? If you wanted a drink, we've passed three better inns on the way here."

"I'm not here for a drink."

Just as she was about to chase off Schaller, the door opened. A tall handsome young man stepped out with long, red, flowing hair. Cerna's attention snapped away from the woman as he stepped in close to hear the whispers of the red-haired stranger. A few heartbeats later Cerna said goodbye to the woman he was chatting with and went inside.

She recognized the red-haired man. He was an apprentice to one of the masters inside. The apprentice necromancer appeared to notice her as well. He waved at her and began to walk their way. He wore a smile on his face but his eyes betrayed his intent. This apprentice necromancer looked at her like she was just one more bug to squash, re-animate, then squash again. She didn't like him one bit.

Reaching out, she grasped Schaller's wrist. "Keep close."

The apprentice, she thought his name was Frantz, slowed his pace. He showed his open hands as he approached. To some, it could appear as a greeting between old friends. To her it was unmistakable, he was showing her that he had no weapons and no ill intents. There was one thing you could count on with necromancers. They were all liars.

"Are you here for Miller?"

"That was my plan. Is he about?"

"No. He has been out at the temple all night with Aileen. He should be back soon enough though' she lied, "Care to come in and wait?"

It was a dare. Frantz wanted her to come in and see whatever depravity they were engaged in. He wanted to cause a rift between Miller and herself. Most of all, he wanted her gone.

"Oh, that would be nice. Would it be all right if my friend came along?" She gazed up at Schaller.

Frantz didn't sound very sure. "Eisenvard?"

It was easy to see if you knew what you were looking for.

Schaller was ready for the play though. "Long ago. Those days are done now that the goddess has returned. I think it best we leave the enmities of the past where they belong—in the past. Don't you?"

She felt Schaller moving his fingers. Was he stressed? No, it felt familiar. She remembered her father's lessons from long ago. Eisenvard knights had disciplines they used to calm the mind and repel magics. Schaller had just used one. He was prepared to battle an apprentice necromancer right here in the street. Schaller towered over Frantz by more than a hand span. Frantz was lithe and in fine shape. Schaller was decorated with hard muscles and the scars from more than thirty battles. The half-smile that he wore seemed to invite Frantz to do something stupid. In her heart, Chamise hoped for the same thing.

"Sure," she said, half-trying to diffuse the situation. "Let's check on Brita. Hopefully, Miller will be back soon."

Frantz stood aside motioning them toward the entrance. "Welcome back."

THE TUTOR

Miller didn't hear the person walk up next to him. He had been staring at the pattern for so long that he had lost track of time. When they sat on the bench next to him, close enough so his leg touched hers, he finally looked up. The first thing he saw was the long brown hair. It was peppered with a hint of gray. She wore a priestess robe. Her face was long, made up of angles and deep concerns. She was probably beautiful once, but time had left her with more strength than beauty. Her eyes seemed kind, but aware of everything around her. This wasn't a woman to toy with.

"Hello," she said.

Miller didn't know what to say. He was well past when he should have left. Time had slipped by him as he stared into the pattern on the floor.

"Sorry. Have I been here too long?"

"I don't know. Have you?" She smiled when she made the comment, turning a barb into a witty jest.

Miller smiled back. "I lost track of time. The pattern just sort of pulled me in. I was trying to trace the flow of lines and I think I got wrapped up in some kind of loop."

She nodded. "That happens a lot. The first time I found this work my sisters had to drag me away from it. I was actually banned from the library for three weeks."

"Three weeks for looking at a pattern?"

"No, three weeks for staring at the pattern for three days without eating. It had quite the effect on me. I tried to make it my focus of study when I apprenticed to the crafter sisters. They banned me, said I was too susceptible."

He chuckled. "Yeah. I understand. I must have been down here four hours. I think I could keep staring at this all night." He pointed at a broad curve that was decorated with shapes that reminded him of teardrops if teardrops could themselves cry. "That part right there had me. I couldn't stop trying to follow the curve to find its end. But the whole time, I could tell that it didn't have one. Crazy, eh? When I look at it directly, it seems to stretch on forever, but if I look at the side, it's just a curve. It has an end at both sides. I swear, it changes based on where you stand in this room."

"Sure. But that's what this room is for, exploring these mysteries. Don't feel bad. It took me two years before I discovered that the loops don't end, they just transform. But every time that I returned here, they seemed new to me."

"Well, I guess my escort will be back soon enough. I've got some tasks to do yet, so I had better move on."

"Your escort came to find you three hours ago. She spoke to you for a good bit, but you were unresponsive. That is when she sent for me."

"Three hours?"

"As I said, it is easy to get lost in the pattern. Don't worry though. The pattern has been here since the library was built. A high priest named Stevenson created it. He was very interested in the history of the ancient magics and First Gods. I'm not sure what he created, but it has a power vastly different than what we understand as magic."

That was true. Miller hadn't felt a hint of power from it, not a channel, not a touch. It felt like the power he had discovered in the arrowhead and the power that lay between the worlds.

"People used to cast magic with these patterns?"

"Somewhat. But they didn't understand magic in the same way that we do today. Back then, it wasn't about the will of an adept or a person's skill as a caster. Somehow magic just was. People interacted with it more than commanded it."

"Like the First Gods?"

"Yes. Only more so."

He began to fidget and rub his hands together. He had just noticed the cold. The fires had been reduced for the evening. He wondered how late it had gotten. The mystery of the pattern called out to him though, unwilling to let his mind go.

"Is there someone here who knows more about this? I would love to talk to them."

"Really? You dabble in spellcraft?" Her voice seemed surprised, but perhaps too much so.

"I have had some exposure, and I have an interest."

"Perhaps I could talk you into joining our order then? We have books and wisdom to spare. We are always looking for those with the talent, no matter how small."

Miller shook his head and recited the words that Aileen had taught him to say when faced with such questions. Many people wanted to find those with the talent. "I'm sorry. That isn't my path."

"No, dear Miller, you are right. If only it could be. Right now, your path is strewn with blood and bones."

His eyebrows shot up. She knew who he was. He instinctively slid away from her, farther down the bench. She slid down, maintaining closeness. She placed a hand on his thigh, uncomfortably close to his sensitive parts, and moved closer, almost snuggling.

Just before he could say something, she interrupted. "Shush. Don't ruin it. I don't get the time and peace to flirt with young men often. Just let me have my moment."

He stopped trying to retreat.

"Flirt?"

"Yes, that is what we are doing. I'm dangling the notion that you could have access to all of our knowledge of this pattern, and you are dangling the idea that you know why Aileen is truly here in Home's Hearth. Neither of us is going to give the other what they want without some form of, well, mutual benefit. Like I said, flirting."

"You know who I am and who I serve then?"

"I do. You serve Aileen and the dark forces that have tempted her. I understand."

Dark forces. He wondered if the stain of the White Hand had grown on him. Perhaps it was obvious to the priests.

"So, what do you want?"

"Me? I want you to know that you just might have a friend in the temple and that Phyllicitus may be having difficulties with Aileen. That does not mean she is having difficulties with you."

Miller was surprised. This priestess was being very kind to a lowly apprentice.

"May I ask why?"

"You may ask all you want, but I probably won't tell you the whole story. But you knew that, didn't you?"

"I suspected. That's more common than I care to admit."

"Oh, poor dear. Let me help restore your faith in fellow man then. I'll tell you my secret purpose and you can decide how threatening it is."

"Uh, all right."

"You are staying in an old inn with a few White Hand masters. At least two, perhaps three."

She waited for him to nod in agreement.

"So normally that isn't much of an issue. But this time Phyllicitus directly prohibited them from coming into Home's Hearth and they ignored her."

He didn't like where this was going. He nodded again.

"So that means we can assume their reason for visiting is sufficiently important to risk disrespecting a goddess. I fear that you may be in the middle of something much larger than you know."

This time it was Miller who had something to lead her on with. "It's a bit more than that. I'm sure you know about the Taken. You've heard the story of how we had to fight a horde on the way here. But did you hear it from Mistress Aileen?"

This time the sister shook her head. She had not.

"Aileen has been avoiding Home's Hearth. Now she needs to speak with Phyllicitus about the Takers, and the danger the townspeople are going to be in. Does Phyllicitus act like a goddess and embrace her former priestess? No. She throws a tantrum like a spoiled girl shunned at the dance."

The sister barked a laugh. "Oh, you've got the right of her. She isn't a cold heart, that one." Then she looked into Miller's eyes, drawing her face closer to his. "That's probably why she is a goddess, you think?"

Her closeness combined with the entirely reasonable question left him without words. Finally, the sister pulled herself away from Miller and stood slowly from the bench.

"Come, Miller. Let me show you out. While Aileen is in residence, The Garden will let you linger more than usual. Once she is gone, I expect your visitation privileges will expire as well. So we should assume that you will be able to visit again, at least for a short while."

Miller didn't want to go. He knew that Aileen would be needing her things soon, as morning was approaching. But he desperately wanted to know more about this pattern and its crafting. "How do I learn more?"

She knew exactly what he was referring to. "Well, there are books in the libraries here. There are a few books back at the temple as well. There is even another Stevenson pattern there."

"I mean, who can I talk to?"

"Oh, the naïveté of the young." She giggled. "You can talk to Aileen. She was fascinated by the different types of magics from the time of the First Gods. It hasn't been that long since she was joining The Garden just to reach this very place."

"Aileen?" The surprises didn't stop coming.

"And you could come find me. I have scant knowledge but I'm willing to share."

He felt embarrassed. "I'm sorry. I didn't ask your name."

She bowed, offering a slight smile. "It isn't a problem. I knew your name so it's only fair that you get mine in return. My name is Sister Fidelity. Come find me if you want to talk."

"Thanks. I appreciate it. But now, I really need to go."

"Yes, you do."

NOT WELCOME

Chamise opened the door to the New Pony Inn. Motioning behind her, she urged Schaller to stay close as she crossed the threshold. Brita's tent stood in the center of the room. She sat on the floor beside it wearing a surprised look as they entered.

Schaller entered the room following closely behind her but keeping an arm's distance from Frantz. Schaller didn't trust him at all.

The words escaped Brita's lips before she could call them back. "Oh dear. This is the wrong party."

Chamise looked back in confusion.

"Can I help you?"

The words came from Chamise's left. A stout man who lost his hair long ago stood there. He wore a rich red woolen robe spotted with what appeared to be gravy stains, along with a pair of mismatched soft slippers and a floppy purple hat. The hat was garish, rimmed with yellow stitchery. At some point in time it would have been luxurious, but it had lost its shape long ago. Remains of the stitches hung down in tassels, having given up their designs.

Chamise turned toward the man. "We are here to see Apprentice Miller. Is he available?" She felt Schaller tense behind her, ready for any action that might erupt.

Schaller whispered in her ear, "I know this one from long ago, the asylum battle. Beware. He's one of the bad ones."

Master Darjeeling frowned before continuing. "I see that you have met my apprentice Frantz. Been playing together well, have we?"

Frantz merely replied with a word to acknowledge the comment. "Master." Frantz continued walking past Chamise and Schaller to take his place beside Master Darjeeling.

"As you expected, Miller has pulled in a few strays."

Darjeeling giggled to himself. "Stray whats? They don't look like cats. Are these dogs?"

"Most likely they are masters. Or they could be worse—rats."

Chamise felt herself go cold. Had Miller led them into a trap? This had the feel of a confrontation long in the planning. Reaching back as if to take Schaller's hand, she made the sign of protection that Schaller had done outside. She would take any protection that she could get right now. Coming here was a mistake.

"Oh, you won't be needing any of that. You see, you came into our house. You gave up any pretense of protection. Right now, your petty crafts are useless, Eisenvard."

He spoke that last word with distaste. "Right now, you live at my mercy, you breathe at my mercy. I suggest you get used to it."

Brita rushed forward, reaching only the edge of the magic circle. "No! You two need to leave now! Don't you understand? He's got bees in his head! All the buzzing buzzing! You don't want to be here!"

Chamise looked about. Runes covered the walls. Some were protective, some were curse runes. A few of the runes were unknown to her and those were the most frightening of all. She felt like an ice pick had gone into her heart. The channels were different here. Something was changing the way that magic itself worked.

It may look like an inn from the outside, but to spellcasters, the White Hand had made this into a fortress.

Schaller took a stance, preparing for a fight that could only end one way. "I know you. You are the White Hand master who built the madhouse. It took the deaths of almost a thousand people to purge that nightmare from the earth."

"Why yes, 'tis I," Darjeeling said with a slight bow. "Now we only have two more to go."

Chamise didn't wait for the next quip. Things and already gotten out of control. "Run!" She turned and pushed Schaller toward the door. His soldier's instincts kicked in and he sprinted, reaching it to pull it open. It didn't move.

Chamise hit the door as well, channeling forces from her spirit, tying them to the planks of the door, to the iron nails that kept the door together. She heard Frantz calling out words in a mystical language that brought the hairs on her back upright. Schaller began ripping at the door handle. Chamise cast her will through the channels, through the hard planks, through the iron nails, encouraging them to age, to shrink, to fail.

She had learned that trick from her Free Mage books. Wizards seldom thought about defending against the passage of time. There was one universal truth. All things fell into ruin eventually.

Schaller turned to face Darjeeling and Frantz just as a bolt of blackness hit him. He screamed in pain as a snake-like cloud of darkness began to envelop him. Chamise slammed her shoulder into Schaller's chest, slamming him into the door. It shattered beneath his weight. They rolled out onto the street, splintered door planks scattered about them. Rusty bent nails cut into her back as she rolled back up, standing, preparing for battle.

Frantz walked out of the door. He appeared calm. The dark snake enveloping Schaller had begun to weaken. Its magic faded away as it was disrupted. Outside of the inn, Phyllicitus's power continued to rule. Within a few heartbeats, the black cloud dissipated completely, returning to the void where it came from.

"What was that about?" Chamise screamed.

"About? You are Eisenvard, and you came to our abode. We were simply defending ourselves. Defending yourself is in keeping with the will of the goddess, isn't it?"

The will of the goddess. Chamise nodded, angry but understanding. The White Hand could not find a way around the holy magic of the goddess. They had to play within her rules. The White Hand seem to have found a way to do just that.

"I'm with Miller, you idiot!"

"You're an Eisenvard, you idiot. Miller is just an apprentice. How much influence do you think he has over the masters? Seriously, you make me laugh."

"But he promised me."

Frantz didn't let her continue. "His promises are worth as much as any other apprentice, which isn't much. Unless you have the promise of a master for safe passage, don't come back here. You are vulnerable without our house. Soon enough, you will be vulnerable anywhere in Home's Hearth. Don't be foolish. Let this one go. The masters have much more important issues to deal with than a few stray Eisenvard, let's not give them an excuse."

Chamise knew he was right. She survived only because she could get through the door. She tried to imagine a way that she could return to Miller and gain his promised secrets. It would never happen within the New Pony Inn.

She nodded, acquiescing to his logic no matter how much it rankled her. Looking down at Schaller lying in the street, she knew that acting against Frantz and his master now would only result in their death. She needed Miller's help now more than ever.

"I'll stay clear of you. I get the message." She reached down to pull Schaller from the street. He wavered, almost losing his balance. Turning away, they staggered down the street, Chamise holding him so he didn't fall.

Five minutes later, Schaller broke the silence. "Do you know what?" he said, his voice dry and cracked.

Chamise kept her hold on him, giving him a steady body to rely on. "What?"

"Those Eisenvard hand charms don't work at all."

She laughed out loud. "No, they never have. They were always based on belief, never on magic."

"I'm starting to think that belief isn't enough to get the job done."

"Welcome to the club."

Miller found Chamise and Schaller walking down the street heading back toward the practice yard. Schaller had recovered enough to walk without assistance, but barely. When Miller called out, Chamise stood in front of him, placing her hand on her knife hilt, as if protecting him from Miller.

He slowed his approach. "What's wrong?"

Miller could hear the anger in Chamise's voice. "What's wrong? Your White Hand master tried to murder us. Is that your idea of some kind of twisted joke?"

Her voice wavered and shook with both anger and fear. Miller didn't know what happened, but it had frightened Chamise to her core. He had never seen that before.

"I'm sorry. I got delayed with some issues involving Mistress Aileen. Was I supposed to meet you?"

Her voice started softly but ended in something close to a scream. Each syllable was stretched, giving it the weight of both an accusation and a betrayal. Every word was spoken slowly, syncopated with her growing emotions.

"You... Were... Supposed... To... Teach... Me... Magic!"

Miller could feel the storm of emotions gathered about her. Schaller just looked at him coldly, as if judging his every motion. He didn't know what to say.

Chamise began to shake. A tear ran down from her left eye, leaving marks against her skin is it cleaned the road dust from its path.

"Where were you?"

Blame. He felt the blame. Somehow Chamise found a way to make his absence the key event. If she would have listened to him, waited for his message, this would have never happened.

Schaller glowered at him. "Well, out with it. She's barely holding together here."

Chamise turned to unleash a verbal attack back at Schaller as well. While she turned, Miller stepped forward quickly and embraced her. At first, she tried to push away, but he held her tight.

"It's over. It's over," Miller whispered to her repeatedly. Tears began to run down her face, as if a waterfall of fear and anger was released. She grabbed his shirt tightly, holding on as if her life depended on it. Miller didn't know what had happened, but he was starting to get a hint.

"Who was there? Frantz? Cerna?"

Schaller walked up beside them. "I don't know Cerna. One of them had some nice long red hair, I think his name was Frantz. The other was a pudgy older master."

Miller didn't let him continue. He pulled Chamise closer, holding her in the closest embrace that he could manage.

"Darjeeling," Miller provided.

"Yes, I think that was his name. For some reason, I'm having a tough time remembering some of the details." Schaller rubbed his head in confusion.

"That isn't surprising. Darjeeling is a master of mind magics. He specializes in driving people completely insane. I'm guessing that's what happened to her."

Chamise turned and wrapped her arms around him, holding on as if for dear life. "What's wrong with me? Oh, Goddess, I'm destroyed."

"You aren't destroyed. This is just a little reminder that Master Darjeeling left you with. It's more a mark of his power than anything else. The worst will pass in an hour or so."

Chamise didn't hesitate. "Stay with me. I got out. I made it." Tears began to flow anew. "What in the name of the crooked gate is wrong with me? Why can't I stop crying?" she screamed in frustration.

"Yes. He got you on the way out. It will pass by tomorrow. Hopefully."

"Get away from me."

He gave her a dry laugh. "I can't leave. You've got me in your crushing grip. I'll be lucky to breathe let alone leave."

Schaller gently placed his hand on her shoulder. "Don't worry. We won't leave you like this."

She nodded slightly, then buried her head deeper in Miller's chest.

Miller looked over at Schaller. Schaller's eyes were bloodshot. He wavered back and forth, having trouble keeping his balance, but otherwise seemed intact.

"You seem to be surviving pretty well."

Schaller gave him a shrug. "I used an old Eisenvard charm before we went in. I didn't think it had worked. Now I'm starting to think that it did."

Miller said, "It was lucky for you then. Master Darjeeling is one of the most talented mind manipulators the world has ever known. He is so good at it that he even drove himself insane.

Come on," he said with encouragement. "Let's try to walk a bit. It will help this pass all the more quickly." He took Chamise by the hand, walking close to her side, never letting her get out of reach. Schaller walked alongside Chamise, always scowling, alert, looking.

After a while, Schaller started to chat with Chamise about playing a game of nets. Miller smiled and enjoyed the easy conversation about simple things. It didn't take long before Chamise returned the conversation to long-promised things.

"I can't go back to the New Pony," she said, indicating her unwillingness to confront Darjeeling again. "You still owe me lessons, and you are late with them. How are you going to keep that promise?"

Miller looked over to her. She hadn't completely recovered, but she was back to being Chamise in every way. Driven, aggressive, unwilling to accept defeat.

He walked for a few more steps thinking about the problem. He needed a place to instruct Chamise, one where the masters would not threaten her.

"As luck has it, I may have a place. I had to go to The Gardens earlier yesterday to talk with Mistress Aileen. While I was there, I found a very quiet place that would be perfect for practicing disciplines and a few light craftings. I'll need to get permission, but I think Sister Fidelity might sponsor me, at least as long as she can get some kind of insight into what Aileen is doing."

Schaller held up a hand. "Are you saying that the temple would give you access if you spy on your mistress?" He was clearly uncomfortable with that idea.

"Not really. The goddess worries about her, even though she left the temple. I think a few reports about her health and happiness would be enough."

Chamise couldn't resist the opportunity. "So how happy is she now that she is a mighty White Hand master?"

"Not very."

They were quiet as they walked the streets of Home's Hearth. Market stalls had begun to break down as they passed. Craftsmen returned home to families and children. They continued their silent walk until Chamise asked him a question.

"That Darjeeling drove himself insane?" The tone of her voice indicated that she didn't believe it. Most people didn't.

"Yeah. He drove himself as mad as a hatter, decades ago. It's amazing what the Order will tolerate in their ranks."

"That explains why Brita said that he had bees in his head."

Miller instantly stopped. "She said what?"

"Bugs in the head. You know." She made a motion swirling her finger along the side of her head to indicate insanity.

"No, that's not what you said." Miller slowed his words

down giving each one weight. "Tell me exactly what she said. It's important."

"Important? She's as crazy as he is."

Schaller scratched his head. "I can't remember."

"I do," Chamise provided. "She said that he had bees in his head, and she could hear buzzing."

Miller remembered his notebook, of dozens of hours trying to get Brita to talk about being taken. He had written an account of someone named Ebber. He seems to have been taken twice. "I'm not sure what that is all about, but Brita kept telling me that he was so messed up by it that she could hear buzzing coming from his mind."

Chamise held Miller's hand tightly. She looked up in alarm. "They can read minds?"

"They can read each other's minds, I think. They seem to be able to communicate over distances, but the communication isn't very good. It's more like feelings than words."

Schaller understood Miller's reaction instantly. "Does that mean that this Master Darjeeling is in communication with the Takers?"

Chamise completed the horrible thought. "Or that he has been taken?"

DECEMBER RETURNS

December stared up at a ceiling, yellowed from decades of neglect. Off-color patching stood out where someone tried to repair leaks and failed. He blinked, trying to adjust his blurry vision. The pain shot through his eyes, into his face. He sucked in a deep breath causing his chest to erupt in agony. He cinched up, raising his head off the fetid pillow.

Coming back from the final black door was getting harder each time, he realized. Every time he passed through and returned, a little more was left behind.

He began hacking. Clotted blood shot out of his throat, showering the bed and wall with the same gore. His hand shook as he began to push himself up.

It didn't work out very well. Clotted blood filled his lungs. He was drowning in his own fluids, again. Coughing loudly, he pushed against the wall, causing his body to spill from the low pallet onto the floor. The coughing began to transform into a deep hack as he rolled onto his hands and knees. Placing his face against the floor, he kept coughing, kept trying to expel the death that had grown inside his body all the months he had been gone.

He looked down at the clotted reddish-brown mess decorating the floor. His stomach heaved. Giving into the sickness, he vomited chunks of months-old, half-digested food. It created a portrait of disgusting, rotted flesh and fluids. The smell burned in his nose like acid. Five minutes later he could pull his head up. He ever so slowly leaned back against the wall. Cold sweat began to run down his forehead, stinging his eyes.

A one-legged man stood across the room leaning on a cane. His paunch hung over his belt like a bag of dead fish. He smelled a little like that as well.

"Welcome back, Master."

December cracked a twisted smile. He gazed up at the wreck of a man. His right leg had been replaced with a wooden peg. His left arm ended with a rusty hook. The man's eyes refused to point the same direction, one always aiming slightly to the left.

"Onion. Good to see you," Master December hacked out. His voice wasn't strong yet, but he tried.

Onion let loose a slow exhale as if choosing his words with care, even though he knew it would be fruitless.

"Indeed. It is a shame that we only seem to meet under these sorts of circumstances."

"That is true. If only we had the time to dally and catch up on old times, eh?"

The thought of old times caused him to blanch, changing his already pale complexion into something resembling the whitest of whites. His attention snapped back to the task at hand.

December began to cackle at the humor of it until a cough took him again.

"I've prepared some mackerel and roots, as instructed."

"Excellent. And the vitalist? Have you procured one?"

Onion shook while he spoke. The idea of the vitalist seemed to give him some sort of twisted pleasure.

"Indeed, I have. As you suggested, I offered a small bag of coin, fourteen silvers, to someone who had just lost a loved one.

It didn't take much to convince them that they could serve a greater purpose in death and that it was easier than ending their own life from grief."

December sighed in weariness. "It seldom is. What have you brought me?"

"I've found a young girl, I think she is sixteen years old if barely. Her love had recently passed in a mining accident. She is bereft, sadly ready to end it all. I offered her fourteen silvers and your eternal gratitude. It seemed enough."

December scowled back at Onion. He hated it when they were that young. Dying for a cause was one thing. Dying because you were stupid was quite another.

"We might as well not postpone it. Send her in." He struggled to sit up. Onion moved forward to offer his arm. December ignored the offer of assistance and kept struggling, eventually succeeding at sitting up. It took all the strength that he possessed.

"The vitalist please," December said with a hint of command in his voice.

Onion's eyes sprung open, returning to the main function in his life, providing vitalists.

Onion spun and left the room. Two minutes passed while December felt every pain, every sick fluid, and every broken bone that his body possessed. Returning from the dead was hard. It took most people weeks to recover from the experience. He didn't have that kind of time.

Onion opened the door of the room, walking in and motioning someone forward. The vitalist was a comely young woman, more likely fifteen years old than sixteen. Her eyes were afraid, darting from the yellowing walls, the horrid mess on the floor, then to December's emaciated body. He didn't give her a chance to back out.

"Before we begin, I'd like to thank you. What you are doing is noble and good beyond measure." December paused for the lie to sink in before resuming. "Rest assured that I will safeguard and treasure this thing that you give me, all in an effort to heal and bring peace to the world," December began, starting the same empty discussion he had been having with different vitalists as long as he could remember. The girl could only nod as she had begun shaking.

"Second, let me promise you that there will be no pain. The process is simple and straight forward. I will be taking just a nibble of energy from you. It will grow back over time. Your energy will quickly restore me, and I will be thankful."

She nodded, still shaking, still unsure. December didn't know what Onion had told the young woman, but it was too late to scold him now. He needed the energy. If his enemies caught him like this, he wouldn't last a second.

"Onion told you of the reward?"

This time she did speak. "Yes. Thirteen silver coins and my family looked after while I recuperate."

December looked over at Onion. "Thirteen, eh?"

Onion tried to look calm but failed. "It's all that we had sir. The orphanage took up all the rest. You know?"

A cracked grin spread on December's face. Onion hadn't changed that much at all. "Indeed, we must always support the orphanage. I believe that this young woman will make the children very happy."

Onion nodded up and down in a panic. "Indeed, very happy."

Motioning the girl to come closer he said, "Shall we do this deed then? Others await my return. I can hardly imagine the bright smiling faces of the children when they see me again." The girl offered a slight smile as she took a step forward.

"Let me have your hand if you would," Master December said. She offered up her hand to him, and he took it in his leathery husk of a limb. He tried to hold it tight, but his grip was weak.

"Now, try to relax. This may seem a little odd, but it is important that you not break contact, and not back away. It would be dangerous if you did that. This magic will only work if you are calm and you don't fight it. It's very important."

She nodded again. December took her other hand in his, then began a recitation. His words opened channels through the spirit realm, binding her very life force to his. For a moment they were closer than any two people in the world. They could feel each other's emotions, see out of each other's eyes. She smiled in surprise, then a frown began to form. The girl saw inside December, she saw what fate awaited her.

Gasping in a breath, she screamed out, "No!"

By then December had her hands in a tight grip. Just that little bit of energy siphoned off the girl was enough to restore much of his strength. While the girl had been investigating all these new feelings and experiences, she hadn't noticed Master December stealing her strength, her vitality, her health. She struggled to pull back, away from the necromancer. She was stuck in place. December's strength had been restored, and hers had wasted away.

Onion began to laugh, amused as doom closed in upon her. She screamed louder and kept screaming. With each beat of her heart, her strength ebbed. Within a dozen heartbeats, she collapsed onto the wooden floor, sobbing with terror. Master December stood above her. His skin had returned to a healthy color. His muscles were well defined and strong.

Onion moved forward, a garrote in hand, ready to finish the day's work. Master December held up a hand.

"No, not for her. I didn't need to take very much of her life-force. She can still recover. Let her live."

Onion looked back, confused. "But we always kill them. We need to keep your secrets, you said. Can't let the others in your order know."

December smiled, thinking about the sick, twisted joy that Onion took when he murdered young girls. There was a reason he had picked this girl to donate vitality. Normally December didn't mind the Onion's twisted behaviors, but not right now. December grew tired of these indulgences.

"But I thought we had a deal," Onion whined.

"Don't worry, Onion. I won't go back on our deal. I had

promised you that every time you brought me a vitalist, I would reward you by returning one of your limbs. Let me have the night to rest, and I'll send you a new arm. Or would you prefer a leg."

He scoffed. "I would have preferred that you not take all of my limbs in the first place."

"Careful. Never forget that I can find another of you, easily. You are not important. You are merely my instrument. If you challenge me, you will be wiped away from this world."

The threat was not lost on Onion. He bowed in submission. "I would be glad to have any of those limbs as you choose, Master."

December smiled. He was back in the world, and none dared oppose him. Onion looked back at him. Only two of his limbs were missing. Tonight, December would regrow his leg so he would only be missing an arm. Next time he came back Onion would be made whole. It was a shame that December would have to kill him then. After all, what use is a servant that isn't in your debt? It was easy to find other amputees for servants. He could always make more.

A THEORY ABOUT RINGS

The New Pony Inn was quiet when Miller returned. The conversation that he had with Chamise and Schaller was fresh on his mind as he scanned for Darjeeling or his apprentice. Neither of them were present.

Brita and Cerna were there. He had interrupted some deep conversation between the two, and Brita looked embarrassed when he approached.

"How goes it, apprentice?" Cerna asked.

Miller offered a smile back to him. Their earlier enmity had faded into the past. "I'm not sure yet. Ask me again when we leave Home's Hearth. Has anything happened here?"

"Aside from Sister Fidelity's visit? Not really. That woman is the coldest priestess of Phyllicitus that I have ever met. How did she ever get that job?"

Miller shrugged. "I spoke with her at the Gardens. She seemed very helpful to me."

"She probably thinks that she can still save you," Brita interrupted, smiling at the ceiling. She began dancing with

275

herself, holding her dress up to her waist like a little girl.

Miller exhaled. Brita was worrisome, and he hadn't done a single successful experiment on her yet. He was starting to doubt that he would ever have the time to work with her. She was mad, but somehow, still connected to reality.

And she could sense the Takers, he thought.

"You two seem to be getting along well."

Brita took in a quick breath. "It isn't like that. I just need someone to keep me company," she complained.

Cerna shook his head. "We're both here, we might as well get used to each other."

"Sure. But one of you is infected by Takers. The other one is the guard."

"You don't have to tell me what my role is here. Master Easter made that abundantly clear when he brought me."

Miller nodded. "Good. Let's not be stupid."

"Speak for yourself, apprentice. I'm not the one indentured for eternity to a group of necromancers."

That comment cut Miller's confidence to the bone. He was right.

"Yet, here we are."

"Here we are," agreed Cerna.

Miller set down his bag of supplies on the floor. He had stopped at the market to purchase a few treats for Brita. Rummaging in the bag, he produced a packet. It fit nicely in his hand. He unwrapped it, showing the two others what he had.

"Oh, Miller! You are a dear!"

Two pastries lay in his palm. Each was cut into a triangle shape. Honey and nuts decorated the top of a dozen layers of dough. Cerna sucked in his breath as he recognized the desert from his homeland. "Where did you find that?"

"A baker stand. I stopped by and saw these, then I thought of you two stuck here at the New Pony."

He channeled an opening in the protective circle, then reached out to Brita to give her the first choice between the two pieces. She placed her fingers on the largest, looked over at

Cerna, then moved to the smaller. Pulling it up to her mouth, she offered a huge smile before she bit into it.

"Oh, this is lovely," she managed to say as crumbs fell out of her mouth. She sighed with joy as she finished the pastry.

Cerna picked up the other pastry from Miller's hand, keeping the paper wrapping that it rested upon. He carefully took a bite, taking care not to smear honey across his mustache. He nodded in approval, clearly enjoying the treat.

Brita's face was covered in honey. She had taken only one bite, then she had shoved the entire triangle into her mouth as a little child would. She sucked on her honey-coated fingers, delighted in their taste.

Cerna finished his food after a half dozen bites.

"What do you need then? I like the treats and all, but it's a pretty obvious attempt at a bribe."

Miller chuckled. "Nothing like that. I just wanted to make sure everyone was feeling valued and happy."

"I do!" Brita supplied.

"I always feel valued and happy," Cerna scowled with suspicion.

"You've figured me out. Today I'm going to do some more experiments with Brita. I was hoping that you could be persuaded to guard outside for the next half hour."

"Outside? Why? Are we expecting trouble?"

"Not from out there. But given some of the masters, I thought it would be wise to have you outside. There would be little reason for Master Darjeeling to read your memories then."

Cerna raised his eyebrows in surprise. "Darjeeling? Why would he do that?"

"Because he is Darjeeling. It happens a lot."

Brita jumped up and down. "I'll guard outside! Please! Pick me! Pick me!"

Miller walked over to the long table. It was a dark wooden piece of furniture they had kept from the inn's original stock. It had room for six to sit comfortably. This table was adorned with chairs instead of benches, and its aged beer-stained surface was still flat enough to write on. Miller leaned over to fetch his journal as Brita moved across the circle, stopping only to pick up a single chair. She placed the chair across from him and sat. They were face-to-face, separated only by the magical circle. An expectant look crossed her face.

Miller paused until he heard the front door open, then close again. Cerna had left the room. He had a half hour. He hoped that would be enough time.

"Are we going to play a game?" Brita asked. Many of their previous interactions had been in the form of a game. This time, there would be no game.

"Not really. I just want to ask you a few questions. Is that all right?"

She smiled. "Do you want to marry me?"

"What? No."

She scowled back at him.

"Yes. Maybe. I mean, well, we have to fix you before we can talk about things like that. Right?"

Brita laughed out loud. "I see you look at me. I know your thoughts even without the Friends."

"Friends?" Miller had heard about the 'Friends' before. Somehow it gave the Taken an ability to communicate with each other. It was frightening, and he was counting on it.

Brita responded. "Yes, no. Like usual, things are hard to describe. It makes me dance."

Miller nodded. "You might need to dance."

Brita didn't understand why, but she found that she could communicate more clearly when she was distracted by moving, dancing, playing.

"I want to talk about one of the stories you had told me. Do you remember the journey to the tower?"

"Yes. Which story?"

"The story about the man named Ebber. Do you remember Ebber?"

She smiled back toward him. "Ebber taught me a lot. He got eaten by dogs. I think they were Master Easter's dogs. I don't like them."

"Do you remember when you told me about the buzzing? How when you talked with Ebber, it felt like bees were buzzing in your head?"

"Sure. He was special like that. I miss him."

His heart began to beat as he approached the next subject. This is where the conversation could become dangerous.

"I met Chamise and Schaller in town. Do you remember them?"

Her lower lip came out in a pout. "Sure."

"Don't be like that. I just ran into them and Chamise told me something that you had told her. She said that you heard buzzing coming from Master Darjeeling. Did I understand that correctly?"

"Sure. He is like a beehive, that one."

That fit, Master Darjeeling seemed to be insane. "Is it the same kind of buzzing that Ebber had?"

She paused, thinking about the question for a long moment. Miller wondered if this strange communication ability the Taken had could be used as a madness detector, or if madness could be used as a sign of being taken. Perhaps, he wondered, a crafter might find a way to listen in on these communications.

Her words were like an iron nail being pounded into his coffin.

"Yes."

He chose his next question very carefully.

"Was Ebber troubled in his mind?"

She smiled. "Oh yes, he had been taken before, and it broke a lot of things inside him. I did like him though. He taught me to dance."

Miller shook his head, not understanding what she was trying to say.

"The buzzing. Do you think that anyone who is troubled would cause that? Or would they have to have Friends?" He took the leap, not completely sure he understood what the term Friends meant to the Taken.

"Oh yes. It's the same."

She gasped, clutching her throat. The chair skidded across the floor as she fell out of it. She began to kick. Blood began pouring out of her mouth. She was biting off her own tongue!

Muttering a channel binding, he opened the magic circle so he could cross. He sprinted to Brita, pulling her head from the floor and opening the channels, forcing her into the gentle embrace of sleep. She screamed, fighting against his channeling. Miller raised his voice shouting the incantations from the disciplines, doubling the magical power of his assault.

The door to the room swung open. Cerna stepped in, curved sword in hand.

"Help me! Hold her down!"

Cerna sprinted over as Miller reached behind him to grab the journal. "Open her mouth! Force it if you have to! Don't let her bite you whatever you do!"

Her eyes rolled up as she fought to stay conscious. Cerna reached down and grabbed a dagger from his belt. Holding it hilt-first, he punched Brita with his empty hand. His fist smashed into her face, knocking her head against the floor. She began to scream as Cerna shoved the dagger hilt into her bloody mouth.

Miller moved fast, channeling all of his remaining willpower to put her to sleep. It didn't work. She was in the grip of something with complete power over her. The Takers had shown themselves. They didn't want her talking about the buzzing sounds. They didn't want her talking about Darjeeling.

"Do something, apprentice!" Cerna's shout awakened Miller to the dire peril of the situation. If the Takers could remove Brita from the world, or at least remove her ability to communicate, Miller would never discover what this new threat was.

"Get ready to run!" Miller shouted as he came up with an idea. He wasn't sure that he could do it, but he knew the principles in detail. He opened three of his five channels, moving the forces of nature into Brita's body, slowing her, making her denser. She began to scream as her body transformed. She grew darker. Her face changed, dark streaks appearing deep in her veins.

"What is happening to me?"

She began to slow. Her motions became jerky and uncoordinated. "I don't feel right. Miller! Do something!"

"It's all right. I'm with you. Just let it take you."

She pushed up against the floor, raising her head up to stare at him, to plead for her life. She never got to say a word. Her skin completed its transformation, becoming solid wood. She was now a wooden statue, frozen in mid-crawl across the floor.

Cerna stared at her, surprise written across his face.

"I'll never get used to you necromancers."

"It isn't necromancy, it's nature-mancy. I picked up some tricks from a Free Mage that I traveled with." He put his hand on the top of Brita's head, gently touching her, offering her comfort. "This form will last less than an hour." He spoke to explain to Cerna, and also to Brita. "The nice part of this trick is that the wood is alive, so we can keep her tethered to life. When her body returns to normal, she should awaken fully refreshed."

"She seemed a bit off before you did this." Cerna motioned to Brita's new wooden form. The dark texture of the walnut stood in contrast to the oaken floor. Even as a wooden statue, she remained beautiful.

"She was in the grip of something. I'm hoping this transformation interrupted it."

Cerna nodded, quietly thinking about what he had just seen. "It would have interrupted me, that's for sure."

Miller stood up, then walked around the circle's edge, assessing any damage. When he completed his inspection, he began to cast, restoring the magical circle to its full functions. Once finished, Miller pulled up the chair and began to wait. Every ten minutes he recorded his observations into the journal. He wrote about what he saw, how Brita looked, and how well his enchantment was working. Just as he was starting to wonder if his experiment had failed, Brita began to move again. She sucked in a deep breath of air, then began to cry. She pulled her knees into her chest and wept like a baby, rocking back and forth, seeking comfort anywhere she could find it.

When she finally looked up at Miller, he offered her a smile. He was genuinely glad to see her recovered, if only partially.

"I have to ask you questions now."

Brita nodded back, pushing herself up into a sitting position. She stared at the floor, preparing for what was going to come next.

"Are there any bees?"

She paused, then looked up. "Just a few. Hornets maybe. I know because they seem angry."

Miller jotted down a few notes detailing her responses.

"Are your Friends trying to talk to you?"

She looked up in astonishment. She slowly shook her head. "It's like I can hear them, but I can't make out their words."

He asked her to open her mouth so he could inspect the damage she had done to her tongue. Retreating back to the set of boxes the masters had brought, Miller fetched a red flask marked with the symbol of body healing. He walked back and set it on the circle's edge, willing it to open just a hand's breadth in width.

"This will make you feel better."

She took it without asking what it was, pulled out the cork stopper, and drank.

Miller looked down at his journal. The transformation seemed to offer some hope, but he wasn't sure how long it would last. He would have to watch her carefully until morning. He closed his journal, hid it beneath a stack of supplies where it wouldn't be obvious.

He didn't need Master Darjeeling or his apprentice Frantz reading this book, especially before he shared what he had discovered with Mistress Aileen.

FIRST GODS

Chamise screamed in terror. The call reverberated through Hurriet's ears. She felt her heart momentarily stop, frozen with fear. She could feel her life fading away as she stared up into the sky. Blood began to bubble up from Chamise's throat as she writhed upon the cold stone floor. Hurriet reached over to her, desperate to help, to save her. She couldn't move. Something held Hurriet in its grip, invisible tendrils wrapping around her arms and legs. She watched as her new friend died in agony.

Hurriet tried to suck in a breath of air. Her lungs would not work. Within seconds her heart began to beat wildly, terrified at the lack of oxygen. She could feel herself slipping into death, beyond the final black door.

No, she thought, this isn't right. None of this is right.

Somehow, against all evidence, she knew that none of this experience was true. Everything she saw and felt was false, a lie. She tried to close her eyes, to shut out what she saw and isolate herself against the visions. The sky seemed to bore down into her soul, sucking hope and joy out of her until it reached the core of her being. She didn't know what was happening to her but she knew that she had to fight it.

A few of Apprentice Miller's words came back to her. He had visited Chamise yesterday for a few moments. She overheard them talking about this thing he called disciplines. He had described a way of quieting the mind and resisting fear. He called it the discipline of quietude. From what she could piece together, the discipline of quietude calmed the mind by focusing on eliminating stray thoughts from one's consciousness. Somehow thinking about stones and rivers could help someone achieve quietude. She had no idea how this was done, but she grasped at the idea. It felt like she was drowning, her body rebelling and desperate for air that would not come. She needed to try something, anything.

She thought to herself, "calm, calm, focus." She tried to follow the advice Miller had given to Chamise and focus on her blankness. She concentrated on the slivers of time between the seconds. Her life's breath felt captured by someone else. Emptying her mind was hard. She calmed herself while blanking out the pain. She kept telling herself to accept whatever fate had in store for her, to seek emptiness.

Three seconds later her eyes snapped open. She gulped down a fresh breath of air. She found herself in the dark room that she had been in when she went to sleep, deep in the labyrinth of the Eisenvard's keep.

Somehow, she knew that Chamise continued to be in danger. Hurriet sprung out of bed with no thought of dressing, pausing only to slip on her shoes. She dashed out the door, her soles pounding on the flagstone. Sprinting along the credo hall, she kept her breakneck pace as she turned left into the entry hall. Her feet slipped and she fell, skidding to a halt against the far wall. With arms and legs flailing, she pushed herself from the ground and restarted her run. She started to breathe hard as she continued her run.

The feeling of danger was overwhelming. Terror began whispering dark thoughts to her. Chamise needed her and could die at any moment.

She saw the outer gate. As she moved closer, details emerged. The door was ajar as if someone had come into the compound and not closed it behind them. Her fear spoke up. Someone had left the compound, and that someone needed her.

She didn't hesitate. She couldn't save Gar when he had been murdered. She swore to herself that she wouldn't let Chamise be killed as Gar had been.

Her breath came in gasps. She tried to scream out to Chamise, but her breath wouldn't come. A pain shot out from her gut, silencing her voice. Only ragged heavy breath emerged from her. She kept running.

She left the gate, traveling across the darkened street. Cobblestones emerged from the shadows beneath. Only three torches lit the street, supplying dim light as they burned in their iron brackets. One of the neighborhood streets seemed brighter than the others. She dashed forward angling left, convinced that she had found Chamise.

As she closed in on the street, she saw light shining from the street entrance. It splayed onto the ground, lighting up the stone and surrounding houses. Dark shadows danced along the edge of the illumination. She turned. Frantz stood in the center of the street. He held a yellow staff in one hand that reached from the ground to just above his head. She froze as she saw the light. It floated above the staff, a single point that shone into the night. It bounced on the top of the staff like a lightning bug, only a thousand times brighter.

Then she noticed the fat man next to him. The White Hand master was portly, wider than two men. The folds of his stomach cast shadows against the walls of surrounding houses, dancing with the movements of the small light source.

The events of the night became clear to her. The dream tricked her into leaving the compound. Now Frantz was here to either kill her or maybe worse. Miller had warned her about how the White Hand liked to take in young children, to raise them up to their own ends. They killed Gar. Anger spiked in her heart as she saw them.

The feeling of searching for Chamise fell away like a cold breeze. Now she understood. It had never been her own intuition. It was something forced on her by magic. She wanted nothing to do with these people.

"Shite!" she exclaimed in panic. Turning sharply, she tried to run back the way she had come. She struck an invisible wall, bouncing off and falling onto the street. She saw a flash of light emerge from the pavement.

The fear had her in its grip. She had ended up in the middle of a magic circle. The spell imprisoned her, at the mercy of the White Hand. At the mercy of Gar's murderers.

She tried again, scrambling forward to escape the circle. Her instincts told her that it was all futile. She didn't know if she could believe those feelings anymore. She found the edge of the circle. It would not let her pass.

"You're quite sure this is the one?" Darjeeling asked.

Frantz pointed a long finger at her. "She's the one. I'm sure."

"Excellent," Darjeeling began. "I'm sure you are curious why I've invited you here tonight?"

Hurriet didn't pause to listen to the master's speech. She knew what was about to happen. They would take her, or they would kill her. It seemed like the kill option was most probable. She moved again, pressing herself against the magic wall that sealed her within, trying to push herself through.

She called out to the necromancers in a panic.

"You can't do this! The goddess won't let you! We're in Home's Hearth!"

Darjeeling offered a slight smile. "Don't be like that. I've long known how to avoid the goddess's wrath. It's very simple, you see? The goddess uses her magic to dilute the desire to do evil. If I don't want to do evil, then it doesn't affect me. Indeed, I only want to do good. I'm here to offer you a life without death, a path to education and enlightenment. Even a role in saving all of humanity. What could be more good than that?"

She continued to look from side to side, desperate to find a way out of this trap. She glanced upward trying to find any way out.

The sky shone down upon her, filled with stars. Her panic began to ease as she stared at the heavens above. She had been convinced there was no escape just a few moments ago, that she would die the same way as Gar. The sky had been overcast and dark when she arrived in the alley less than a minute ago. Now it stood cloudless with thousands of stars shining down upon her.

"Ask my apprentice Frantz here. He will tell you how easy it is to overcome Phyllicitus's power, even in her own city. The goddess is a fool, but no worse a fool than most people. She forgets one of the fundamental truths of the universe. Frantz?" Darjeeling could not resist testing his pupil.

Frantz replied back with a string of words, memorized across the years, used on multiple occasions.

"Because all lies are truths to some people, and all truths are lies to others."

"Indeed, well done," Darjeeling responded. "Now it's time for your truth, or your fiction, whichever you prefer. We won't take you in if you are unwilling. We won't let you live and be a danger to others if you are not. You need to make up your mind. While I do have all night to wait for you, I just don't care to." Darjeeling waved his hand in the air, flippantly. "This is all so annoying, and so very tiring."

The conversation felt unreal to her. The stars shone down, offering hope, an escape. Her gut instincts shouted at her. She knew that something was up there, something that could save her. She felt it calling to her, some force of the universe. She couldn't hear words or understand it, but she wanted it nonetheless.

The sky lit up in streaks of blue. It illuminated the street as bright as daylight. A horse appeared within the circle. It stood almost twice as tall as the mare had. Jet-black hair coated it. Its eyes looked down on her, communicating with her using pure feelings in a way she had never experienced before."

"By the final door, what is that?" Frantz shouted out in a panic. The horse towered over him. Even if he stood on his toes, he would not be able to reach its head.

"Huh," Darjeeling said with surprise. "Don't poke it, you'll spook it."

"Spook it?" Frantz asked, unsure what was happening around them.

The horse walked to where Hurriet lay on the ground and dipped its head to her. She understood what it wanted, even though no words had been spoken. She stood from the cobblestones and set her hand upon its barrel chest.

She heard an additional set of hoof beats. The mare emerged at the entrance to the street. After a few moments of silence, the gigantic horse began to walk away. It crossed over the edge of the magic circle and it erupted in sparks, fading away as quickly as it began, the magic having been drained away. Hurriet followed after. The mare joined their group and they turned left to continue down the street, walking away from the necromancers.

Frantz began to walk forward, to stop them from leaving. Darjeeling set his hand on his shoulders.

"Wait for it," the White Hand master said.

Dutifully, Frantz stopped and simply watched them walk away. The blue light cast from the sky faded away. Darkness returned to the streets. Frantz opened his magical channels, trying to understand what this horse was.

"Don't bother," Darjeeling said. Just as he uttered those words, Hurriet, the massive horse, and her original mare faded into darkness, like fog dissipating on a warm morning.

"Master, what did we just see?" Frantz asked.

"Nothing to worry about. It's just a First God, come to claim the girl as his own. They do this now and again. It keeps the First Gods supplied with shamans."

"We just tried to bring her into the Order. Shite, I killed her brother. Should we worry?"

"Me? No. Nothing for me to worry about here. It's just

nature taking its course."

"How about me?"

"Oh, you? Probably. Either way, I'm hungry. Let's go eat." The stars continued to shine down upon the pair as if the universe itself was watching them closely.

NOTE FROM THE AUTHOR

Thanks for reading my second book, Enemies Within. This book has been a labor of love over the past year. I'd like to thank those who supported me and cheered me on. My gaming group provided much of the inspiration for writing this book. I thank my wife, Laurie, for being the most patient editor and beta reader ever, and all of my friends that connect with me through Facebook, or at Ravencon. I would especially like to thank all my writing friends (Catherine chief among them) that kept my head in the game.

Just a note - If you liked this book, please review it online! Also, look out for book three soon. A Flaw in the Master's Ring should be out by 2020. The first draft has been finished, now it's time for the hard part, editing.

Best Wishes

Brian P

Brian@brianphillipswriter.com
http://whitehand.brianphillipswriter.com

ABOUT THE AUTHOR

Brian Phillips lives in Northern Virginia, writes books, plays games, and lives life to its fullest. He has been in turn a sailor, a student, a Doctor of Philosophy, an engineer, and an author.